"A Jill Shalvis hero is
are made of, and Pac
—*New York Times* bestsellin

Not for

The next day, she still hadn't heard any news from Pace, or about Pace, and she wondered what the final outcome on his shoulder injury was. She wondered how he was.

If he was doing okay . . .

Going stir-crazy, she grabbed her camera and headed to the Heat's facilities. She told herself that she needed some pictures of the team, but if she ran into Pace, so much the better. They had a few things to discuss.

Okay, maybe it was just her. *She* had a few things to discuss.

And she wanted her underwear back.

Praise for Jill Shalvis and Her Romances

Double Play

JILL SHALVIS

BERKLEY SENSATION, NEW YORK

THE BERKLEY PUBLISHING GROUP
Published by the Penguin Group
Penguin Group (USA) Inc.
375 Hudson Street, New York, New York 10014, USA
Penguin Group (Canada), 90 Eglinton Avenue East, Suite 700, Toronto, Ontario M4P 2Y3, Canada
(a division of Pearson Penguin Canada Inc.)
Penguin Books Ltd., 80 Strand, London WC2R 0RL, England
Penguin Group Ireland, 25 St. Stephen's Green, Dublin 2, Ireland (a division of Penguin Books Ltd.)
Penguin Group (Australia), 250 Camberwell Road, Camberwell, Victoria 3124, Australia
(a division of Pearson Australia Group Pty. Ltd.)
Penguin Books India Pvt. Ltd., 11 Community Centre, Panchsheel Park, New Delhi—110 017, India
Penguin Group (NZ), 67 Apollo Drive, Rosedale, North Shore 0632, New Zealand
(a division of Pearson New Zealand Ltd.)
Penguin Books (South Africa) (Pty.) Ltd., 24 Sturdee Avenue, Rosebank, Johannesburg 2196,
South Africa

Penguin Books Ltd., Registered Offices: 80 Strand, London WC2R 0RL, England

DOUBLE PLAY

A Berkley Sensation Book / published by arrangement with the author

PRINTING HISTORY
Berkley Sensation mass-market edition / July 2009

Copyright © 2009 by Jill Shalvis.
Excerpt from *Perfect Game* copyright © 2009 by Jill Shalvis.
Cover art by Jim Griffin.
Cover design by Diana Kolsky.
Interior text design by Laura K. Corless.

ISBN: 978-0-425-22868-5

BERKLEY® SENSATION
Berkley Sensation Books are published by The Berkley Publishing Group,
a division of Penguin Group (USA) Inc.,
375 Hudson Street, New York, New York 10014.
BERKLEY® SENSATION and the "B" design are trademarks of Penguin Group (USA) Inc.

PRINTED IN THE UNITED STATES OF AMERICA

10 9 8 7 6 5 4 3 2 1

Acknowledgments

To JR Murphy, one of the cutest, nicest minor league pitchers out there—thanks for all the patient answers to my endless questions on absolutely everything in baseball, from rules to what you guys talk about in the bullpen to what really goes on in the clubhouse.

To Stacy Joyce, an old, dear friend who works for the Anaheim Angels, who also came through for me with answers to all of my panicked questions, and there were many.

To Sarah and Adam, for the first draft read and the invaluable input. Couldn't have done it without you.

Chapter 1

A guy's definition of *baseball*: you don't have to buy
the other team dinner to get game.

If Pace Martin had the choice between sex and a nap, he'd
actually take the nap, and wasn't that just pathetic enough
to depress him. But his shoulder hurt like a mother and so
did his damn pride.

Go home and rest, Pace.

That had been his physical therapist's advice, but Pace
could rest when he was old and far closer to dead than thirty-
one. In the locker room, he bent down to untie his cleats and
nearly whimpered like a baby.

This after only thirty minutes of pitching in the bullpen. Thirty minutes doing what he'd been born to do, playing the game that had been his entire life for so long he
couldn't remember anything before it, and the simple art of
stripping out of his sweats had him sweating buckets.
When he peeled off his T-shirt, spots swam in his eyes. An
ace pitcher in the only four-man starting rotation in the
majors, and he could hardly move.

Pushing away from the locker, he made it through the
Santa Barbara Pacific Heat's luxurious clubhouse—thank
you, Santa Barbara taxpayers—and into the shower room,

grabbing a can of Dr Pepper on his way. Lifting his good hand, he probed at his shoulder and hissed out a breath.

Sit out tomorrow's game.

That had been his private doctor's orders. Pace had managed to escape the team doc all in the name of not being put on the disabled list. Being DL'd would give him a required minimum fifteen-day stay out of action.

No, thank you.

Not when they were nearing the halfway mark of their third season, and as a newbie expansion team, they had everything to prove. Three seasons in and anything could happen, even the World Series, *especially* the World Series, and management was all over that.

Hell, the players were all over that.

They wanted it so bad they could taste it. But to even get to any postseason play, Pace had to pull a miracle, because as everyone from ESPN to *Sports Illustrated* loved to obsess over, *he* was the Heat's ticket there. Sure the team had ten other pitchers in various degrees of readiness, but none were putting out stats comparable to his. Which meant that everyone was counting on him. He was it, baby, the fruition of their hopes and dreams.

No pressure or anything.

Reminding himself that he hated whiners, he stepped into the shower. Under the hot spray, he rolled his shoulder, then nearly passed out at the white-hot stab of pain. Holy shit, could he use a distraction.

Wild monkey sex.

That had been Wade's suggestion. Not surprising, really, given the source. And maybe the Heat's top catcher and Pace's best friend was onto something. Too bad Pace didn't want sex, wild monkey or otherwise.

And wasn't that just the bitch of it. All he wanted was the game that had been his entire life. He wanted his shot at the World Series before being forced by bad genetics and a strained rotator cuff to quit the only thing that had ever mattered to him.

He didn't have to call his father to find out what the old man would suggest. The marine drill instructor, the one who routinely terrified soldiers, whose motto was "Have clear objectives at all times," would tell his only son to get the hell over himself and get the hell back in the game before he kicked the hell out of Pace's sorry ass himself for even thinking about slacking off.

And wouldn't that just help.

Tired of the pity party for one, Pace ducked his head and let the hot water pound his abused body until he felt slightly better, because apparently he'd gotten something from his father after all. He had fourteen wins already this season, dammit. He'd thrown twenty-four straight scoreless innings. He was having his best season to date; he was on top of his game. Lifting his head and shaking off the water, he opened his eyes and found Red standing there.

The Heat's pitching coach was tall, reed thin, and sported a shock of hair that was the color of his nickname, though it was also streaked with grey that came from four decades in the business. He had a craggily face from years of sun, stress, and the emphysema he suffered from because he refused to give up either his beloved cigarettes or standing beside the bullpen surrounded by the constant dirt and thick dust.

Red's doctors had been after him to retire, but like Pace, the guy lived and breathed baseball. He also lived and breathed Pace, going back to their days together at San Diego State. Wherever Pace had gone, Red had followed. Red always followed. Truth was, he'd been far more than a coach to Pace.

All the guy wanted was to see Pace get a piece of the World Series. That was it, the culmination of a life's dream, so Pace's arm would have to be literally falling off before he'd admit that he couldn't play.

"What are you doing here?" Red asked, taking Pace's Dr Pepper from the tile wall and tossing it to the trash before replacing it with a vitamin infused water, the same brand the whole team drank so much of that they'd been given their own label. "Usually you guys are all over a day off."

"I was drinking that."

"Soda makes you sluggish."

No, his bum shoulder made him sluggish.

"Why are you here?" Red pressed.

They didn't get many days off. Pace pitched every fourth game, and in between he had a strict practice and workout schedule. "Maybe I just like the shower here better than my own."

"The hell you do. You throw?"

"A little."

Red's eyes narrowed. "And?"

"And I'm great."

"Don't bullshit me, son. You were favoring the shoulder yesterday in the pen."

"You need glasses. My ERA's 2.90 right now. Top of the league."

"Uh-uh, 3.00." Red peered into the shower, all geriatric stealth, trying to get a good look at his shoulder, but Pace had cranked the water up to torch-his-ass hot so that the steam made it difficult to see clearly.

"It's fine." Pace didn't have to fake the irritation. "I'm fine, everything's fine."

"Uh-huh." Red pulled out his phone, no doubt to call in the troops—management—to have the multimillion-dollar arm assessed.

It was one of the few cons to hitting the big time: from April to October, Pace's time wasn't his own, and neither was his body. Reaching out, water flying, he shut Red's phone. "Relax."

"Relax?" Red shook his head in disbelief. "There's no relaxing in baseball!"

Okay, so he had a point. The Heat had been gaining momentum with shocking speed, gathering huge public interest. With that interest came pressure. They were hot, baby, hot, but if they didn't perform, there would be trades and changes. That was the nature of the game, and not just for players.

Red was getting up there and not exactly in the best health. Pace didn't know what would happen if management decided to send the old guy back down to the minors instead of letting him walk out with his dignity intact and retire on his own terms. Well, actually, Pace did know. It would kill Red. "Just taking a shower, Red. No hidden agenda."

"Good then." Red coughed, wobbling on his feet at the violence of it, glaring at Pace when he made a move to help. When Red managed to stop hacking up a lung, he lay Pace's towel over the tile wall. "You've had enough hot water. You're shriveling."

When Pace looked down at himself, Red snorted. "Get out of that hot water, boy."

Boy.

He hadn't been a boy in a damn long time, but he supposed to Red he'd always be a kid. Waiting until Red shuffled away, Pace turned the water off and touched his shoulder. Better, he told himself, and carefully stretched. Good enough.

It had to be.

Red had a lot at stake. The Heat had a lot at stake.

And knowing it, Pace had everything at stake.

Reporter Holly Hutchins prided herself on her instincts, which hadn't failed her yet. Okay, so maybe they routinely failed her when it came to men, but as it pertained to work, she was razor-sharp. And given that work was all she had at the moment, she really needed this to go down correctly. She was waiting to interview Pace Martin, the celebrated, beloved badass ace starting pitcher she'd just watched in the bullpen.

He probably hadn't been aware of her observing his practice. There'd not been a manager or another player in

sight, certainly no outsiders, including reporters or writers—
of which she happened to be both. She'd sat on the grassy
hill high above the Heat's stadium, surrounded on one side
by the Pacific Ocean and on the other by the steep, rugged
Santa Ynez Mountains, and studied Pace from the shadow
of an oak tree.

She hadn't used her camera. That would have been an
invasion of privacy. She might be the epitome of a curious
reporter, but in spite of her ethicless, demanding ass of a
boss, Holly had a tight grip on her own personal compass
of right and wrong. Taking pictures when Pace hadn't been
aware of her even being there would have been wrong.

Which was a shame, because he'd looked pretty damn
fine in his warm-up sweats. Not a surprise, really, since he
was currently gracing the cover of *People* magazine's "Most
Beautiful People" issue.

But what *had* been a surprise: his pitching had sucked.

She hadn't wanted this assignment, had fought against
it—hell, she'd known only the basics about baseball before
spending the last two weeks cramming—but Tommy had
forced her to do this or quit. Since she'd grown fond of eating and having a roof over her head, she'd agreed.

Reluctantly.

And since she did nothing half-assed, she was in this,
for better or worse. She knew Pace was the best of the best.
He had two Cy Young awards and a Gold Glove, and routinely won a minimum of twenty games a season. She also
knew that the Heat needed a fantastic year and that the
pressure had to be enormous. Holly understood pressure;
she wrote under enormous pressure on a daily basis.

She wasn't tabloid. No, making up tidbits and taking
racy pictures didn't turn her on. The truth turned her on, a
throwback from a disillusioning childhood. Tommy White,
the editor-in-chief for *American Online Living*, had given
her a weekly blog on his site, where she picked subjects of
national interest, then profiled that subject in depth for three
months at a time—with an interesting angle. Secrets. As she

knew all too well, everyone had one and people loved to read about them, and since she was the master of digging them up—thanks, Mom—it was a natural fit.

Her last ongoing series had been on space travel. It'd garnered her awards for exposing the dangerous use of inferior, cheaper parts, which had resulted in two tragic accidents . . . and a bitter breakup when her boyfriend had turned out to be one of the rocket scientists on the wrong side of the law.

Before that, she'd blogged about the ghost towns of the great wild, wild West, using her own photographs to document what had been left behind when those towns had failed and what the cost had been in terms of human suffering. That one had ended up getting her a segment on *60 Minutes*.

Yep, secrets had both once destroyed her and served her well.

She looked down at her watch, then eyed the clubhouse door. Women were allowed into the locker room but by invite only. She had one for the upcoming game but not for today. If she had a penis, she could just walk right in and interview him in his element. Not that she wanted a penis. No thank you, they were way too much trouble. In fact, given the fiasco with her last boyfriend, she'd given up penises.

Or was it *peni*?

It didn't matter, singular or plural, they were a thing of her past. Not a huge loss, as they'd never really done all that much for her other than give her brief orgasms and a whole lot of grief.

Where was her phenom? She looked at her watch and assured herself that she had time. Months of time, which she'd be using to profile the Santa Barbara Heat in depth. Her plan was to start easy, taking a personal direction for her first article. She could have picked any of the young, aggressive, charismatic players. Joe Pickler, the second baseman who'd given up medical school to play AA ball and then spent five years working his way up to the majors. Or Ty Sparks, the relief pitcher who'd overcome childhood leukemia and was trying to work his way into the starting rotation. Or maybe Henry Weston, the left fielder turned shortstop who'd left the Dodgers where his twin brother played in spite of it causing a major family rift. There was also the reputably charming rogue Wade O'Riley, the Heat's catcher, who'd come from abject poverty, something Holly knew all too much about.

But always a sucker for a challenge, she'd chosen to start with Pace, a player three years into his fifty-million-dollar, five-year contract, who'd oddly and very atypically for a ballplayer turned down millions more in alcohol and cologne ads, a guy the tabloid reporters loved to try to dig up dirt on.

She glanced out to the parking lot. Pace's classic apple red Mustang GT was hard to miss. Nope, he hadn't skipped out on her; she wasn't worried about that.

But she was curious.

Why had he pitched for thirty minutes, pushing hard in spite of the fact that he'd clearly been having an off day, and then suddenly dropped to the bench, shoulders and head down, breathing as if he'd run a marathon? He'd just sat there, very carefully not moving a single inch. Only after many minutes had passed had he pushed to his feet and escaped to the clubhouse.

Was he nursing a heartache?

A hangover?

What? She could *feel* his secrets, and the part of her that needed to get to the bottom of everything, to hurry up and expose the bad so she could relax and get to the good, reared its head just as the clubhouse door finally opened and she caught a quick glimpse of tall-dark-and-attitude-challenged in the flesh.

Pace Martin.

"Hi," she said, gripping her pad of paper and pen, perfectly willing to forgive his tardiness if he made this easy on her. Not that it mattered. Sure, he'd made a secondary career out of being tough, cynical, edgy, and for a bonus, noncommittal. Luckily for her, she specialized in tough, cynical, and edgy. She thrust out her hand. "I'm Holly Hut—"

"Sure. No problem." He grabbed her pen and leaning over her, quickly wrote something on her pad.

As he did, she took her first up-close look at him, searching for that elusive "it" factor that seemed to make men want to be him and women want to do him. Granted, he owed much of that to his packaging, but she'd already known that. He had still-wet-from-his-shower dark hair and movie-star dark eyes, and a face that could have been descended directly from the Greek gods, but she wasn't moved by such things. As a writer and a people watcher, Holly knew his pull had to go far deeper, that there had to be more to his charisma than genetic makeup.

Or so she hoped.

But the good looks sure didn't hurt. He hadn't shaved, though she could smell his shampoo or soap, something woodsy and incredibly male that made her nostrils sort of quiver. Which meant *People* magazine appeared to be correct on the beautiful-people assessment—he clearly had genuine appeal.

Since she barely came up to his broad shoulders, she had to tip her head up to stare into his face as he straightened and handed her back her pad, giving her just enough time to see that his eyes weren't the solid brown his bio claimed, but rather had gold swirling in the mix. They weren't smiling to match his mouth, not even close, and if she had to guess, she'd say Mr. Hotshot was pissed at something.

Then she glanced down at her pad and saw what he'd done.

An autograph. He'd just given her an autograph.

And then, while she was still just staring at the sprawling signature in shock, he handed her back her pen and walked away, heading down the wide hallway with his steady, long-legged, effortlessly confident stride.

"Hey," she said. "I didn't want—"

But he'd turned a corner and was already gone.

Chapter 2

You spend a good chunk of your life gripping a baseball, and in the end it turns out that it was the other
way around the whole time.

—Jim Bouton, professional baseball player and writer

Unbelievable, Holly thought, stunned enough to stand
there while Pace got away. Okay, so maybe she *had* looked
like a fan girl hanging around outside the locker room.
And she'd obviously been holding a pen and a pad of paper, just as she imagined the hordes of people who hounded
him on a daily basis did.

But there was something faintly embarrassing about him
thinking that all she'd wanted from him was a signature.
And for the first time since she'd taken on this assignment,
instead of thinking of killing her boss, she thought of Pace
Martin as someone more than an overpaid athlete. He was
flesh and blood, no doubt complete with a myriad of complex emotions driving him. As a writer she should have
known that—which would be her first and *last* mistake. At
least today.

Shoving the pad in her purse, she hurried after him,
through the wide hallways of the multimillion-dollar facility that housed and bred the Heat. The walls on either side
of her were adorned with pictures and awards. The imagi-
native, aggressive team was a multimillion-dollar marketing

and merchandising gift from heaven. Posters, collector's cards, T-shirts, memorabilia . . . and the county of Santa Barbara enjoyed it all, soaking up the love and raining it back down on the players in spades. Especially Pace.

It fascinated her. And also worried her. She'd been perfectly comfortable when writing about space travel and faulty parts, about what happened to abandoned old West towns, but honestly she wasn't all that comfortable with beloved athletes, especially potentially knocking them off their public pedestals. Maybe she wouldn't find a secret to expose this time, but the truth was everyone had one. She'd learned that early enough, and she'd learned it the hard way.

Plus, there was the fact that two players had been quietly traded from the Heat before the start of this season and then just as quietly suspended for testing positive for illegal enhancers.

Not that anyone wanted to talk about *that*.

She caught up with Pace as he headed through the outside doors, where she was blasted by blinding So-Cal sunshine and blistering heat. Ignoring it, she pulled a file out of her purse.

Her *Heat* file. She also grabbed her media pass and slipped it around her neck to prove she wasn't a groupie, and when she looked up, she found that Pace had stopped and turned to her, his gaze glued to her opened file and the eight-by-ten publicity photo lying on top.

Which happened to be of him.

"Fine," he said, dropping his duffel bag and rubbing a hand over the stubble on his jaw, looking tall, broad, and undeniably weary. "I'll sign that, too, but only if you promise not to sell it on eBay. I hate seeing myself on eBay."

She'd gotten the photo from Samantha McNead, the Heat's team publicist, along with some articles already written on the team. The picture had made her blush when she'd first looked at it, and now was no different. In it, Pace was shirtless. He was leaning back against a brick wall, wearing only a pair of threadbare Levi's so low on his hips as to be almost indecent. His feet were bare, and he had a thumb hooked in his jeans, causing the denim to sink even lower, gaping away from the most amazing set of perfectly cut abs she'd ever seen.

And that torso. *Holy hot tamales, Batman.* When she'd first laid eyes on it, she'd actually squirmed as if she'd personally caught him in an intimate act.

Then she'd drooled.

Her reaction had disturbed her. She preferred men who made a living with their brains not brawn.

And yet look where that's gotten you . . .

Pace glanced at the photo again, then into her face, his own simmering with something she couldn't quite put her finger on, but given his dark edginess, it certainly wasn't a fairy tale. His eyes were opaque, and beneath his inky black lashes and the straight line of his brow, they swirled with her favorite thing—secrets.

Interesting. And a little disturbing. If she'd met a dead end, she could have gone back to Tommy and gotten a different assignment, something that would maybe somehow fulfill the empty spot deep inside her, eradicate the odd sense of restlessness that had been dogging her.

But she had a feeling this was no dead end.

Pace's hair was longer now than in the picture, his face more tanned, but other than that, he looked the same, no digital doctoring required. He was, she found herself a little surprised to note, every bit as gorgeous in person. "It's not for your autograph," she said. "It's research. I'm a writer."

"A writer." Crossing his arms, he leaned against the railing of the walkway and looked at her while she tried not to notice how tightly and leanly muscled he was, or how his arms appeared to be ripped and corded with strength.

"I'm doing a series on the Heat for *American Online Living*," she said. "Your publicist made an appointment with me for an interview and pictures."

He didn't respond, but she could almost hear the resounding "no" come from him nevertheless. "I watched you pitch today," she said, figuring that might warm him up. People, especially men, liked to talk about themselves. Another lesson from good old mom—or more accurately, from the myriad of men she'd gone through.

But Pace didn't warm up. In fact, it was as if he vanished. One moment he was standing there willing to sign his picture for her, and the next he'd completely closed himself off, eyes cold, mouth grim.

"That was a closed practice," he finally said, sliding on a pair of mirrored Oakleys that probably cost more than her entire outfit. "You were trespassing."

"I sat on the grassy hill outside the facility."

"So you didn't trespass, fine. You were still out of line." He reshouldered his large duffel bag but then went still. Very still.

In *pain* still. And she instinctively took a step toward him. "You okay?"

Grinding his teeth, he held her off with a lifted hand. After letting out a careful breath, he turned and resumed walking.

There were other cars in the lot, including two cop cars. The police station was just up the street, and she'd learned that sometimes on breaks, the officers came to watch practices. Apparently *that* was okay. "Is it your arm?"

He kept walking.

"Your shoulder?"

More of his silence.

Huh. Sensing a pattern here . . . "When Samantha arranged this time for us to meet, she said you'd be happy to do so."

"Happy is the wrong adjective."

"I'd settle for resigned."

"I told Samantha to cancel the interview. I have another appointment." His voice was low and husky, with a whisper of the deep South.

Which meant they had something in common. "Is it your doctor?"

"Why would I need a doctor?"

"Because something made you pitch like crap today."

He let out a sound that might have been a laugh and stopped again. Behind his sunglasses, he gave nothing of himself away, just a wry amusement. "You know, most reporters try a different approach. A softer one."

"Yes," she said. "I imagine you get kissed up to quite a bit."

"I do." He pulled down his sunglasses and slid her a long look. "You could try it."

A little furl of something dangerous slid into her belly as she looked into his face, at the lines etched around his dark eyes, his strong jaw, the stubble . . . "I don't kiss up." But her knees wobbled. *Dammit.* "All I want is the interview."

He let his gaze run over her, and just as she knew he was trying to distract her, she also knew what he saw when he looked at her. Average brown hair, average body, average everything, including clothes. She wore a simple skirt, jacket, and athletic shoes, which she happened to be grateful for since he'd made her run through the lot. She wasn't exactly a fashion plate. Her budget didn't allow for it, but even if it had, she wouldn't have spent more. Her wardrobe made a statement, one that had started out as a protective gesture when she'd been very young but had become hard habit, and that statement said that she was smarter than she was pretty.

Unlike her, he hadn't dressed with a budget. He wore a pair of brown cargoes and an untucked white button-down, both clearly made for him, both revealing taste, sophistication, and just enough of that tough athletic body that he demanded so much of on a daily basis.

And it was a very nice body, she could admit, not that it mattered. His body wasn't what interested her. Okay, so it did, but it shouldn't. *Wouldn't.*

Be sweet but firm and distant. That's what she'd learned in her twenty-eight years, and it was all she'd ever needed to know when dealing with a man, any man. Be sweet but firm and distant, with everything, and ignore all sexual innuendoes unless she planned to get naked—which she most definitely did *not*. "I'll make this painless, Pace, I promise."

He shot her yet another look, this one with that disconcerting flare of awareness, but also filled with something else she recognized all too well—annoyance and exasperation. Yeah. She got that a lot.

"Look, any of the other guys would love the press," he said. "Seriously. Joe. Joe would probably buy you a five-star dinner. Or Henry. He sent the last reporter who interviewed him a bouquet of flowers the size of her car."

He was trying to get rid of her. Again, not a new feeling. "I can feed myself, and I'm not much of a flower girl. Besides, I plan to get to them. But you're first up."

"Fine." He let out a rough breath. "You've got five minutes."

"Now?"

"Or yesterday. Take your pick."

"Now, thank you." She once again reached into her purse for her pen and tore the cap off with her teeth while attempting to catch her breath.

Of course *he* wasn't breathing like a lunatic, but then again, he worked out for a living. "Okay, so how do you feel about the reports that the Heat has such great pitching because the ballpark is so hollow and vast that at night the heated, thick Santa Barbara air floats in from the ocean and prevents the fly balls from traveling too far?"

He made a sound like a tire going flat. "They've been saying the same thing about Dodger Stadium for years. People are going to believe what they want, and if they want to believe it's the stadium and we're cheating, whatever. Fact is, we win. Period."

"You don't mind that rumors like this take away from those wins?"

"No. Because it doesn't."

Instead of putting her off, his easy confidence had her

taking another, longer look at him. He took up a lot of space and suddenly seemed to be standing close, close enough to be affecting her pulse, and she wasted a few precious seconds trying to unscramble her brain. "By all accounts," she said, "you're a close-knit team."

"Yes."

"How difficult was it when Jim Wicks and Slam Rodriquez got traded, then suspended for testing positive for illegal enhancers just before the start of the season?"

He arched a brow. "Going for a lighthearted tone, are you?"

"This is my job."

"Well, your job sucks. And losing Jim and Slam sucked."

"Are there more of you on the team who are using?"

His jaw tightened. "Trick question."

"How so?"

"Jim never admitted to anything, and Slam claims innocence."

Yes, she'd read all the reports. And he was right. The question hadn't been kind. Or easy. That was also her job, unfortunately, and it was never kind or easy. "So are there? More of you using?"

He stopped at his car. "Three and a half."

"Three and a half what?"

"Minutes left in this interview."

"What about you personally," she said without missing a beat. "Did you—"

"No personal questions."

She considered him for a precious few seconds, how he stood there tall and silent and tense with what she'd bet her last dollar was pain. That softened her unexpectedly, and she had the oddest urge to touch him. "People want to read about you, Pace."

"They can read about me already. You can, too, just Google me."

"Already have. There's very little known about you other than your ball play, which is by all accounts amazing. You have world-class velocity and control, both reflected in your stats. You always use your head, and you're never without a game plan." She pulled a couple of magazines from her file to quote from. "You can pitch in any situation, you have the stuff to make it work, and you have guts. *Newsweek*." She shifted to another. "Batting against you is just about impossible, the balls come out of nowhere, no one can judge your rotation, speed, or the break of the ball. *Sports Illustrated*."

"Sounds good," he said. "Use that. You can add that my sexual prowess is unrivaled, if you're so inclined."

She laughed, even as a small part of her wanted to say "Prove it." "Come on. Give me more."

"Like?"

"Like what's wrong with your shoulder?"

"Nothing."

She stared at him and he stared back, stoic and tough as nails. "Wow, Pace. I don't know how I'm going to fit all this great new info into my article."

He smiled tightly. "You look capable. I'm sure you'll manage."

"Okay, let's try something easier."

He looked at her from behind those dark glasses, eyes hidden, thoughts inaccessible. "Let's," he said softly.

"What would you say makes your team so strangely beloved in the public eye?"

"Strangely? A real fan, huh?"

Actually, she did enjoy baseball, and in junior college she'd even made extra money running the scoreboard for home games. The money she'd earned had paid for her books and the Top Ramen noodles that had sustained her through those lean years, which had been virtually rich compared to her childhood. "What I think isn't relevant here."

"Given that you're the one setting the tone for your article, I think it is."

"Articles. Plural. To be run throughout the summer. What is it about your team that the public loves so much?"

"We win. One more question, that's it."

"And then I go away?"

"That would be great," he said with such feeling she laughed.

And as impatient as she might be, she also knew when to back off. "Fine. Last one—tell me what happened to you out in the pen today."

When his eyes lit with something that looked suspiciously like triumph, she knew she'd been had, that he'd successfully distracted her from something else. "Wait—"

"Oh no. Too late." He had his cover-boy smile in place. "Just a bad day. We all have them." He spread his hands. "Okay then, thanks for your time, buh-bye." He turned, and his bag fell off his shoulder to his forearm, jerking a wordless sound of pain from his lips.

Bad day, my ass. "You're in pain, Pace. A great deal of it."

"Yes. Doing interviews is fucking painful." Pale now, he let out a tight breath. "But I answered your single question. We're done here."

She touched him when he would have moved off, just a hand on his arm, and felt the heat and strength of him beneath her fingers. "Would you like some Advil?"

"No. Thanks."

His car was shiny and undoubtedly fast, and as a lead-foot herself, she felt a twinge of envy. "Would you say that your personal life often collides with your professional one?"

"Anyone ever tell you that you're relentless?" His color hadn't come back, but she was still breathing hard from their run out here, and it didn't escape her that he wasn't. "Or that you might want to consider cardio exercise?"

She was never insulted at the truth. "Maybe we could talk during one of *your* cardio workouts," she suggested.

His expression burned with challenge, even right through his dark lenses. "I run five miles every day. Feel free to join me."

A dare, uttered with the utmost confidence that she

wouldn't even try. But Holly never backed away from a dare, especially one spoken with the certainty that she couldn't measure up. He could have no idea that she'd spent a lifetime practicing at measuring up, and she was getting damned good at it.

Clearly confident he'd scared her off, he fished his keys from his pocket as she eyed the Mustang, itching to give it a spin. "Nineteen sixty . . . ?"

"Eight," he said.

"Nice collision of professional and personal." She'd bet this baby never conked out on him on Highway 1 during morning traffic—unlike hers, which had done exactly that only two weeks before.

"Yeah. Still not going to comment on my personal life."

Dammit.

Looking amused at her expression, and maybe at himself, too, he tossed his bag into the car, where it landed on one of the soft leather seats, then sucked in a breath at the movement.

Yeah, he was in bad shape, not that he wanted her to know given that trademark smile he managed to keep in place, the one that was designed to melt away a woman's panties.

Good thing she was immune.

Mostly.

Okay, she *wanted* to be immune, she really did, but he'd been lucky enough to be born one of those guys who brought certain things to a woman's mind, especially one who hadn't had any of those things in a while.

A long while . . .

"Time's up," he said with mock regret.

She smiled back, giving him her own brand of charm. He might be hot and charismatic and able to bend a woman's mind like Superman bent steel, but she was unflappable and stubborn to a tee. "Your publicist wants these articles written, and so does my boss, which means we're stuck with each other. So why don't we go grab a drink and you play nice and give me what I need in order to do my job?"

He studied her for a beat. "The last reporter really did offer to sleep with me."

"A fact that makes me shake my head at my entire gender." Certain portions of her anatomy quivered, making her a liar.

A corner of his mouth quirked as if he knew. "Okay, here's the thing. I know what Sam wants. I even know what you want. But it's not going to happen. Nice meeting you—"

"Woo hoo, Pace! Oh, *Pace* . . ."

At the voice behind them, a look of utter panic crossed his face, which was so odd and misplaced on his six foot two frame that Holly turned to see who'd put it there.

A young woman, barely five feet tall, was running through the hot day toward them, wearing only what appeared to be Pace's white home-game jersey, which fell nearly to her knees. In her hands was a large notebook covered with baseball cards—all Pace's—her flip-flops slapping the asphalt, her wild, curly dark hair poking out from beneath a Heat cap.

"Pace!" she called out, waving. "I caught you! I caught you! Ohmigod, luck is *finally* on my side!"

At that, Pace muttered something beneath his breath, which rhymed with that luck the fan claimed to have, and Holly choked out a short laugh.

Stopping just in front of them, the woman put a hand to her heaving chest and beamed up at Pace. "Are you free for dinner tonight to look over the scrapbook I made for you? I've brought all the recent clippings—well, except for that nasty one from *Sports Life* because they didn't put you in their fantasy lineup. They think you're too old to anchor their rotation. So are you?"

He blinked. "Too old?"

"No!" She laughed gaily. "Free for dinner, silly." Her voice was high and bubbly, sort of like Marilyn Monroe on helium. "Because last night you said no, and the night before you said no, and the night before that, too, so I was hoping—"

"Tia." Looking torn between running and wishing he could vanish into thin air, Pace took off his sunglasses and scrapped a hand down his face. "You're not supposed to be here, remember? Your doctor told you that, and so did the police. You promised."

"I know, but you never got a formal restraining order on me. I checked. I know you wouldn't want to do that to your future wife, because if I get arrested again, I can't afford to pay for the bail, not after I hocked my Great Aunt Dee's pearls for the last two times, so . . ." She finally noticed Holly, and all the air seemed to deflate from her lungs, coming out in one unhappy whoosh. "Who are you?"

Holly opened her mouth, but Pace spoke first. "My girlfriend," he said, shocking both Tia *and* Holly when he put a proprietary hand on Holly's arm. His hand was huge and warm, his palm calloused. He looked into Holly's eyes, his own suddenly not nearly as cold and distant, or even wryly amused, but . . .

Desperate.

Pace Martin looked desperate, which was dumbfounding enough, but then he tightened his grip and said, "Hurry up, honey. We'll be late."

Honey?

Before Holly could process that, he shoved her none-too-gently toward his bad-boy car.

"I—"

"Shh," he muttered in her ear.

Oh no, he didn't. He didn't just shush her, and she sent him a glacial stare, but he shot her one of those hey-baby smiles, the one that matched the picture he'd taken for *People* magazine, while hissing out the corner of his mouth, "I'll pay you a thousand dollars not to argue with me right now."

A thousand dollars? That'd make a nice addition to her never-be-poor-again fund. "You've got to be kidding," she whispered.

"Okay, two. Two thousand," he grated out. "Jesus, just hurry."

Two thousand dollars.

Holy smokes.

And he clearly *wasn't* kidding. Another shove and she was in his car, and he was locking the doors, accelerating them out of the lot with an impressive exhibition of speed as she twisted to look back. Tia stood there hugging her scrapbook, staring after them, looking forlorn.

"Don't look at her," Pace directed. "Trust me on this."

Holly gawked at him. "You've got to be kidding me," she repeated.

"No, seriously. Looking at her only eggs her on."

She laughed in further shock, even as her stomach quivered at the hair-raising turn he was executing at speeds better suited for a racetrack than the narrow, curvy lanes of the highway. She gripped the console. "You're more afraid of that little tiny thing than me?"

"Only very slightly."

She tightened her grip as he took them into another hair-raising turn with shocking ease. It gave her a thrill, a kick of adrenaline. "This is going to cost you."

He sighed, long and weary sounding, downshifting into the next turn. "Don't I know it."

Chapter 3

Things could be worse. Suppose your errors were counted and published every day, like those of a baseball player.

"**I** figure the price for this abduction should fit the crime."

Pace took his eyes off the road and glanced at the reporter in his passenger seat. She wasn't beautiful. Irritating people couldn't be beautiful, not in his opinion, and all reporters were irritating. Besides, she was too . . . careful looking. Yeah. That was it. She wore . . . efficient business clothes over some more than decent curves—which he happened to be a sucker for—but there was that whole annoyance factor. She had light brown hair carefully pulled back, matching light brown eyes that carefully saw everything, and a careful smile she'd attempted to manipulate him with.

He figured that was standard reporter issued.

He wondered if it gave her a headache, all that carefulness. She was certainly giving him one, and given the pain he was fighting in his shoulder, that was saying something. "Abduction?"

"Yes," she said. "That's what it's called when one person takes another against their will."

"I offered you two thousand dollars, and you jumped into this car so fast my head spun."

"Well, you were combining my two favorite things. Money and getting my interview."

"I never promised you the interview."

"It was implied," she said sweetly.

Ha! If she was sweet, he'd eat his shorts. "No, it wasn't implied. I purposely *didn't* imply it."

"I'll be happy to offer a trade. I'll reduce the fee from two grand to one," she said magnanimously.

"You'll—" He laughed in disbelief as his cell phone buzzed an incoming text from Wade:

Three reasons to get down here. Brandy, Cindy, and Sweet Pea. Hand to heaven–SWEET PEA, that's her real name.

"You're not supposed to text and drive in California," his reporter said from the next seat. "It's illegal."

Pace tossed the phone to the console. Sweet Pea. Over the years he'd seen or heard it all, from the crazy Hollywood underground clubs to the White House. But as ridiculous as it sounded even in his own head, having women want him for the sake of how fast he threw or how big his bank account was had gotten old. "I can't text and drive— I'm not that talented."

She didn't reply, thank God. Silence. One of his favorite things. He took in the Pacific Ocean on their left, the Santa Ynez Mountains in all their dramatic and rugged summer glory on their right, casting gigantic shadows on the highway and water. Midsummer was a great season, and not just because of baseball. The weather was fantastic, hot and nearly rainless, and the sage and scrub terrain was mind-soothingly beautiful as the late afternoon sun made its way down toward sea. Pace opened his window, adding the noisy warm wind to the mix, which he hoped would keep her from asking any questions.

"Do you get out of speeding tickets because you're famous?"

Or not. When his cell phone rang at that exact moment, he considered it a gift and reached for it without even looking at the ID, a huge risk on a normal day, but he desperately needed the distraction. "Go," he said, hitting the speaker button, leaving the phone on the dash so his passenger couldn't complain about the risk, and also so he couldn't get his second ticket of the month.

"Not answering your texts?" asked Wade.

Pace had to roll his window back up to hear him. "I'm driving."

"Good. I'm at Jax, and you owe me a beer. Get your ass over here."

"Can't." He glanced at Holly, who was soaking up the conversation with open curiosity. "Got a situation."

Holly rolled her eyes.

"You getting laid?" Wade asked.

"Hey," Pace said quickly. "On speaker, and I'm not alone here."

"Sorry." Wade paused. "So are you?"

"No!"

"Man, do *not* tell me you got a bunch of screaming women surrounding your car again."

"One time," Pace said on a sigh as Holly snorted. "That happened one time."

"And I saved you. I keep telling you that edgy, brooding thing you've got going on is never going to cut it with the ladies, but you don't listen—"

"Okay, what part of *not alone in the car* don't you get?"

Wade laughed. "Who's with you?"

"I am." Holly leaned forward. "Holly Hutchins."

"Well, hello, darlin'," Wade purred silkily. "You as gorgeous as you sound?"

"She's a reporter," Pace said. "So watch your mouth."

"I'll watch whatever she wants me to watch."

Obviously, Wade was Pace's virtual opposite. The guy had practically grown up on the streets, seeing more as a kid than anyone should see, and he still always had an easy smile on his face. His motto was work hard but play harder. His California-surfer good looks didn't hurt either, but it was his laid-back nature that had women flocking to him wherever he went.

Holly would flock to Wade, too; it was just a matter of time . . .

"I'm doing a series of in-depth articles on the Heat," Holly said to the cell phone. "From a personal angle. What makes you guys so popular, what makes you tick, who you are . . . I'd love to set up a time to meet with you and get your thoughts."

"Just say when," Wade told her. "I'll be there."

Holly sent a smug smile in Pace's direction that said, *See how easy that was?*

"He's a publicity slut," Pace said in his own defense. "And an attention slut, too."

"Hey," Wade said. "True. But hey."

"I want to hear more about Pace and the women surrounding his car," Holly said to the phone. "Sounds like a good story."

"No." Pace didn't need a recap of how he'd been spotted at the grocery store and besieged. Wade had come to his rescue, happily answering questions and signing autographs, ending up with a date every night for two weeks running as a reward.

They'd been best friends for years, and Pace still had no idea how Wade handled all the attention the way he did, letting everything bead off his back.

But Pace didn't need saving now. He could handle one damn woman. The wind had whipped her hair, making a mess of it. She was trying to smooth it back into place, but failing miserably. Inexplicably, she looked softer with it all wild, and more approachable. Even pretty.

Clearly, the pain in his shoulder was going to his head.

"So about that drink," Wade said. "Bring Holly. There's a nice crowd, not too many bunnies."

"Bunnies?" Holly asked, giving up on corralling her hair to look at Pace.

"A group of fans."

"*Female* fans," Wade amended. "They follow our season. They appreciate our talent and enjoy our . . . great attitudes. One's named Sweet Pea."

Pace felt Holly studying him, taking mental notes. "I see the talent," she said. "But only a bad attitude."

Wade laughed.

"Nice," Pace said, nodding at her. "Thanks."

"Hey, I say that about you all the time," Wade told him. "Great talent, bad 'tude."

Pace rolled his eyes. Some wingman. "Say good-bye, Wade."

"Come on. Drive over here. Prove you haven't forgotten how to have fun."

But he very possibly had. "I have stuff."

"Stuff? What could be more important than wooing that pretty lady in your car?"

"There is no wooing going on."

"See now, *that's* why you never get laid anymore—"

"Reporter," Pace said, pinching the bridge of his nose. *"In my car."*

"Which is why you should—"

Pace reached out and shut his phone.

"That wasn't very nice of you," Holly said.

"He'll get over it."

"So . . . you get stalked by women a lot?"

He opened his window again, which didn't stop her from talking.

"I'm just making conversation, Pace. Being friendly. You should try it sometime."

They were on a stretch of highway where he had nowhere to turn around, and nowhere to dump her out. Which meant he was stuck with her. "I'm not feeling all that friendly."

"Should have taken the Advil."

The wind was working wonders on her again. Besides

her hair—which had rioted completely now—her cheeks were tinged pink. Her jacket was whipping around, too, opening a little, making her look a whole hell of a lot less buttoned-up. Oddly disoriented by that, he glanced at the clock on the dash. "Listen, I really do have to be somewhere." Several somewheres. It'd been a long while since his time had been his own. "I'll call you a cab, have it meet up with us to take you back to your car." He reached for his cell phone. "I'm sure Tia's gone by now."

"I can't believe you're afraid of her."

She could be amused by this all she wanted, but Tia was more than just a five foot pain in his neck. Twice she'd gotten into the practice arena and climbed onto the field during home games. She'd attempted to break into the clubhouse as well, and he'd swear under oath that she'd been at his own house, walking the perimeter of his yard trying to find a way inside there, too. "Just do me a favor and stay clear of her. For your sake. Now I really have to—"

"How about this . . ." She pulled the cell phone from his hand and shut it. "I just come along to wherever you're going."

Yeah. Hell. That's what he'd figured she'd say.

"Did you know that baseball players, pitchers especially, are usually blessed—or cursed, depending on how you look at it—with a natural physical prowess and acute mental agility? It manifests into self-confidence and mental toughness. Or, as some would say more clearly, arrogance."

When he didn't respond, she slid him an amused look. "It seems to be most prevalent in successful players. It stems from the desire to make things happen."

"Good to know."

"Did you also know you have to be one in two million to have the total package of physical and psychological abilities required to succeed in baseball at its highest level of competition?"

No. That was a new one.

"What's fascinating about that is you've climbed this

incredibly steep pyramid of players to make it to the top of a highly selective and narrow pool, which means you're incredible under pressure, and yet you crumble like a little girl at the thought of an interview. Interesting, Pace. Very interesting."

He stared at her in bafflement. "What do you want from me?"

"The interview."

"I really did ask Samantha to cancel." Well, actually, technically, he'd asked his manager to get Sam to cancel. But now that he thought about it, Gage had been surrounded by women at the time, at a high-powered fashion show event they'd all attended for the Heat's 4 The Kids charity, and Gage's eyes *had* been sort of glazed over when Pace had made the request. It was entirely possible Gage hadn't heard a word Pace had said.

"No worries," Holly said. "This has worked out for me so far. After all, I got to learn all about your women problems, getting stalked, surrounded—"

"Funny," he said, and found her smiling at him.

And damn if there wasn't something contagious about it, about her. She was actually quite sharp, and pretty. But he didn't want to be amused, or attracted.

He wanted to be alone.

Given how much of his life was spent in the spotlight, he really liked being by himself. At this level of his life, there were two types of ball players: those in it for the money, and those in it for the love of the game. He was in the latter, definitely. He loved the game, period, and would play it with or without the money, preferably also without the reporters, pretty or otherwise.

He just wanted to play. He loved everything about baseball—the feel of the ball in his hand, the whizzing of the air as the ball left his fingers at ninety-plus miles an hour, the smell of the field right after it was cut, the sensation of standing on the mound, watching the batter walk up

to the plate, having Wade send him a cocky smile and a sign
for the next pitch . . .

Everything.

It was his passion, it was his heart, it was his entire life.
So he understood why people wanted to watch.

What he didn't understand was people wanting to watch
him *outside* the game, as if he were a movie star. It made
no sense, and plus, it bugged the hell out of him. "What if
I promised you that aside from the game, there's nothing
out of the ordinary about me?"

She arched a brow. "That's not what *Playboy* said."

"You read *Playboy*?"

"Did you see last month's cover story, the one where
they asked their readers which professional athletes would
make the best lovers?"

Ah, Christ. He knew what was coming. "No."

"You were in the top five, big guy."

When he shook his head, she laughed. And when he
didn't join her, she sighed. "Trying to lighten the mood
here, Pace. Specifically your mood. How come no one ever
thinks I'm funny?"

"Because you're not?"

"I'll have you know, I was voted class clown."

Now *he* laughed. "Sorry, but no. No possible way."

She was frowning at him, still trying to keep her hair
out of her face. "Why do people say sorry before they say
something rude?"

"Admit it, you were the bookworm who did the football
players' homework for manicure money, right?"

She crossed her arms, lifted her nose to nosebleed
heights.

"Oh yeah," he said. "I'm right."

"Basketball team," she muttered, looking away. "I did
the *basketball* players' homework."

He could picture her, all carefully buttoned up and serious, nose buried in a stack of books doing work for a

bunch of lazy, entitled jocks. He'd been one of those
jocks.

"And I didn't do it for manicures either," she told him.
"I was never that shallow."

Now that he believed. She might be a pesky know-it-all,
but nothing about her said shallow, trite, or conceited. "I
was shallow in high school."

And more, probably.

"Was?" she asked, looking pointedly around the leather
interior of his obviously expensive car.

Yeah, yeah. On the outside looking in, he had it all: the
sizzling hot pro-baseball career, women leaving panties
with their phone numbers on his hotel room doors . . . a
shallow lifestyle.

Sue him.

But ever since his shoulder had started to go and he'd
realized he was nothing outside the game, it'd all started to
crash down on his head. It was humbling.

Demeaning.

And, if he thought too much, devastating.

He exited the highway and drove down the twisting,
narrow roadway now entirely shadowed by the mountains
that isolated the city of Santa Barbara from the rest of the
world. He pulled into a small, out-of-the-way park and took
in the athletic field, the low-lying creek next to it, and felt
his heart lighten slightly. The field was rundown. The
empty lot next to the park had been abandoned long ago,
with grass growing through the cracks in the asphalt and
graffiti on the walls of the abandoned store that was nothing but a shack now. A For Sale sign had come unnailed on
one side and was tipped, hanging to the ground.

The place had been up for sale for years. The last time
Pace had checked into it on a whim, his attorney had told
him only an idiot would buy it.

"Oh God." Holly turned to him suspiciously. "You're not
bringing me to a drug deal, are you?"

"Yeah. Because I always bring nosy reporters with me

when I buy my drugs." He sighed when she didn't smile. "That was a joke. Because I *was* the class clown. Wait here."

"But—"

"Wait, or call a cab." He pulled some cash out of his wallet for the ride back. "Nice meeting you," he added in case she bailed.

Which he was betting on.

Hoping on.

Chapter 4

If a woman has to choose between catching a fly ball and saving an infant's life, she will choose to save the infant's life without even considering if there are men on base.

—Dave Barry

Pace's mind was still on Holly as he pulled his duffel bag from the back of his car. Okay, so she'd turned out to be far more pretty than annoying; he still didn't have time for her. Gritting his teeth at the movement of his shoulder, he strode toward the field under the late afternoon sun, meeting the guys on the pitcher's mound.

They were a ragtag team of middle school kids who played here every single day. They didn't belong to any school team; no one would have them. There was a rec center league, but it was too far from here, closer to the center of town, and these kids didn't have the means to get there, much less pay the fees to join that league. They needed something here, on the edge of the county, to keep them busy and out of trouble, and he'd made that something baseball.

He'd discovered them one day after a particularly tough game of his own, where he'd pitched like shit, hurt like hell, and had come here just to stand on a field where talent didn't matter, only heart did.

"You're late," Chipper said, tossing Pace their ball. Chipper was their catcher, a term used quite loosely since

mostly the only things he ever caught were Ding Dongs.
Literally. He could catch Ding Dongs in his mouth. He was
the park champ.

"Don't worry, Pace," River piped in, slurping from a
soda, making Pace's mouth water. "We won't make ya take
a lap." River was their pitcher. Another loose term, as River
had a helluva time getting the ball anywhere near home
plate, much less over it.

They were working on that. "I brought you guys something." Pace's fingers actually twitched to yank that soda
away from the kid and down it. Christ, he missed Dr Pepper
like he'd miss a limb.

"Chocodiles?" This from a hopeful Chipper.

"Better." Pace let the bag drop and crouched down to
unzip it, revealing a pile of brand new leather gloves, all
infinitely higher quality than what they'd been using.

The guys hit their knees to get a closer look. "Dude : . ."

"Sweet . . ."

"Tight . . ."

Pace watched them all grab a glove and marvel over
them with more joy that he'd gotten out of his last three
wins. He rubbed his shoulder absently, wondering what
was wrong with him that he was brooding about . . . hell,
he didn't even know. "When you get home, put a ball inside each glove and wrap it with a rubber band or string to
break them in." He rifled through the bag. "And Chipper,
I brought you a new bat."

"I have that aluminum one."

Pace shook his head. "Wood. Wood is better."

"But I have a huge sweet spot on the aluminum—"

"Yours doesn't ring when you hit anymore."

"It's because he doesn't hit anything," River quipped, and
Chipper might have launched at him but Pace straightened
and gripped him by the back of the shirt just in time.

"He's right," he told the kid. "You need batting practice.
When your bat doesn't ring anymore, it means it's dead.
It's not your fault."

"It's not all the way dead, not yet—"

"Wood," Pace repeated stubbornly, and handed it over, which produced more oohs and aahs. "This baby's sweet spot is all hickory. You're going to love her." Wood was more expensive, but it was required in the pros, and Pace wanted them to get used to the feel of it. He rose to his feet. "I can't stay."

This was met with a bunch of groans and protests, but Pace just shook his head. "Sorry, I've got a—"

"A chick," Chipper said.

"Doctor's appointment—"

"Don't look now," Chipper whispered loud enough for the living dead to hear. "But you have a chick getting out of your car. She's walking along the creek, coming this way."

The "chick" smiled at the guys as she came close. Holly's hair was carefully tucked up again, and she'd buttoned her jacket, but her eyes sparkled with life as she crossed the patchy weeds masquerading as grass and came to a stop right in their midst. "New equipment," she said with a smile.

"Pace brought it all," Chipper said. "He's the best."

The others all nodded emphatically.

"He's always bringing us stuff," River added. "He's like our skipper."

"That's what a team manager is called by the guys," Chipper informed her.

"I know." Holly was looking at Pace with a speculative curiosity in her sharp light brown eyes. "I think that's lovely."

"When he gave up Dr Pepper, he brought us the cases he'd had stashed at his place so he wouldn't fall off the wagon," Chipper told her. "Oh and he takes us for pizza, too."

"Well that must be fun. And he coaches you."

"Yeah. He's the best pitcher in the majors right now."

"Chipper." Pace shook his head. They were trying to sell him like a used car.

Chipper ignored him. "Did you know he packs high heat? It means he's got an unusually fast fastball. So technically he could be a closer, but he's an ace starter."

Great. His own personal cheering squad. "She doesn't need to hear—"

"Are you Pace's girlfriend?" Chipper asked her.

She laughed, a sweet musical sound that had Pace taking a second look at her.

"Definitely not." She sounded extremely amused at the question, so much so that he found himself taking offense. What the hell. He wasn't a bad boyfriend—when he chose to be a boyfriend, that is, which, granted, he didn't do a lot. Women liked his wallet but usually not the fact that for seven months out of the year he was pretty much physically and emotionally unavailable.

"His date then," River guessed.

Another laugh from Holly. "No."

"You don't have to sound like it would be so distasteful," Pace muttered.

"To date you?" She was still smiling. "Really?"

Okay, now he felt downright irritated. "What would be wrong with dating me?"

"I'm not sure we have enough time to cover it all."

And what the hell did *that* mean? He opened his mouth to ask, but she dropped to her knees next to the boys with utter disregard for her skirt and was oohing and aahing over the gloves. His cell phone rang, distracting him. It was Samantha, the bane of Pace's existence at the moment. "You didn't cancel my interview," he said, stepping away from the gang so he couldn't be overheard by one nosy reporter and a bunch of even nosier kids.

"I didn't, no," Samantha said. "Was I supposed to?"

"Hell, yes." Behind him he heard Chipper asking Holly if she was a baseball groupie. Jesus. He strained his ears to catch Holly's response.

"No," she murmured. "I'm not much of a groupie type."

"Do you play baseball?"

"Pace?" came Sam's voice in his ear. "You still there?"

"Yeah. I'm still here."

"Holly Hutchins is a reporter who's known for the nitty-gritty. The owners want her to do this series to give us some good publicity. She's supposedly a little uptight and reserved . . ."

Gee, he hadn't noticed.

"But she's fair, and very good, so be nice."

"Uh-huh." At the moment, Holly didn't seem quite as uptight and reserved as she had back at the facilities, not with her knees in the dirt, smiling and laughing with the kids, telling River that she'd grown up in a rough neighborhood, where hanging around outside on a field hadn't been such a good idea, so no, she'd never learned to play baseball.

"Sucks," Danny said, their shortstop. Which was also his nickname, given that he hadn't had his seventh-grade growth spurt yet. Or any spurt.

"Pace?" Sam said in his ear.

"I never wanted this interview, Sam. Give it to one of the other guys who'll love it. Wade, maybe." Who'd get into Holly's pants in thirty minutes. "No, wait. Give her to Ty." Ty didn't have sex during the season, ever, which made him safe. Though why Pace cared, he had no idea. "He's been wanting more press now that he's having a strong year."

"It's good publicity," Sam repeated. "For *you*. You're our star, Pace, and you know it."

"It's only good press if she spins it that way, and trust me, I haven't made the best impression."

"Oh for God's sake." Samantha sighed, the sound of female exasperation personified. "How hard is it to smile and make nice for the pretty lady?"

Harder than she could imagine.

On the mound, Danny was still trying to sell Pace to Holly. "I bet if you dated him," the kid said, "he'd teach you how to play."

Holly turned and gave Pace the serious once over. She didn't look too impressed, so her next words didn't surprise him. "I tend to date a more cerebral type."

"I'm cerebral," Chipper told her eagerly. "I got an eighty-one in science."

"Do the interview, Pace," Sam said in Pace's ear. "It won't kill you, I promise." She sounded amused, and hell if he wasn't getting a little tired of amusing females at his expense.

And dammit, he was plenty cerebral.

"I'm going now," Sam told him. "Just be nice. Women respond to nice. She's a tough one, I'll give you that, but I doubt you've ever met a woman you couldn't crack. Flash her that million-dollar charm and give us some good press."

He sighed. "I always give good press."

She laughed, but he could hear her fingers already clicking over her keyboard, as always multitasking efficiently and effectively. "Oh, and if you could *not* sleep with her, that would be really great."

Sleep with her?

Fuuuuurthest thing from his mind.

Not even a possibility.

Not even a spec of possibility.

Even if her hair was suddenly catching the sunlight, looking like spun gold. And her smile, as she aimed it at the kids, wasn't for his benefit. Hell, she wasn't even looking at him. Nope, she wasn't playing them to get into Pace's good graces; she was being heartwarmingly genuine. She had some sweet curves on her for such a careful thing, too, curves that would be even nicer with less clothing.

Okay, so maybe he'd given the *briefest* thought to sleeping with her.

The kids were walking her farther out onto the field, fawning all over themselves to try to impress her, and she was impressed.

Or at least acting it.

She was talking to them, not down to them as so many stupid adults tended to do, but *to* them, in a way she hadn't with Pace. Yeah, she was definitely much more open now, and he felt as though he was getting his first real glimpse of her as she nodded, listening to everything Chipper said. She walked with confidence and smiled with compassion.

Two of his favorite things in a woman.

Danny handed her a glove, turning her to face River, and Pace straightened. No.

Oh no.

Oh shit. *"No!"* he yelled just as River let one fly, low and screwball as usual.

And hard, very hard.

Pace ran toward them but not fast enough, and Holly caught the ball.

With her forehead.

Chapter 5

People ask me what I do in winter when there's no baseball. I'll tell you what I do. I stare out the window and wait for spring.

—Rogers Hornsby

Holly flew backward and hit the ground hard enough to rattle every thought right out of her head. *"Fother mucker,"* she muttered, lying still on the prickly crabgrass, listening to the creek beat up the rocks as she took mental stock.

Arms? Still in place.

Legs? Also still in place.

Her head? Not quite sure–

"Did we kill her?" came a horrified whisper.

"Back up, guys." This was Pace's low, calm voice. "Give her some room to breathe."

"Are you sure she's breathing? Pace, give her CPR!" Chipper said urgently. "Hurry!"

Holly had the strongest urge to keep still just to see if he'd really do it, but her body wouldn't play along, because what if there were ants on the grass? Plus she could feel her hair was a complete mess again, and worse, it was entirely possible that her skirt had flown up. She opened her eyes and locked gazes with Pace, his dark with all sorts of things, with concern leading the pack. His hair was wind-blown and tousled, and he was frowning, and . . . and she had to admit, he sure was something to look at, even with all that bad attitude.

"Anyone have a sweatshirt?" he asked over his shoulder.

When everyone just shook their heads, he unbuttoned his shirt and, oh good Lord, shrugged out of it, bunching it up to slip beneath her head like a pillow.

Don't look at him, she told herself. Don't look—

She looked.

Sweet Jesus.

Smooth tanned skin. Hard sinew. And those shoulders were broad enough to block the sun from piercing her eyes. And then there were those six-pack abs . . .

"CPR?" he asked politely with a hint of irony, the lean, carved lines of his face making him look incredibly tough, and incredibly handsome.

Yes, please, she thought. "Don't even think about it."

"You about done napping then?"

"Ha." What was it about his voice? And those eyes . . . Now that she was lying still and he was staring at her, she could see they weren't filled with just that sharp edge and a good amount of trouble, but something else, too. Something dark and soulful, something that she couldn't quite put her finger on, but whatever it was, it mesmerized.

"You have a good goose egg going," he murmured. "Your head hurt?"

Yeah, now that he mentioned it. As she sat up, he slipped his arms around her to help. Arms that were warm and hard as they tightened on her to hold her still.

Against him.

Oh boy. His chest was smooth and warm and hard as stone, and she wanted to both touch and nibble.

And lick. Could she pretty please lick?

"Holly?"

"Yeah?"

"Are you all right?"

She could hear genuine worry in his voice. Interesting.

As was her body's reaction, which was an urge to curl in and cuddle.

Cuddle.

She never cuddled.

She was too busy to cuddle. "Yes. I'm fine." She struggled to get up, but again he held her still.

"Give yourself a minute." He was also irritated, which was really unfair, because she'd almost had that ball.

Okay, she hadn't almost had that ball. "I'm really okay."

"Good." He leaned in very close. "Fother mucker?"

"There are kids present." Embarrassment blocked her throat until he ran a surprisingly gently finger over her forehead. *"Ouch!"*

He frowned, and she said, "I'm okay."

"Tell me what your name is and why you're such a pest, and maybe we'll agree that you're okay."

She lifted a hand to his face. "Did you know when you're irritated, you have a very slight Southern accent? Actually, it's more of a drawl. Texas?"

His gaze narrowed. "Your name," he said tightly.

"Holly, and I'm just doing my job."

"Not playing ball like that, you're not." But he let her slide out of his arms. "A reporter writing on the sport should be able to play it."

She rolled her eyes, decided it was a gift that she even could, and got shakily to her feet. Ignoring the throbbing ache between her eyes, she smiled into River's terrified gaze. The poor kid was pale, and looking like he'd just killed a puppy. "I'm okay, River, I promise."

"I'm sorry I threw so hard. I mean, who knew I even could? And you took it right dead center, too." Giving her an instant replay, he poked himself between the eyes. "Bull's-eye. And then you went flying backward like you'd been shot, and hit the ground solid."

Yeah, she remembered that part all too well. "In my research about baseball players, I've learned they have faster reflexes than the norm."

"If that's the case, I don't think you're a baseball player," Chipper said solemnly.

She sighed. "I think you're right. Well, I hope I was at least entertaining." She rubbed her temples and wished she hadn't been in such a hurry to get up, because her legs felt wobbly.

Pace was watching her carefully, slipping back into his shirt, which was really a shame.

"What's my name?" he asked her.

"Hot Arrogant Baseball Stud?"

He blinked.

"Sorry. I think the hit loosened my tongue. But I'm fine," she said quickly when she saw the boys' horrified reaction. "Really."

"Good, cuz it'd have sucked to kill Pace's girlfriend," River said with huge relief.

"I'm not his girl"—but they'd all begun to move off, spreading out into the field with their new gloves— "friend." She absently rubbed her butt, realizing that hurt, too.

"Need a hand with that?"

She glanced up as Pace smiled. And it was the oddest thing. The good humor changed his face, making him look like one of the kids, both younger and far more carefree than she'd seen him except in pictures. His eyes sparkled, fine lines fanning out from the outer corners. His mouth was curved, and even though he was having fun at her expense, she felt her own smile reluctantly tug at her mouth as they stared at each other for several long beats.

"Hot Arrogant Baseball Stud?" he repeated softly.

"Are you objecting to hot or stud?"

"Arrogant, actually."

Okay, so he had a quick wit and a sense of humor to go with those looks and, she guessed, more than the average smarts. And in spite of her best efforts to remain immune, she felt drawn to him.

Which was not good.

Not good at all.

They were still standing practically hip to hip. In fact, he was still supporting her, gaze still locked on hers. His smile slowly faded.

And so did hers.

Her heart gave a good hard leap against her ribs because suddenly she felt . . . hot. Very hot. A heavy beat passed, and then another, each filled with . . . well, she wasn't quite sure what.

Okay, that was a lie.

She knew exactly what. Anticipation. And a reluctant attraction. And enough heat to have her palms going damp, which was odd because the mountain peaks were shading them and there was the nicest sea breeze brushing through the trees, through her hair, brushing her face and her aching head.

"I've got to go," he said quietly. "I really do have somewhere else I'm supposed to be."

"It's okay."

"You sure?"

"Yeah."

"Then maybe you could stand on your own?"

"Oh!" Oh good God. She was leaning all over him. She rectified that by pulling free and backing up a few steps. Turning, she eyed the kids, thinking maybe she'd stay and hang out for a few minutes, chat with them some more. Sometimes her best stuff came from unexpected sources. Besides, it might be a nice human touch to her article on Pace . . . But damn, she was dizzy. Yeah, she was just going to sit for a minute, right here, right in the grass—

With a low oath, Pace immediately crouched at her side, brushing the hair from her face to look into her eyes. "Holly."

"I'm good."

He let out a rough breath. "You're such a liar."

"Hey." She blinked her vision clear. Sort of. *Dammit.* "I never lie."

"Everyone lies."

"Not me."

His gaze turned speculative. "So if I asked you, say, what you really thought of me, you'd say . . ."

"That you're a little full of yourself, but you do have more redeeming qualities than I'd counted on. Such as being nice to stupid reporters who catch with their foreheads."

He arched a brow. "An honest woman. Imagine that."

"You look so surprised."

"I am."

"Then you're hanging out with the wrong women."

"That's undoubtedly quite true." Still looking at her very closely, he shook his head. "I can't leave you here."

"Sure you can." She managed a smile. "I'm just going to sit here in the sun and write up some notes. It's a gorgeous day. And I'm not dizzy at all. At least not now as much as I was."

"Okay, that's it. Come on." He pulled her upright with him, keeping his hands on her when she wasn't quite steady on her feet. "I know you had your heart set on grilling the kids, but I can't let you do that."

"Why, what do they know?"

"Holly."

"Just kidding, I wouldn't do that."

"No?"

She grimaced guiltily. "Not grill, precisely. But maybe speak gently with . . ."

He looked into her eyes. Then his gaze dropped, slowly taking in the rest of her features, and when he got to her mouth, she felt another of those odd flutters low in her belly. He didn't step back, he didn't step away. Nope, he stayed right in her personal space, which normally would have bugged the hell out of her, but she didn't feel bugged so much as . . .

Jittery.

It was the bump on the head. It had to be.

"I can see those wheels turning, Holly."

"I'm just thinking that maybe you're not quite the jerk you want me to believe."

"Yes, I am," he said. "A big jerk. An asshole."

"You run from stalkers rather than call the police. You play baseball with kids and bring them new gear. You help stupid reporters who catch with their foreheads. There's a soft side to you, Pace Martin."

"Hell no, there's not."

He looked so insulted, she laughed. "Oh yes, there is." She put her hand on his chest. The hard, warm muscles there did not escape her notice, no sirree, they did not. "A big old softie, deep down inside." Very deep, past all that delicious sinew.

Shaking his head, he turned her toward the car. "Let's go, Sherlock."

"Where to?"

"To get your damn head checked. And probably I should have mine examined while we're at it for even putting you in my car in the first place. Sorry guys," he called out. "We've got to go."

Chipper just waggled his eyebrows and gave a thumbs-up. "Gotcha."

"Stop that. I have an away series, but I'll be back in a few days."

"Phillies," Chipper said. "You're going to kick ass."

Pace narrowed his eyes. "Are you allowed to say *ass*?"

"Not at home, but we're not at home. Don't forget to tell the flight attendant that you can't have Dr Pepper. They make you feel like crap. Oh, and pack some spare uniform pants. He always busts his zippers," he explained to Holly.

"Sounds like a problem." She thought it was adorable how the kids seemed to take as good care of him as he did of them.

"Stay out of trouble," Pace said to each of them and took Holly to his car, keeping his hand on her the whole walk back, which she found both disconcerting and unexpectedly sweet. It was a big hand, warm and calloused. Very male.

Yeah, she really did need her head checked. She slid in his car, put on the seat belt and met his dark gaze. Poor baby, he looked so uncomfortable that he'd ended up with her again.

"What's so funny?" he asked when she couldn't hold back her smile.

"You. You're afraid of me."

"What? I am not."

"You so are."

"Maybe a little." He pulled out of the lot with more speed than required, and hit the highway. "Look," he said, "I'm sorry about the hit to the head."

"Sorry enough to give me the interview?"

He sighed. "I've already admitted that I'm an ass. You, however, neglected to mention that you're a pain in the ass."

She laughed, but that hurt her head so she leaned back, enjoying the sparkling ocean, the ridge of the mountains so dramatic in the late sun, the warmth of it on her face, the speed of the car, not to mention the way he handled said car. "You're right. I am a pain in the ass. I should have disclosed that up front. Disclosure is important to me."

"Why?"

The question surprised her. "Childhood trauma," she quipped. "Involves Santa. It's not pretty."

She couldn't hear his answer over the roar of the wind, but she did catch the quirk of his lips, and for a quick beat, she experienced that odd flutter low in her belly again.

Probably just her brains being scrambled by the ball. But she wasn't scrambled enough not to realize they were still going in the opposite direction of her car. "We're going the wrong way."

"Uh-huh. Since you accused me of abducting you, I thought I'd make it for real."

They came into town. Holly knew Santa Barbara was sometimes called the American Riviera, but it never failed to surprise her how beautiful it was with its intriguing and

charming mix of colorful Old West and Spanish cultures.
Pace pulled off the highway and drove down a few tourist-
filled streets before pulling into a parking lot behind a
three-story glass and steel building that overlooked the
ocean. He climbed out of the car and walked around to
the passenger side. "Let's go, Nosey Nose," he said as he
opened her door.

"Where to?"

"Just come on."

"How very passive-aggressive of you."

He just reached for her hand and pulled her toward the
building. "It's called pleading the fifth. And it's a constitu-
tional right."

"A kidnapper *and* a scholar."

He slid her a long look behind his shades. "Haven't you
ever heard the saying that you get more flies with honey
than vinegar?"

She might have answered, but then she read the sign
on the door he held open for her: *Santa Barbara Medical
Group.*

"Don't be silly," she said, dragging her feet. "I don't
need to go in there. I'm good."

He shoved his sunglasses to the top of his head. His
eyes were calm, and very amused. "Don't be scared. I'll
hold your hand."

For some reason, that sounded incredibly intimate, and
her brain went to a naughty place.

Clueless, he tried to nudge her none too gently inside, his
hand at the small of her back, but she stood on the threshold, a little overtaken by the odd and yet secretly thrilling
beat that seemed to pass between them every time they
touched.

What was going on? She'd given up penises! "This is a
waste of your apparently in-demand time, Pace. I'm *fine*."

"Okay. Let's just prove it." But in opposition to the
amusement in his voice, he lightly squeezed her waist.

Reassurance.

He cared. Good to know. Because she cared back. And that . . . well, that wasn't nearly as good to know. "I don't want to waste your money."

"I'll take it out of the grand I owe ya."

"Two. You owe me *two* grand."

They were still standing close, very close, and he was taking up a whole hell of a lot of space. Her space. He had one hand on her, the other above her head, holding the door open, and that felt intimate, too.

And suggestive.

His shirt was stretched taut across his shoulders, and with his arm raised she could see the delineation of the muscles along his forearm, which should have been no big deal, so why she looked, then kept looking, she had no clue.

But God, he smelled good, and was still smiling in reassurance. And before she could register the thought process, she leaned in to give him a kiss on the cheek. A thank-you-for-caring kiss—except that he turned his head to look at her and . . .

Their lips collided.

Gently connected.

Held . . .

A beat of shock reverberated through her system. She waited for the awkwardness to hit, but that wasn't what hit at all as he pulled back a fraction and stared at her, clearly as completely thrown as she.

"In or out," a woman behind them said, sounding irritated—until she got a look at Pace. "Hey. Hey, are you . . . Pace Martin? Ohmigod, you are! You're him!" Irritation gone, she flashed a wide grin. "You had an amazing season last year, what was it? Twenty-four and six?"

"Something like that."

"Twenty-four wins." She sighed in pleasure. "With, what, almost two hundred strikeouts, right?"

"Not quite that many," he said modestly.

"Well, it was a fantastic run, whatever it was!" She turned to Holly. "He led the National League in wins, ERA, *and* strikeouts on his way to the Cy Young Award!" She grinned at Pace. "And you had the NL's record in strikeouts the year before, too, don't think I forgot that! We've got a bet going that you're good for at least 225 strikeouts this year. We *love* you in our house."

"Thank you."

She grinned, then gasped. "Ohmigod, you have to sign something for me."

Holly watched, head spinning, as the woman searched her pockets and came up with a pen but no paper. "It's okay," she gushed. "Just sign me." With that, she tugged her tank top off her shoulder, low on her breast, which nearly, but not quite, popped out. "Here," she demanded, tapping herself with her finger, flesh bouncing all over the place. "Right here."

Pace didn't even blink as he obligingly leaned in to sign the woman's breast.

"My husband is the hugest fan," she said to the top of his head, beaming. "He's going to go nuts when he sees this!"

Pace handed her back her pen and held the door open for both women to precede him in.

Inside, the happy fan rushed off.

Holly looked at Pace. "She knew your stats. By memory."

"Some do." He took her arm, but she dug in her heels.

He looked at her from those dark brown eyes fringed by darker, thick lashes and waited.

"You sign a lot of breasts?"

"Body parts are a fairly common request," he admitted.

"It's an interesting life you lead, Pace."

"So I've heard."

"I really don't need a doctor."

"Humor me. And when the doc tells me you're fine, I won't feel bad dumping you back at your car and pretending this past hour never happened."

"Okay," she agreed. "But only if you promise to sign a body part afterward."

Chapter 6

There are three things in my life which I really love:
God, family, and baseball. The only problem—once
baseball season starts, I change the order around a
bit.

—Al Gallagher, 1971

That night Pace skipped his usual five-mile run to give
his body a rest. He also skipped the Dr Pepper he wanted
more than his next breath and drank water as he packed for
the three-game run in Philly.

Since prepping for travel was as familiar as breathing,
his mind wandered as he threw clothes into his bag. Holly
was going to be fine. He'd made sure of it before driving
her back to her car. He hoped—in spite of her having the
most compelling eyes he'd ever had the discomfort of being leveled by, and in spite of that very intriguing hot kiss
they'd shared—to never see her again.

But he was fairly certain he wouldn't get that lucky. She
wanted his secrets, and given that her picture was probably
in the dictionary next to *tenacious*, not to mention *stubborn* and *ornery*, she wouldn't be discouraged by a ball to
the forehead.

She was going to be a pain in his ass, and he knew it. But
she was also sharply funny and sharply smart, and damn
if when she'd pitted her wits against his, he didn't forget
to feel sorry for himself—something he appeared to have

down to a science tonight, thanks to the news from his doctor.

When his cell phone rang, he considered ignoring it, but the display revealed it was Gage, and it was never smart to ignore the manager. Not if he wanted to play, and he was scheduled for tomorrow. "Hey, Skip."

"I hear you clocked a reporter in the head."

Pace dropped to his bed and stretched out, staring at the ceiling, picturing Holly and her pretty hair and amazing eyes, and how she'd felt in his arms when he'd scooped her off the grass after taking River's pitch.

And then there'd been that kiss . . . "Not exactly. Is she suing or something?"

"Or something." Gage was a hands-on TM. He loved the game, he loved the guys, and because of it there was little of the usual management-versus-the-players attitude on the Heat. At thirty-four years old, their "Skipper" as they called him was the youngest MLB team manager in the country and possibly the hardest working, a fact that everyone on the Heat wholeheartedly appreciated. Gage was loyal to a fault, calm at all times, and utterly infallible when it came to supporting the Heat in every possible way, including, apparently, helping one of his players get out of a mess created by his own stupidity. "What the hell happened, man?"

"It was an accident," Pace told him. "I took her to the doctor and she checked out. Is she not okay?"

"You could ask Ty, Joe, and Henry, all of whom she met for dinner. Or better yet, ask her yourself."

The guys had probably charmed the hell out of her. And he'd been worried about Wade. "I don't have her number."

"Well lucky for you, I do."

Shit. He took the number, then spent a few minutes procrastinating with his TV remote, but when the local anchor questioned Pace's stats and said he was "getting up there" in age, it was drink a Dr Pepper from his private stash or call Holly. Up there his ass, he thought as he pounded in her number. He was thirty-one. A damn *young* thirty-one, too—

Holly answered her phone in a soft, sleep-roughened voice, and he immediately went from pissed off to concerned. "Hey, you shouldn't be sleeping after a bump to the head." He shouldn't have just dumped her off. He should've—

"You paid the doctor bill, Pace," she said calmly. "You know I'm not concussed. But that you're worrying like a mother hen is very sweet. And interesting, as I've never seen *sweet* on any of your bios. I'll have to make sure to put that in any article about you."

"I'm just afraid you're going to sue. How's *that* for sweet?"

"Aw." She laughed. "You're so full of shit. I met your teammates tonight. They were great company, full of stories."

He just bet.

"But oddly enough, when I tried to get the scoop on you from them, they all clammed up."

"It's called friendship."

"Well, I have to admit, as a reporter, it's annoying." Her voice softened. "But as a person? Also incredibly sweet."

"So you're saying the entire team is sweet." Now he laughed. "Good luck with your credibility if you print that. We're not exactly known for the sweetness, Holly."

"No," she admitted with a smile in her voice. "You're not, are you? I'm hoping to figure out what makes you guys tick."

"Why?"

"Because that's what I do. I like to furrow deep."

"And expose secrets."

"Yes, when they need to be exposed." She was quiet a moment. "But to ease your mind, I haven't found any yet. Oh, and the only reason I was sleeping is because we have an early flight. You can stop worrying about me, sweet or otherwise."

His gut tightened as a very bad feeling came over him. "We? *We* have an early flight?"

"Didn't anyone tell you? I'll be traveling with the Heat." Christ. "Seriously?"

"Seriously. How's your shoulder? And don't bother trying to give me the standard line. This isn't Holly the reporter asking but the friend who rescued you from your stalker."

He let out a low breath. "A little sore, that's all."

"Okay, we'll stick with that for now, since you don't trust me."

"You're still a reporter."

"Which is what, synonymous with bad guy?"

"No, of course not." He ran a hand through his hair and looked at his open duffel bag. Why had he called her? "I just don't want it plastered all across the Internet that I'm in trouble."

"Are you?"

"No."

She was quiet a moment, as if taking the time to read right through him. "I understand the Heat has a lot riding on this next series."

"Yeah." In Pace's life it was fact that people always said *he* had a lot riding on the next game, *he* had a lot riding on the next series, or whatever they were facing. Not the Heat, but *him.* Pace had always hated that. Yeah, he was a good pitcher, maybe even at times a great one. But he was also part of a damn team.

And in only a few words, Holly had just made it clear that she was one of the few who recognized that. Pace would like her for that alone—if he hadn't already decided not to like her at all. "Okay, well, I just wanted to check on you, so . . ."

"And you're already sorry you called."

Yes. Yes, he was.

Sounding amused again, she said, "That's okay, Pace. You can take me off your list of things to be concerned about. I'm not going to hold it against you that I have a lovely black-and-blue bruise in the center of my forehead."

He winced for her. "In my experience, women tend to remember these things."

"We've already agreed you've been hanging out with the wrong women. 'Night, Pace."

"'Night." He closed his cell phone and stared at it for a minute, debating whether or not to hunt up her address and go over there to check on her in person. But he had to be honest with himself. If he did that, it wouldn't be just to look at her bruise.

And that, more than anything else, made the decision for him.

He wasn't going anywhere near her.

When Red knocked on the door only a minute later with the tapes of the Phillies' last game and some sub sandwiches, the decision was all the easier. Watching tapes before an away series was a tradition. Often Wade came, too, and some of the other guys as well, but tonight it was just Red and his son Tucker, who had baseball in his blood the same as his father.

Tucker and Pace went way back as well. They'd played against each other at their respective rival high schools the one year Pace hadn't had to move to accommodate his father's military career. That'd been the same year Tucker had made a string of bad choices including mixing alcohol and street racing, and had ended up with his car in a ditch and several pins in his right leg. Unable to play baseball but equally unable to shake loose his love for the game, Tucker now repped for a vitamin company, the one which exclusively supplied the Heat with their own vitamin enriched water.

Father and son were mirror images of each other. They had matching carrot-top, trademark messy hairstyles, stark green eyes that saw everything, quick smiles, and two big, warm hearts.

Tucker limped across Pace's large, undeniably plush

living room, and Pace couldn't help the twinge that always hit him. If not for some shitty choices made all those years ago, Tucker might be right where Pace was, with the MLB contract and fat retirement account.

Tucker wouldn't want the pity, but knowing that didn't assuage Pace's discomfort. They sat in front of the TV and watched the tape. Usually it was a good time, the calm before the storm, but tonight, it felt like an effort to be social. So did listening to Red point out the Phillies different pitching idiosyncrasies.

"Pace, watch his foot, see? He's not pushing off with his back leg. He's leaving the fastball up and his curve's flat. You don't do that. You're too smart to do that."

Pace didn't feel so smart. If he'd been smart, he'd have figured out how to avoid his injury.

"Look at that." Red poked a bony finger toward the TV. "The way he changed his grip right there, see?"

"Pace knows how to win, Dad," Tucker said with a laugh. "He's done it a time or two."

Yeah. What Pace didn't know was if he could *keep* winning.

Tucker helped himself to Pace's refrigerator and shook his head at the six-pack of Dr Pepper in the way back. "Thought you gave this shit up since it made you feel like—surprise—shit."

"I did." He just liked to look at it sometimes. Like a junkie.

Tucker pulled out a bottle of water instead and slapped it to Pace's chest, along with a vitamin pack. "Our newest stuff. One a day. It speeds up healing and promotes strength, both of which you need. Gives you energy, too."

Pace raised a brow. He really hated taking anything, even Advil—a throwback to the old man who'd always believed such things showed weakness. "Sounds like HGH."

Human growth hormones were banned, with a strict MLB ruling that required a fifty-game suspension for a first-time offense. A second offense was a one-hundred-game suspension, which was nothing next to the third offense—life banishment from the majors.

Harsh, but extremely effective. The MLB was just as hard on banned stimulants. A second test for those resulted in an automatic twenty-five game suspension.

Red, a firm old-schooler from the days before the commissioner had stopped the steroid use, rolled his eyes. "The new regulations are shit."

"Oh boy," Tucker muttered to Pace. "Here we go."

"Well, Jesus on a stick," Red griped. "They put athletes on the cover of the Wheaties box and say the cereal gives you strength, but a guy can't take something to promote that strength? Should we ban Wheaties then? Hell, let's also ban Tylenol while we're at it." He said this so vigorously he started coughing.

Tucker sighed and smacked him on the back. "Maybe we should ban your cigarettes, Dad. How about that?" He turned to Pace. "The vitamins are all natural. Nothing manufactured, no drugs in the mix. Ty's been taking them and his energy level is way up."

Ty occasionally had a problem with his energy levels, something left over from the leukemia he'd faced as a teen. Or more correctly, the meds he'd taken to fight the disease.

In any case, in theory Pace understood the appeal of enhancers. Pro athletes were paid to be strong. If there were drugs to help build strength and muscle, then that's what some would choose to do. It was life. It just wasn't for him, simply because while he believed certain drugs absolutely could make him stronger, he didn't believe strength was what made a pitcher. Pitching came from a complexity of arm and shoulder movements combined with the science involved in directing the baseball.

"Just try them for a week," Tucker said at the look on Pace's face. "I swear you'll feel like a new man."

With his doctor's prognosis ringing in his ear, Pace

nodded. A little extra boost, whether real or perceived, couldn't possibly hurt.

"What's the matter with you?" Red asked. "You seem off."

"Just tired."

"Yeah?" Red's sharp gaze ran over him. "Or maybe you have a late date and want us out?"

"Jesus, Dad," Tucker muttered.

"What? Women throw themselves at him in every city we go to. Did I tell you in Dallas someone left their panties on his hotel room door?"

"Well, lucky him." Tucker rolled his eyes in sympathy at Pace. "Sorry. He actually still believes sex takes away from a guy's game."

"It does!" Red insisted.

A sentiment Pace wholeheartedly disagreed with, but it wasn't as if sex was on the table for the evening anyway.

"Fine. Get your rest, Sleeping Beauty." Red took his tape and, heading to the door, added, "If you keep winning, I just might get my pennant yet."

"You mean if *we* win this series."

"That's what I said."

"No, you said if *I* win."

"Well, what the hell's the difference?"

"I'm not the whole team."

"This year you are."

Pace's doctor would disagree. He'd remind Pace what he'd said just this afternoon, that his rotator cuff was possibly beyond strained, that it might be torn, which meant that it needed to be repaired. He had two choices: laser surgery now, or stick with physical therapy and hope it didn't get worse.

Two perfectly reasonable and perfectly shitty choices.

Tucker tapped the plastic bag of vitamins he'd pushed into Pace's arms. "Take these, daily. *Especially* if you have a hot date."

"The only hot date he needs is with his own bed," Red

muttered. He nudged Pace, which equaled a hug in Red's world. *"Alone."*

Pace just sighed and kicked them both out.

Unable to sleep after Pace's call, Holly alternately paced her condo and stared at her blank computer screen. She was trying to write her first article, but every time she wrote a sentence, she considered hitting Delete instead of Save.

This might have been because she'd kissed her subject. *God.*

She paced some more, obsessed some more, then called her best friend, Allie.

"About damn time, chica," Allie said. "I've been worried."

They hadn't touched base all week, which was all Holly's fault as Allie had called several times. "I'm sorry. I'm starting a new series."

"Which means you're pacing in front of your computer, cursing Tommy and life in general. One of these days, maybe you'll try it my way."

Which involved yoga, health food, and a complete lack of stress. Unfortunately, Holly fell over whenever she attempted yoga, she had an ongoing love affair with junk food, and she lacked the ability to live stress free. "My way is fine. Or it would be if Tommy would trust me to pick the series ideas."

"Interesting that you want your scumbag of a boss to trust you, when you don't trust anyone."

"I trust you."

"When you trust so few," Allie amended. "Yeah, you write about secrets, chica, but remember, not all secrets mean someone is cruel and neglectful. Not everyone with a secret is your mother."

Holly sighed. "Yeah." She and Allie had met in a college creative writing course, and despite their differences, they'd bonded over their horrible teacher. They'd roomed together for two years, Allie and her tofu, Holly and her chocolate. They'd become close, with Allie turning into Holly's first true friend.

Now Allie lived in LA working as a housekeeper for the rich and famous while writing a screenplay on the side. They saw each other as often as Holly got to LA, which hadn't been much lately. Allie was Holly's one tie, the lone string on her heart, and she depended on it to keep her grounded.

"I hear your baseball phenom hit an RBI double and a sacrifice fly to go along with his seven innings of no-hitters in his last game," Allie said. "He's expected to do at least that in Philly."

"I didn't know you were into baseball."

"I looked it up so I'd sound smart. Did it work?"

"I'm impressed."

"Good. Mission accomplished." Allie had a smile in her voice. "I was beginning to think maybe you'd fallen off the planet. Or better yet, found a hot guy or something."

"Or something."

"Are you kidding me? I'm right?"

"No," Holly said on a laugh. "You're not right. I'm swamped with getting this series started, that's all." Or not, she thought, staring at her laptop. "I just wanted to check in."

"Aw, you miss me."

"Yeah." Holly felt a smile cross her face. "I really do."

"Then stop running around like a chicken without a head. Stand still and grow roots. And if you could do that here in LA, with me, that'd be great. This is where it's at, chica."

"For you maybe, but I write nonfiction. I need to travel to the stories."

"So switch to fiction. So is he on the Heat?"

"He who?"

"He, the hottie distracting you who."

"Stop it." But she caved as she sank to her chair and

stared at the computer. "He's the phenom. Phenoms don't tend to like bossy reporters."

Allie laughed. "I love it. You always did aim high."

"You heard the nothing's-going-to-happen part, right?"

"Call me when you have details."

"There won't be any."

"Uh-huh."

Holly thunked her head on her desk. "Well I don't *want* there to be details, how's that?"

Allie laughed and Holly hung up. She looked around at the condo she'd rented for the next month and let out a breath. Another condo in another city.

She had no idea where she'd go next.

Contrary to what Allie thought, that was actually the fun part of her job, nothing tying her down . . . Or it had been, until recently, when this odd sense of restlessness started hounding her. Maybe Allie had a point, maybe she should think about settling. She didn't have to do it the way her mother had, with all the various addictions in play— the men, the shopping, the lying . . . which when combined had destroyed her, and nearly Holly as well. It'd certainly left them in the poor house.

Or more accurately, a single-wide in south Georgia. Not that there was anything wrong with that. Nope, if they'd been a real family, it'd have been fine. But Holly's mom had always blamed Holly for her problems, and Holly in turn had blamed her mother for . . . everything.

They'd never been a real family.

Talk about being tied down. Poverty was the worst of ties. The memories were harsh, but Holly had raised herself and gotten out. The days of being so poor she couldn't pay attention were over.

And yes, maybe now she was a little tough, a little jaded, and a whole lot mistrustful, but she had her morals firmly in place, instincts honed sharp.

Which is how she screwed up enough courage to call Tommy.

"Finally," he grumbled. "I was getting ready to send out a search party. You don't return calls now?"

"I'm sorry. I need to talk to you."

"Well, I need to talk to you, too, doll. I need you to get me your article ASAP. I'm running it tomorrow."

"It's not due until Monday."

"I know, but Alicia crapped out on me and now I have a spot to fill. You're it."

"I need some more time."

"What do you mean you need more time?"

"Actually," she said with a glance at her blank screen, "I need to change subjects. I'm thinking ice dancing."

He laughed good and hard. "Oh no you don't."

He had no idea. She *had* to change subjects—she'd kissed hers! "I have a little conflict of interest." A six foot two conflict of interest . . .

"Huh?"

Tommy had given Holly a chance when no one else would, so she felt she owed him for that, and she gave him the truth that meant so much to her. "It's possible that I'm developing a very small . . ."

"Zit? Parasite? *What?*"

"Crush. On one of the players."

"So?"

"So . . ." The last time she'd dated someone related to her work, it had ended badly. Very badly. So badly Alex was probably still wishing her dead, and she was still wishing she'd never faked an orgasm for him.

She didn't intend to date Pace, or to kiss him again for that matter, but she had to face one fact. "It'll be hard to be objective."

"I'm not paying you to be objective," Tommy said. "This isn't a series about baseball facts. This is a personal commentary. Your opinion matters, so if you're getting close to them, then so much the better. And hey, I hear the players all do tons of charity work with kids. Get me pics of that, pronto. It'll go good alongside whatever tough-hitting stuff you write. We'll tug on the heartstrings, then rip out their guts."

"You are one sick man, Tommy."

"I know it. Now send me the damn article."

She looked at her blank screen again and winced. "And if it's biased?"

"I'll un-bias it. *Send it.*"

"Tommy—"

"Look, we've done this. Send it or quit."

She gave one brief thought to doing just that. But two things stopped her. One, her fear of being poor again, and two, quitting in shitty economic times because of a guy she'd spent one hour with had to be the definition of *stupid female*, and she hated *stupid females*.

"What'll it be, doll?"

Dammit. "Give me a few hours. I'll write your damn article."

Chapter 7

There's no crying in baseball!

—Jimmy Dugan in *A League of Their Own*

For the first time in recent memory, Pace slept like the living dead. When he woke up, he stretched and felt another first: no aches, no pains. In fact, he felt damn good. He eyed the empty vitamin pack by his bed. If Tucker's stuff had done this, then it was worth its weight in gold.

He got up, showered, and checked his e-mail. Samantha had sent him the link to *American Online Living* and Holly's first baseball series article on her blog. She'd profiled their close-knit team, highlighting the friendship of Ty, Joe, and Henry. They were a threesome now, but she wrote about how they'd once been a fivesome, before Jim and Slam had been traded. The guys had put a positive spin on the situation for her, and Pace found the article nonjudgmental and thoughtful, but also a little on edge.

She was on the hunt for secrets, and he knew it. The Heat hadn't had any bad press lately, and that was always a good thing, but none of them were angels and it wouldn't take much digging to find dirt.

* * *

Holly sat at the private gate at the airport waiting for the Heat's plane to be ready for boarding. Tommy was so excited about this Philly trip that he'd called three times since she'd gotten to the airport, and she knew if he could have somehow switched positions with her, he would have.

"Find any secrets yet?" he demanded to know.

"Nope."

"You losing your touch?"

"I told you I didn't want this assignment."

"It's a great assignment. Oh, and if the Heat go all the way this year, I want a signed ball."

"If I dig out any secrets, no one's going to want to sign a ball for either of us."

"Yeah." Tommy sighed. "But since you tend to sell advertising space like crazy, I'll have to live with a fat bank account instead. So . . . which one are you sleeping with?"

"What? None of them!"

"You said you had a crush."

"That doesn't mean I'm *sleeping* with him."

"Maybe you should. Get the inside scoop. Yeah, do it!"

Holly hung up on him and boarded.

When she'd been invited by Sam on this trip, she'd had no idea what to expect, maybe a luxurious trip from start to finish, with maids and butlers to serve the players every whim. Instead they flew on a relatively no-frills chartered jet with a single steward onboard. The Heat players wore suits and looked good while they were at it. They also smelled good. The support staff was there as were coaches, management. Sam's brother, Jeremy, was aboard, too. He was Sam's equivalent at the Charleston Bucks, and the two of them often co-chaired publicity events for both teams together.

Holly looked at the testosterone filled cabin. All around her was the scent of big, built men—deodorant, soap, aftershave. She'd never seen such concentrated . . . maleness in one place before, and it was distracting to say the least.

But she was here for a job, and she would use her time wisely. Forcing herself to get to work, she pulled out her computer, booted it up, and opened Word. Then stared at it for a while. Yeah, look at her, hard at work.

Two rows ahead of her, Ty and Henry were playing cards, Henry's head bopping to some beat from his iPod. Just to her left, Wade and Pace were talking and laughing, amusing each other with the ease of old, tight friends.

Then Pace turned his head toward her. Wade was saying something to him, but Pace didn't take his eyes off her as he slowly nodded a greeting, his gaze dark and assessing and . . .

Warm enough that she needed to adjust the overhead fan right onto her face. Whew. The guy was edible. No other word need apply. She looked at her blank screen and tried to concentrate, which turned out to be impossible, so she clicked open her Sudoku program.

Five minutes later she had a good portion of the puzzle done when a deep male voice in her ear said, "Four." This was accompanied by a long, tanned finger pointing to one of the squares. "Four goes there."

She tipped up her head and found Pace. Her mouth went dry. He wore a dark charcoal suit cut just for him, a French blue shirt with a sexy as hell tie and an easy smile.

"Working hard?" he asked.

"Very." As she answered, she shut the Sudoku program, inadvertently revealing the Word program behind it.

And her blank screen.

"Ah," he said. "Invisible font."

With a sigh she gave up and sat back. "I don't do idle very well. I like to be on the move, and I'm usually in a hurry as well. Sitting sucks."

He surprised her by folding his long, leanly muscled body into the empty seat next to her. "It's called relaxing."

"Yeah, I don't do that so well either."

"It's hard for me, too, since I gave up soda."

She turned back to him. "Why did you give it up?"

He patted his flat-as-a-board belly, and she laughed. "Come on."

"Hey, you hit thirty and your metabolism changes."

"You're worried about your girlish figure?" Which was anything but girlish . . .

"It made me sluggish. But I miss it, especially when I'm just sitting. There's a lot of hurry up and wait in baseball, emphasis on the wait. You'll get used to it."

She nodded, then shook her head.

"Or not." He eyed the bruise on her forehead, the one she'd not been entirely successful at covering up. "Ouch."

"It's not as bad as it looks."

"Just do me a favor and don't offer to play catch with any of these guys," he said, gesturing to the guys around them. "The last woman who did was a quote 'dancer' from some underground club, and she played in the nude."

She laughed.

"Seriously. TMZ took pics."

"You're making that up."

"Google it." With a flash of a quick, rare grin, he pushed out of the chair and left her alone.

She let out a long breath—her version of relaxing—and wished she had an Internet connection as she went back to her blank screen, where she absolutely did not fantasize about playing catch.

With Pace.

In the nude . . .

The team checked into the Philadelphia hotel together, Holly included. The atmosphere in the lobby slowly changed as people realized the Heat had arrived, and the players were sought out by autograph-seeking fans. Though Holly had read about baseball divas, not a single player seemed to mind as they stood around a few extra minutes making nice.

Even afterward, things remained simple. A few of the

guys went to the hotel bar for a drink, others caught a movie. Some stayed in.

No one got wild and crazy.

They were a united group, yet respectful of their individual differences. It fascinated Holly, who found Mike and Kyle, the third baseman and right fielder, in the bar with Ty and Henry, and sat with them for a while. They talked about baseball's place in history and how the perception of the game had changed, especially from a kid's standpoint. These days, so much more was demanded of the players, and the guys were definitely feeling the pressure.

Mason, the first baseman, joined them, as did Joe. The discussion was blog-worthy, and as the bar began to fill up with women, Holly left the guys to go write up some notes. But the late afternoon sun drew her, and she stepped outside the hotel for some fresh air, eyeing a nicely built runner heading her way as the fading sunlight reflected off his sunglasses.

Pace.

He wore running shorts and a white T-shirt, moving along at a stride that would have killed her in under thirty seconds. She wondered if maybe he would keep going, pretending not to see her, but someone had raised him right. His footsteps slowed, then stopped altogether as he pulled out his earphones. He'd been running hard and his breathing was labored as he drew air into his lungs. He lifted his sunglasses to the top of his head and swiped at his temples with the back of his arm. His shirt clung to him. His shorts did the same.

He was sweaty all over, and she shivered.

Wow.

The single word was a completely involuntary reaction. She couldn't help herself as she stared at him, all intelligent thought flew right out of her head, because from head to toe the man was freaking gorgeous.

"You settled in okay?" he asked.

"Yes. Thank you."

With a slow nod, he kept looking at her with that steady gaze, his brows knit together as he stepped a little closer, his gait easy and relaxed now, as if preserving his energy for other things, like chucking a ball at a batter at ninety-five miles an hour.

Or maybe having sex . . . Good God, what was wrong with her? "I was just getting some air," she said a little weakly. "I'm good now."

He held the hotel door open for her, and as she brushed by his damp, hot body, she had to restrain herself from leaning in and touching.

Pathetic. She was pathetic.

But knowing that didn't stop her gaze from drifting over him, down his damp throat, down the T-shirt covering his broad chest, or from remembering how in the last doorway they'd stood together, they'd kissed. When she looked up, she found that dark gaze locked on hers, his solemn and quiet. "In?" he asked when she didn't move.

"Yes," she murmured. "Thanks." She managed a smile, and with a nod, he moved off, heading toward the elevators. It wasn't until he was out of sight that she realized she was standing there in the center of the lobby, mouth open, staring after him.

"He does seem to have that affect on women."

Holly turned to face Samantha. "Hi. I was just—"

"Don't try to talk until you've had a healthy dose of chocolate." She nodded with her chin toward the café, just off the lobby. "Dessert?"

"Sure," Holly managed. "Dessert sounds good." In lieu of sex, it would have to do.

As it had for far too long now.

They seated themselves and ordered fudge brownies, which came pronto, warm on their plates and then melting in their mouths.

"So," Samantha said after a mutual moan-fest over the deliciousness. She was a tall, willowy blonde who was as attractive as some of the players she represented. Today she wore a yellow business suit revealing mile-long legs, making Holly feel like a run-down Pinto standing next to a brand-new BMW. "What do you think about the guys?"

"I'm wondering if they always behave so well on the road, or is it a show for my benefit?"

"They don't do shows. What you see is what you get." Sam dug into a brownie with clear relish. "It's why I love them. My brother, Jeremy, is the publicist for the Bucks. They're a logistical, diva-run, trouble-filled nightmare. He has his hands full. Not me. They're all good guys here on the Heat. The best."

"So far, I'd agree with you. So no problems?"

"Like?"

"I don't know. Drugs?"

"No. Nothing like that," Sam said firmly. "There're no secrets here, Holly."

Holly liked these guys, and she wanted to believe Sam, but experiences had taught her one thing: no one was as they appeared to be, especially not with the sheer amount of money and fame they dealt with on a daily basis. "What about jealousy?"

"Jealousy?"

"Pace Martin, for instance, one of the highest ranked pitchers in the league and the ace in your starting lineup. How do the other pitchers on the team feel about playing second fiddle to him? Like Ty, a strong up-and-coming player, and yet he's Pace's relief pitcher, maybe not getting the playing time he might somewhere else because Pace is so good. Does he—"

"Honey." Sam smiled like pure melted butter as she reached out and squeezed Holly's hand. "It's been a long day and we're far from home. We're eating a thousand-calorie dessert together. Now I know you like to dig, but all you're going to come up with is a bunch of holes and tired arms. So don't you think we might enjoy ourselves instead of trying to find problems that don't exist?"

Holly blinked. "Oh. Okay, sure."

Sam laughed at her. "You're allowed to take a breather, you know. And do nothing. I won't tell anyone."

Holly let out a self-conscious smile, a little startled that Sam had read her so easily. "It's going to take some practice, this sitting-around thing. I don't usually have so much downtime."

"Well, we'll reform you yet."

The next day, in the packed Philly stadium, Holly sat in the stands with a sense of anticipation and excitement as Pace jogged out to the pitcher's mound looking tall, leanly muscled, and focused.

In his element.

"He's my fantasy pick," a teenage boy said reverently, sitting just behind her.

Hers, too, she thought, watching Pace through her camera lens—but not necessarily for his competitiveness, focus, dedication, or pitching ability. No, her fantasy was much more female based than that . . .

The late afternoon was steaming hot. The air smelled of popcorn, hot dogs, and freshly cut grass, and shimmered with the heat.

Pace put on his glove and adjusted his cap. Game face on, he turned to view his outfield, and Holly experienced a little frisson of thrill at the sight of his name stitched across his back.

Good Lord, she thought, lowering her camera. She'd turned into a rabid fan.

The first batter stepped up to the plate to wild cheers from his home crowd. Holly knew that a successful batter got a hit only thirty percent of the time he went to bat, less when Pace was pitching.

She held her breath.

Pace wound up and let the ball go, where it promptly whizzed right into Wade's mitt with a loud *smack*.

"Steeeee-riiiiike!" the ump yelled.

"Fastball," someone said behind her. "Fastest fastball in the league."

Wade threw the ball back to Pace, dropped into a crouch, and sent Pace a sign between his spread thighs.

Pace nodded. His next pitch arched, making the batter leap back from the plate with an oath, but then the ball arched again, sliding right into the strike zone.

"Steeeee-riiiiike!" the ump yelled again.

The batter looked pissed off.

The Philly crowd booed.

"Jesus, did you see that curveball?" someone on Holly's left said in disbelief. "It must have curved a foot and a half!"

Holly had no idea how low it really curved, because she couldn't take her eyes off Pace. He went on to pitch a textbook no-hitter, and if he felt any of the pain she'd sensed the other day, he didn't let it show. In fact, he let nothing show. He was a solid, tough rock of determination from the start to the seventh inning, when Gage pulled him to save his arm for the next series.

Ty went in, allowing several runs, but still holding their lead, and the Heat won eight to four.

The informal after party was set in one of the bars of the hotel, free drinks on management. Holly found herself with a lingering headache, probably from the hot sun, not to mention the cheering she'd done. She thought about escaping to her room to work on her next article, which she'd decided would be about the public's view of baseball, from past to present, focusing on kids and how much the game and the players meant to them.

But looking around at the growing crowd, she decided to stay a few more minutes in case she heard anything interesting.

Which was really just an excuse.

She wanted to see Pace. Knowing it, she made her way through the gang to the open bar and tried to get the attention of one of the two pretty, young bartenders, one blonde, one brunette, spending more time looking at the players than making drinks. She waited.

And waited.

"You don't have a penis, so I'd give up." Samantha smiled at her and opened her purse to pull out a flask. "It's Scotch. I carry it when I fly because I'm such a wuss. Take it."

"Oh, no, I—"

But Sam had moved on. Holly shook her head and tried once more in vain to get a much lighter drink from either of the bartenders. "I'm invisible," she finally decided.

"Aw. Not to me, darlin'." Wade nudged her shoulder with his as he worked his way in next to her, all three-day scruff and Prada sunglasses.

She'd learned several things about the Heat's star catcher. For one, he was a world-class flirt and yet somehow, when he looked into her eyes, he made her feel like the only woman on the planet.

That he looked like a surfer didn't hurt. Nope, all that sun-kissed beauty from head to toe really worked for him. Like the others, he was gorgeously built, but beneath that laid-back exterior was a sharp mind, a quick wit, and a fierce loyalty to those he cared about, making him about as easy to crack open as a brick wall. He was both cocky and discreet, a paradox she'd learned while trying to ask him some hard-hitting questions; she'd gotten nowhere. Nope, those deep sea green eyes of his had gone from sparkling to closed up tighter than a drum in a single heartbeat.

The entire team had that in common—tight lips.

"What can I get you to drink?" Wade asked her now.

"A wine cooler, if you can get it, thanks."

He gestured to the closest bartender, the cute little blonde one, who ran over to him so fast she nearly killed her coworker.

Holly had been a bartender in college. Actually, she'd been a lot of things in college, since it had taken many, many jobs to pay her way. But she'd served quickly and efficiently, with a nice but distant smile, ensuring that she'd get tips but not hit on. The tactic hadn't always worked. Sometimes she'd gotten stiffed, sometimes she'd gotten hit on in spite of her distance, and sometimes she'd gotten both stiffed *and* hit on, which had always pissed her off.

Wade winked at the blonde as he gave their order, then grinned at Holly as the woman rushed to get the drinks. "They like us here. We tip well."

"I bet."

He studied her while reaching for the bowl of mixed nuts on the bar. "You know, I didn't peg you for a pansy-ass drinker. I'd have guessed you'd drink beer. Maybe a Scotch. Something tough anyway."

She thought of Sam's Scotch in her purse. Maybe she should have stuck with that. "You think I'm tough?"

"Well, not as tough as me, but close. Hey, Skipper," he said to Gage as the manager bellied up to the bar with smooth ease, gesturing with a nod of his chin to the bru-nette bartender.

Gage was built like his players. Plus, he had the rugged dark looks of his Latino heritage going for him, along with a smile that could slice an ump—or charm a reporter. Holly should know. He'd charmed her at the continental breakfast that morning, where she'd gotten almost nothing out of him except stats and a detailed account of how much volunteer work the guys did with their 4 The Kids charity.

"You getting lucky tonight?" Wade asked him.

"I already did with the win," he said as the pretty bar-tender brought him a beer and a smile as he turned to Holly, gesturing to the makeup-covered bruise on her fore-head. "How's that bump Pace got you?"

"Better, thank you. Speaking of Pace, where is he to-night?"

Look at her, all casually working that into the conversa-tion.

But Gage saw right through her as he took a pull of his drink, and offered an easy smile. "Oh, around, I imagine." With a friendly clap on Wade's shoulder, he moved off, heading for a pretty woman waving at him from across the room.

The first bartender was finally back with their drinks. Holly's came without a backward glance. Wade's came on a napkin with a phone number on it. He pocketed the napkin and winked at Holly, who rolled her eyes and turned to eye the crowd, which had doubled, filling with locals and fans who wanted to see the players.

And still no sight of Pace. She really should go to her room and take some Advil. Sleep. Write . . .

Ty and Joe pressed in close to the bar near Wade and Holly, trying to get a drink, but both bartenders were now at the other end, even more slammed than before. Since the drinks were free, Holly simply moved around the bar and filled their order, to their eternal gratitude.

"You're handy," Wade noted.

"I really am." With an easy camaraderie, they sat there and people-watched, and there was a lot of watching to be had. The women were everywhere, in all shapes and sizes—big and petite, sexy and cute, beautiful and not—and they all had one thing in common: they wanted to be with the players, wanted to see them, meet them, talk to them.

Sleep with them.

Several, in fact, were eyeing Wade as if he were sin on a stick. "Am I cramping your style?" she asked.

"Nah." He shot her an easy smile. "I'm taking a break."

"Aw. You get your heart hurt, Wade?"

That caused a deep chuckle to rumble from his chest, as if the idea was utterly laughable. "I meant I'm taking a break for the next hour or so." His gaze snagged on one of the women staring at him with naked desire all over her face. "Maybe half an hour."

She shook her head, then her own gaze caught on Pace as he finally walked in. He was looking rough and tumble, ready for anything, and from across the crowd and above all the noise, their eyes met.

A little shiver of thrill went through her. Actually, a big shiver.

Like the other players, he was dressed nice, wearing a jacket fitted to his athletic body as if it'd been made for him, and it probably had. He looked expensive, cultured, gorgeous, and on top of his world—which by all accounts, he was.

And he headed right for them.

Wade gestured to the cute blonde bartender for a drink for Pace, then said when he got close, "I was getting worried I was going to have to fly solo, no wingman."

Pace smirked and shook his head. "Like you need a wingman."

Wade grinned. "Remember our first time at one of these things? New York, right? The place was loaded with beautiful women. Good times."

Pace nodded. "For you especially. You had two homers that night."

Wade shrugged modestly. "Possibly."

"After the game, we walked into the hotel bar," Pace told Holly, "which was packed with fans. One of the women dancing with us asks Wade if he's gay. Wade says no, and then she asks if his contract is really multimillions, and since it's public knowledge, he says yes. And then she hooks her arm in his and pulls him away. And that was the last I saw of him that night." Pace shook his head and took Wade's beer with an ease that said just how comfortable these two were with each other, but after a swallow, he lowered the bottle and took a second, longer look at her.

Her pulse had bumped up the minute he'd appeared, but now it went into cardiac-arrest territory. "What?"

Reaching out, he ran a surprisingly gentle finger over her forehead. "Still hurting?"

She'd cultivated a lifelong habit of being stoic and sucking it up, and she'd gotten damn good at keeping people out of her head. But somehow he kept leaping right in. By all accounts, he should have been nothing more than a big, sexy jock. Someone she needed to interview. But every time she looked into his steady gaze, that same heart-stopping sensation hit her. Even odder, everything else faded away, as if they were completely alone. She struggled to ignore the flare of heat in all her good spots, but since he didn't even try to hide the matching heat in his gaze, it was all but impossible.

Leaning in, he put his mouth to her ear. "Advil?"

She felt his warm breath on her skin, and she drew a shaky one of her own. He was so close for privacy's sake, not intimacy. She knew this, but her brain didn't seem to process the memo and instead sent her body an overload of pleasure waves. Bad brain. "I'm fine, thanks." Especially if he stayed right there . . .

He looked as though maybe he planned on doing exactly that, but Red came up behind him and clasped a hand on his shoulder. "There you are, son. My God, you were a sight out there tonight. The most beautiful thing I've ever seen." He grinned with sheer joy, his eyes crinkling, his face tanned and leathered from long years on the field beneath the harsh sun. "This is the year, all the way to the pennant. I can feel it." He laughed, which made him cough, deep and hard.

Pace reached for him. "Where's your inhaler?"

"I don't need it."

"Yes, you do."

"I'm fine!"

But he clearly wasn't, and because Holly was looking right into Pace's deep, dark eyes, she saw the love, the affection, there.

The worry.

Unlike her, he had strings on his heart, lots of them, whether he liked it or not. And she wished, just a little, that she'd cultivated more strings in her life. She was a grown-up now, she reminded herself, not a scared little kid. She could make her own choices. She could make strings if she wanted.

It wasn't too late.

Question was, did she want Pace to be a string . . .

Chapter 8

A baseball game is simply a nervous breakdown divided into nine innings.

—Earl Wilson

The Heat took the Phillies two out of three and then flew straight to Atlanta. As usual, the players gathered in the guest clubhouse five to seven hours before the game, where they ate, hung out, played video games, and practiced.

The sounds of Advil being shaken into hands and athletic tape being ripped into strips filled the air, as did the scent of muscle cream, along with the commotion from the support crowd, which included a horde of press and the GM's family, who'd flown in for his birthday.

Pace sat in front of his locker absently rubbing his shoulder as he watched Holly work the group with ease, taking pictures with her ever-present Canon. She did that, made things look easy. Charming the guys, charming the staff, having fun. Making herself at home in his world . . .

There was no reason to care, except he did.

He cared that he not allow her to make herself at home in his head, because for some reason he didn't understand, didn't *want* to understand, he knew that she could.

She'd put out another article—still not about him.

Apparently she'd given up, which relieved him. This entry had been a thought-provoking piece about the youngest fans of baseball, the kids, and how they worshipped the players, emulating their behaviors and actions. Those behaviors and actions were mostly honorable, she'd written, but since the athletes were only human, they were susceptible to the same downfalls as everyone else, and when they screwed up, kids also screwed up. She'd concluded with the pressures on the athletes today as if she really got it, with a nice little section detailing the Heat's volunteer work with 4 The Kids, and how they were doing their part to try to remain positive role models.

The entire blog had gotten picked up by several ESPN sports shows, and also highlighted in the Santa Barbara local press, and—

Henry's sweatband hit Pace in the chest. "Wake up, man. You're pitching in an hour. What planet are you on tonight anyway?"

Planet Holly. Pace simply held up the sweatband, nearly passing out at the smell. "You could clear out the entire stadium with this thing. Open a new pack."

"Can't. It's my good-luck charm. You might be having a hot season, but some of us are cold."

Pace grabbed a water bottle. It wasn't his, and he didn't care because as he drank, he heard Holly laugh, and he turned back to his locker, telling himself he had other stuff to be thinking about than how contagious her laugh was. Tonight's game, for one.

Or how she looked all careful and pretty in her daisy yellow sundress and white cropped jacket . . .

Next to him, Red stood talking to another of their pitching coaches. "In that game against the Rockies," he was saying, "he struck out twelve and walked one. Come on, who does that consistently?"

He did. He did that consistently.

Gage was on his other side talking animatedly with the third-base coach. "Last time we were here, he was hit on the upper right leg by a line drive for a single in the first inning. I don't want that happening again."

More of him. Jesus, he was really tired of himself.

"It's the only reason we lost," Gage said. "He was hurting too bad to throw."

Not true. Well, he *had* been hurting, but that's not why they lost. He'd been pitching like shit before the hit. It happened.

Hopefully it wouldn't happen tonight.

"Hey, that's mine." Wade snagged the water from Pace's hand and tipped it up to his mouth, but it was empty. With a shake of his head, he tossed it aside as the crowd in the visitors' clubhouse began to thin out. Joe and Henry were nearby, getting ready to go back out for the pregame field practice. Across from them were Mike and Kyle, now flirting with Holly, who looked good enough to gobble up whole. Pace opened his mouth to remind them to get their asses out for warm-up, but he gritted his teeth instead. *None of your business*, he reminded himself, and bent to tie his shoes–

And split the zipper on his grey away-game uniform pants. His third this season. *"Shit."*

Wade turned, took in Pace's opened fly, and shook his head. "You know, I've never seen a guy with less body fat go through more zippers. Maybe you ought to ask for Magnum-sized pants."

"It's not the pants."

"You wish."

Pace considered Wade's smug smile. "Have *you* ever burst your zipper?"

The guys around them cracked up, and Wade rounded on them until they shut up.

"Holly can fix it," Ty said. "Hey, Holly. Emergency here."

"What are you doing?" Pace asked him incredulously.

"She used to be a seamstress. Hol, look. Our poor pitcher's sail is broken at half-mast. Think you can help?"

Holly slid Pace a look, her gaze curiously dropping

down the front of him to figure out what Ty was talking about. He knew the exact moment she caught on because her brows shot straight up so far they vanished into her hair.

"That looks . . . problematic," she ventured.

Ty laughed. "Nationally televised game in one hour? You think?"

"I have an extra pair." Pace pulled open the locker. "Probably—"

"I can fix it." Holly pulled her purse off her shoulder and began digging through its mysterious depths with one hand while gesturing to Pace for the pants with her other.

"Seriously," he said. "I can just . . ." But he trailed off as she came up with a small sewing kit. "You sew?"

"Uh-huh. And I can also own property and vote. Want your pants fixed or not?"

He met her challenging gaze. She was nothing like any women he'd ever met, which was to say the kind of women one wouldn't bring home to their mother.

But he didn't have a mother and wouldn't have brought a woman home to her if he did.

Yeah, Holly was different. She was pretty damn perceptive, for one thing.

And pretty damn . . . pretty.

It was useless to deny it. She had those light brown eyes, round and soft and big enough to drown in, but she wasn't vulnerable. Not one little bit, not with her sharp tongue and sharper wit.

She had a small spattering of freckles on her nose, making him wonder where else she had freckles, and then there was her mouth. It was a little too big, and right now it happened to be curved in a smirking, smug smile. He'd had some interesting dreams about that mouth, and all the things he'd like her to do with it.

Yeah. Lots of dreams.

Honestly, he had no idea why she got to him. Or, hell, maybe he did. Maybe it was the combination of that sharp good humor and unmistakable dare in her eyes. Maybe it was the way she stood there in *his* world, so damn sure of herself when even *he* wasn't, when he hadn't been since his shoulder had made him realize exactly how damn tenuous his life really was. And she wanted his pants.

"What's the matter?" Henry asked. "Shy?"

"Shut up." Pace unbuttoned and jerked down his pants to the tune of the laughs of his supposed friends.

Holly kept her eyes on his as he handed over the pants. Then she sat on the bench, her head bent as she worked, her hair slipping in a soft, silky looking curtain around her face, her fingers moving nimbly and ably while he stood there in his compression shorts.

Feeling . . . exposed.

And not just physically. Annoyed at himself, at his ridiculously juvenile teammates, at everyone including the smooth, unruffled, and unknowingly sexy Holly Hutchins, he took his pants-less self off for a moment alone.

Holly fixed the zipper, then went looking for Pace, trying to avoid the area where guys tended to be naked and scratching things that she didn't need to see scratched or otherwise.

The visitors' clubhouse was much smaller than the one at the Heat's complex. In Santa Barbara, they had a huge facility, where anything the players could possibly want was readily available—flat screen TVs, a state of the art sound system, a refrigerator full of goodies, a whirlpool, video games, leather chairs all over the place.

A baseball player's self-contained biosphere.

But here, on the road, there was little of that. Just the guys and their gear. And most interesting, the overwhelming levels of testosterone, male camaraderie, and genuine sense of affection and good humor.

If it'd been filled with women, Holly doubted the atmosphere would be the same. These guys spent more time in close, confined quarters with each other than they spent in their own homes. In fact, she knew that more teams had been brought down by in-team fighting than poor play, but that didn't seem to be an issue with the Heat.

She found Pace alone in the shower room, staring off into space. She'd caught him rubbing his shoulder several times in the locker room, and she wondered if he was in pain. The urge to reach for her camera was strong. He could have walked off a glossy magazine ad. His jersey open over a clean, softly worn white T-shirt, both clinging to broad-as-a-mountain shoulders; tight compression shorts that hit mid-thigh and looked like something a cyclist would wear, revealing legs longer than a country mile. His feet were bare, and she had no idea why, but that was sexy as hell. Yeah, he could have been a model, but she'd never seen one with that hard of a gaze and that much going on behind it.

He was so deep in his own thoughts that he didn't hear her enter, giving her an extra moment to stare at him, which frankly, was enough to make her start to perspire.

The man was beautiful, though she could admit to wondering just how deep that beauty went. She could try to find out, but that hadn't worked out for her so well in the past, and in spite of being willing, even hopeful, she was feeling a little gun-shy. "Hey."

He didn't move, just let out a breath, making her realize he'd been aware of her all along. She cocked her head. "You okay?"

"Off the record?"

"Of course."

He didn't move an inch, but she sensed him relax. "I'd be better if I had a Dr Pepper," he admitted.

"I thought you gave them up to watch your girlish figure." She smiled when he slanted her a look. "I could get you one, if you'd like."

"No, thanks. I'm fine."

Though he was being friendly enough, he was still speaking in the polite tone he reserved for the press and pushy fans, which she knew all too well because it'd been the very first tone he'd used with her. "I'm not looking for a canned response, Pace. You don't have to be fine with me."

The look in his eyes sent a little lust-ridden thrill racing along her spine. He was tall, dark, and full of attitude, with tension coming off him in waves. She wondered if it was the upcoming game or something else. She tossed over his pants, which he caught in midair but didn't move to put them on.

"You're not what I expected," he finally said.

"Ditto. But curiously speaking, what did you expect?"

"For you to be more on guard for one thing. And as bossy as you were at first. You know, a typical reporter."

She smiled. "First appearances are rarely accurate."

"I don't know." He smiled back. "I called you for nosy, too. And you're definitely that."

"I was nosy long before I was a reporter." The shower room was clean but a little dark and damp. It felt humid and musky.

Intimate.

Pace pulled on his pants and buttoned up his shirt. He slipped his hand in his opened waistband to do a half-assed tucking in of his shirt, which seemed to further rev her engine.

She was out of control.

Completely. Out. Of. Control.

"Are you . . . blushing?" he asked, and with a curious light in his eyes, stopped tucking. "Yeah. You are."

And possibly drooling again, too. And as if all that wasn't enough, he smelled amazing. "I'm not."

He traced a finger over her cheekbone. "And lying." He tsked softly, his gaze dipping over her face. "Thought you never lied."

"I—" She broke off when the pad of that finger, calloused and very warm, slid over her throat, stopping at the very base where she imagined her pulse was drumming out of control. Suddenly, she felt extremely aware that his pants were unfastened. "Pace, I . . . I'm—" She let out a breath and shook her head.

He was still looking at her, his expression almost grave. "You're attracted to me."

"Which is obviously a mistake." She wrapped her fingers around his forearm to pull his hand away from her, but he shook his head and stepped closer.

"I'm attracted back, Holly."

She went still, then tipped her head up at him.

"Yeah." A small smile curved his lips. "And I'm no more happy about it than you are."

Her own accelerated breathing echoed in her ears, an admission that maybe she wasn't so unhappy about it.

His smile faded. Slowly, he shifted so that they were brushed up against each other, and though she hadn't been the one to walk around without pants, she felt exposed.

Raw.

And more than a little wary.

Especially since he didn't want to be attracted, and knowing it had an old insecurity rising to the surface, the one stemming from always having to push for what she wanted, and damn if she wasn't more than a little tired of that. Someday, just once, she wanted a man to push for her. "Well, you could just ignore . . . this," she said. "I'm sure that will help—"

Snagging her wrist, he pulled her back around, closer now in the dimly lit room.

"Pace—"

"Shh a second." Hand low on her back, he dipped his head so that their lips were only a fraction of an inch apart.

Oh God.

"Maybe," he whispered huskily, his gaze locked on her mouth. "Maybe there'd be no real chemistry."

Her knees wobbled, and not because she'd taken a ball to the forehead. They were still barely touching in this strange and erotically charged embrace and yet her nipples were hard and achy, her thighs quivering.

No real chemistry?

Ha.

He smoothed his fingers along her throat, then the curve of her jaw, his gaze following his every movement. "There's something that's been driving me crazy."

"What?"

"Do you always kiss as careful as you look?"

"I kiss careful?" She blinked. "I *look* careful?"

"It's the craziest thing. And sexy," he murmured. "Really sexy. Because all I keep thinking is how much I want to ruffle you up."

Her heart took one good hard leap into her throat, further compromising her breathing. His breathing wasn't all that steady either, which was an odd comfort.

She turned him on.

Just the thought made her want to float on air, or do the happy dance, except she'd lost control of her limbs.

He was going to kiss her. She thought about what else he might do, how it would feel, how he'd actually thought there might be no chemistry—

Which was as far as she got with her obsessing before he bent his head and opened his mouth over hers.

Chapter 9

Baseball was made for kids. Grown-ups only screw it up.

—Bob Lemon

Chemistry, Holly thought as Pace kissed her. Oh God, lots and lots of chemistry . . .

In apparent agreement of that, Pace let out a low, rough rumble deep in his chest and slid a hand into her hair, cupping her head, holding her to him. His other hand squeezed her waist, drawing her in even tighter before gliding up her back, slowly fisting in her shirt as his tongue touched hers.

And in less than two seconds she knew this little experiment was only going to fuel the fire, not extinguish it. In the next two beats, she knew she wanted more.

Lots more.

He gave it. His mouth was warm, giving, and quite talented, and she let out a helpless little hum as desire and hunger crowded her brain, squeezing out all that carefulness he'd accused her of. Needing to touch, needing to feel the heat of him radiating through his jersey, she slid her hands up his chest, absorbing the hard, sinewy lines of him. Through it all came the steady beat of his heart, steady but picking up speed, and she thought maybe it was that more than anything else that reeled her in.

He took a step into her, urging her back as his tongue delved in long, lazy strokes that were having a serious affect on her brain capacity. Another step and he'd backed her against the tile wall, holding her there with his deliciously built body as he continued the sexy, hot assault on her mouth.

If it wasn't for the fact that this was supposed to be just a little test, a one-time deal, she might have let it all go, thrown down the gauntlet—or her clothes—and completely lost herself in him as he kissed her as though she were his greatest fantasy come true. Because there, between the hard wall and his equally hard body, she felt desired. Beautiful.

Wanted.

It staggered her, literally staggered her. For so long she'd been by herself, on her own. Strong, independent, *fine*, and yet with just one kiss, that unraveled a little bit, and she knew that this man, this one man, was going to shake her to her very core. Which meant that she should step free and—

"Mmm," he murmured huskily, gliding a hand up and down her back, fingers spread wide as if he wanted, needed, to touch as much of her as possible. His other hand was still tangled in her hair, his big palm cupping her head for the kiss that was quickly becoming the mother of all kisses, hot and wet and deep, and she changed her mind about stepping free. She wanted it to never stop.

Never.

Beneath her fingers, his heart was no longer even close to steady, but thudding in a heavy, erratic beat that matched hers as he dragged his hands over her, cupping her bottom, squeezing as another rough moan of raw need rumbled from his chest. Then his hands went on the move again, heading north, thumbs brushing her ribs, so close to her breasts she caught her breath and wished.

Touch me . . .

Instead, he stopped. Stopped kissing her, stopped

moving, just remained utterly still with his mouth on hers, sharing air, his fingers nearly but not quite touching her breasts.

She tried to collect herself and failed. "Huh," she finally managed.

A low sound escaped him, a half laugh, half groan, and he dropped his hands to her waist, touching his forehead to hers. "Yeah. Huh."

"That was . . ."

He lifted his head, meeting her gaze. "Unexpected?"

"To say the least." Her breathing was still ragged, her body still trembling, and all she could think was, he had to go out there and play in front of tens of thousands of fans and she wanted another kiss. His eyes were so dark now, so dark they were almost black, and filled with so much heat she nearly melted on the spot. "So," she said. "No chemistry, right?"

"Right."

At his lie, *she* laughed and dropped her head back so that it thunked against the wall. "This is crazy."

"Agreed." He slid one hand up to cup her head again, protecting it from the wall, and it was that, that one little gesture more than anything else he'd done, that told her the truth.

He was sexy, smart, funny, and hot. *Very* hot.

But he was also kind.

Dammit.

She could resist a whole hell of a lot of things, but a basic kindness wasn't one of them. The guy ran from stalkers instead of having them arrested. He helped out kids. He took stupid writers who got conked in the head to the doctor for X-rays . . .

And he kissed so amazingly that she knew she'd be dreaming of him for days.

Weeks.

"Pace."

"Holly."

She let out a small smile when what she really felt like doing was stripping him naked and eating him for dinner. "That had more than a tad bit of chemistry to it."

There was something about the way he looked at her that made the backs of her knees sweat. "Yeah," he agreed. "It did."

"Maybe . . ." She tipped up her head and looked at his beautiful mouth, still wet from hers. "Maybe we didn't try hard enough to *not* want each other."

His other hand tightened lightly on her waist as a slow smile curved his lips. "Great minds," he murmured, and oh God yeah, once again covered her mouth with his.

It was insane to wrap her arms around his neck and go for it with more gusto than she had anything in recent memory. But she'd been so . . . restless. Bored. Unsettled, and missing something.

And yet here in his arms, his tongue dancing to hers, she wasn't restless or bored.

Not unsettled at all.

And missing exactly nothing . . .

In fact, she wanted to crawl inside him and keep feeling like this, for as long as she could, and given how he had her backed up to the wall, a certain portion of his anatomy pressing into her belly, she knew he felt the same. So she gave herself over to it, lost herself in his scent, his taste, the feel of him—

Until someone behind them cleared his throat.

With a startled gasp, she yanked her hands off Pace, peering around his wide shoulders.

Red stood there, clearly unhappy. "Goddamn, Pace." He pulled out his inhaler. "Before a fucking game?"

Pace sighed. "We need a minute."

"Yeah, we do," Red said, glancing meaningfully at Holly.

"I meant Holly and me," Pace said.

Red tossed up his hands. "Jesus."

"A minute," Pace repeated.

At that, Red stalked off, leaving a deafening silence.

Through it, Pace reached out and stroked a strand of hair from Holly's jaw, tucking it behind her ear. "I have no idea what to do about you."

That much she knew. "I suppose you could pretend that there's no chemistry, that you got it out of your system."

"Could we?"

"We? No." She shook her head. "I'm not all that good at pretending anything."

His lips quirked, but he didn't smile. "Good thing I am then."

Holly found herself seated next to Samantha for the game. The publicist was dressed in her usual princess-with-a-Nordstrom's-account style, in a fitted business suit that dripped sophistication and elegance. She'd topped it off with a straw hat that had a Heat orange flower stuck in the band.

It would be easy to underestimate Sam, easier still to chalk her off as a trophy piece given that her father owned the Heat and that her uncle owned the Charleston Bucks expansion team, where her brother worked as well, but beneath that beauty beat a heart of steel—and she had the will to match.

Besides, in Holly's book, anyone who loved fudge brownies and didn't judge her for being a reporter was a keeper as a friend.

It was a gorgeous but steady hot day. Holly inhaled the afternoon air and the scent of freshly cut grass as she and Sam stuffed their faces with hot dogs, peanuts, and lemonade. They talked stats, about the game itself, and best of all, the guys.

"Aren't they cute in their uniforms?" Sam asked as the Heat took the field.

Oh yeah, Holly thought, keeping her eyes on Pace as he jogged to the mound, though she wasn't sure *cute* covered it. As he began the inning, she found herself once again mesmerized by the process that went into each throw. Gage stood just inside the dugout, giving signs to Wade, long, complicated gestures that Holly couldn't begin to follow. Wade then repeated the signs to Pace, who'd either nod or shake his head or give a sign of his own. Lifting her camera, she caught his expression as he wound up and released one of his famed fastballs.

"Ah," Sam said at the next pitch. "He pulled the string."

"What's that?"

"An off-speed pitch, which after that first high heat, was genius. Keeps the batter off balance."

By the end of the fifth inning, Holly was in awe. "Oh my God—he's got a no-hitter going—"

"Shh!" Sam cut her off by motioning the sliding of a finger across her throat. "Don't talk about it. Don't even *think* about it."

"Why not?"

"It's bad luck. You'll jinx him—I'm serious," she said when Holly laughed. "Haven't you noticed? Even the announcer hasn't mentioned it. They're all superstitious, every last one of them."

"No."

"See Mason out there, the toughest first baseman in the league? He's wearing the same pair of underwear he wears to every game."

"Come on."

"And Henry? He drinks a soda after the bottom of the sixth inning, watch him. And Gage has to wear his lucky cap and touch it a certain way after each pitch. Hell, even Wade's superstitious. He's been rumored to sleep with his bat, though it's never been proven. No one messes around with this stuff, trust me. They've all got something."

And just like that, Holly knew she had the idea for next week's blog. "What's Pace's?"

"He keeps things pretty close to the vest. You'll have to ask him yourself."

"I'll do that." She took some more pictures and listened to Sam's ongoing commentary. It was all positive, of course. It was Sam's job to spin things that way, especially given what Holly did for a living, but she knew the publicist's affection for each and every player was real.

If there were secrets within the Heat, Holly was not going to learn them from Sam, so she concentrated on the game. Okay, she concentrated on Pace, on watching him pitch with that easy but intense concentration. How he stood on the mound and surveyed his opponent, his every muscle taut and ready before he nodded to Wade, then executed.

The whole process mesmerized her completely, and by the seventh inning she couldn't believe he could still be throwing so strong, with no sign of needing to be taken out for the closer. She used her camera as an excuse to watch him through her lens. His uniform was dirty from the top of the third when he'd hit a double, then tussled at second base, and he had a long streak of dirt down one hip and over a great set of buns. He was sweating.

She had no idea how they'd get that uniform clean for the start of the next game, which set her mind to thinking about how he'd look without his pants, how he'd look without any of it, all six-plus feet of tough, hard muscle naked and—

"Are you?"

She blinked and turned to Sam, horrified to realize she'd obviously missed a question. "I'm sorry, what?"

Fully aware of what Holly had been busy staring at, Sam grinned. "Are you getting everything you need from the guys?"

Well, wasn't that a loaded question, one she was momentarily distracted from when Pace struck out his batter, ending the inning.

"I'm still hoping for a one on one with Pace," she admitted. She'd had a one on one, and it'd been amazing. "A one-on-one *interview*."

"You haven't gotten that yet? Pace, Pace, Pace . . ."

Samantha sighed with a fond smile. "He's a tricky one—" She broke off when the eighth inning began and the announcer called out Wade's name as he came up to bat.

Holly watched Wade take a warm-up swing. "Maybe you could remind him he owes me an interview—"

"Oh God. *Look at him*." Samantha's gaze was locked on Wade in the batter's box, who swung at a wicked curveball and missed.

"Dammit." Samantha stood up and cupped her hands to her mouth and yelled at the top of her lungs, "Come on, Wade O'Riley, show us what you're made of."

Holly blinked at the heretofore completely put-together, sophisticated, elegant publicist, who was suddenly looking like a rabid fan.

Wade swung again and this time connected with a solid line drive right up the middle.

Samantha screamed, *"Yeah!"* so loudly she nearly pierced Holly's eardrum, and then jumped up and down, holding onto her hat with one hand and the hem of her skirt with her other. "That's the way, baby! That's the way! Go, go, *go!*"

The second baseman missed his catch, and Wade rounded the base, heading for third.

"Yes!" Sam screamed. "Ohmigod yes!"

Wade stopped at third, safe, and Sam sank back down to her seat and chewed on her thumbnail, her eyes locked on Wade waiting lithely on third for the next batter.

"So," Holly said, lightly amused, "you're a quiet fan."

"We need a big hit now!" Sam yelled at Mason, who was at bat. "Bring him home, Mas. Bring him home!"

Mason singled, and Samantha leapt back to her feet when Wade headed for home just as the shortstop nabbed the ball and threw.

"Oh God." Samantha slapped her hands over her eyes, then peeked through her fingers as both the ball and Wade raced for the plate. "I can't look, I can't look!"

"But you *are* looking," Holly pointed out.

"Tell me what's happening!"

"Safe," Holly told her, watching as Wade slid into home a fraction of a second before the catcher snatched the ball out of the air and dove onto Wade. "He's . . . buried, but safe."

Samantha dropped her hands from her eyes to her mouth as she stared at the tangle of limbs over home plate, not moving a single muscle until Wade pushed clear, adding an extra adrenaline-fueled shove for good measure as he got to his feet, dirty but safe.

Samantha fell back into her seat, blew a strand of hair from her eyes, and let out a long breath. "Jesus. This is exhausting."

"Yes." Holly put her tongue firmly in her cheek. "Does it hurt, too?"

"What?"

"That horribly painful-looking crush you have going for the Heat's sexy catcher."

"Shh!" Samantha whipped her head right and then left. "Do you want everyone to hear?"

"I hate to break it to you, but you were the one yelling your head off for him."

She looked horrified. "Was I that loud?"

"I don't know. The people in China might not quite have heard you."

"Oh my God, I know! It's ridiculous." She covered her face. "*I'm* ridiculous."

"Why? You're smart, funny, beautiful. He's smart, funny, beautiful. Why is it ridiculous?"

"Oh no. You're not going to interview me. No way. I'm not my publicity whore brother. I set up the interviews and that's it." Sam folded her hands in her lap and returned to the formerly prim, in-charge professional Holly had first sat with. "What were we talking about?"

Holly smiled. "You mean before you revealed you wanted to jump the catcher's bones?"

At Samantha's growl, Holly laughed. "Come on. It's true. Off the record, I promise."

"It's complicated." Sam let out a gusty sigh. "We . . . sort of have a past."

"Yeah?"

"Yeah." Samantha looked away, the tips of her ears sending out enough heat to light North America. "I don't want to discuss it."

"Okay." Holly could understand that all too well. "Well, we were talking about you possibly helping me get that interview with—"

"We got stuck on an elevator for two hours once," Sam burst out.

Holly blinked. "That sounds . . . traumatic. Anyway, I was wondering—"

"We'd just flown into Atlanta. We had those little bottles of Scotch. I definitely blame the Scotch, but let's just say we made damn good use of the downtime and leave it at that."

Holly looked at the misery on Sam's face. Misery, and remembered lust. "Huh."

"We had wild drunken monkey sex!" Sam clapped her hand over her mouth. "I really don't want to talk about it."

"Yeah," Holly said with amusement. "I can see that."

"Oh my God. Sorry. Clearly, I've been holding onto that for too long." She shook her head. "We've been pretending it didn't happen. And I *really* need to shut up now. *What were we talking about?*"

"Nothing as good as this."

Sam closed her eyes when Holly laughed. "You are lucky, Holly, so damn lucky, that you get to pop in and out of people's lives without getting involved."

Holly paused. Is that what she did?

"You get to keep yourself distanced, disengaged. I really need to get the knack of doing that, let me tell you."

Once upon a time Holly would have taken great pride in

that most accurate assessment of her character. But this past week or so, surrounded by the people she was beginning to think of as friends, watching those people live their lives to the fullest in a way she'd never managed, she suddenly realized how much she was missing.

Chapter 10

I'm convinced that every boy, in his heart, would rather steal second base than an automobile.

—Tom Clark

After the win, Pace poured out of the dugout with the others, telling himself things were good. That they were going to stay good. That the unnamable ball of uneasiness sitting on his chest was ignorable.

The guys with family in the stands were rushed and hugged and congratulated, and with that odd ache still in place, Pace turned away.

And then was nearly bowled over by a soft, warm body. Holly.

"I just wanted to say congratulations," she whispered in his ear, her lips brushing his earlobe, and right there, surrounded by tens of thousands of people, the adrenaline that lingered after every game was whipped into something else entirely, and suddenly he felt like a knuckle-dragging Neanderthal who wanted to drag his woman off to his cave and have his merry way with her. *Me want you now . . .* He let his arms tighten on her, hauling her against him.

Oblivious to the sharp need slicing through him, Holly grinned up at him, the woman he hadn't been able to stop thinking about through nine innings, the woman with the expressive eyes and soft lips, the woman who'd panted when he'd kissed her neck, making him want to do it again.

"You're good at that," she laughed, pulling free. "Putting up with people hugging you."

Not so good with it, not usually.

"Your shoulder okay?"

He felt himself tense. "Why?"

"Because I want to put out the scoop before anyone else." She shook her head, sarcasm in her eyes. "Because you look like you're favoring it."

"No, I'm good."

"One of these days you'll learn to trust me." She nodded toward Red. "Looks like you have to go. Coach's gesturing at you."

Yeah, he was, and looking apoplectic while he was at it, wanting Pace to get back to icing his shoulder, which wasn't as okay as he'd pretended it was.

With one last sweet smile, Holly moved off, and Pace headed to the usual postgame signing. Typically, this was actually fun, especially after a win, but tonight a large group of drunken assholes showed up in line, causing a commotion. After Samantha was harassed when she tried to step in and shut them up, the police were called, and the players were quickly bused back to the hotel and ushered into a private room at the restaurant for the postgame team dinner.

Well used to the occasional mob riots, Pace and the guys were unfazed and happy to eat. Pace grabbed his plate and looked for a seat. Wade was getting an earful about something from Gage. There was a spot next to Red, but Pace didn't feel like talking shop.

Besides, the empty seat next to Holly seemed to be calling out his name, and telling himself it was the closest open one available, he took it.

"What?" he said to her surprised expression.

"Nothing. I was just expecting you to do the ignore-me thing, especially after I nearly strangled you on the field with my congrats today."

He looked into her eyes and was instantly transported back to the clubhouse, where she'd held on to him as though she were drowning and he was the only thing that could save her. "I just took the closest empty kiss—er, *seat*. I meant *seat*," he said a little weakly.

She took a bite of pizza, studying him as she chewed. "I knew that kiss made you uncomfortable."

"I wouldn't call it uncomfortable."

"What would you call it?"

He looked into her eyes and had to take a breath. "Turned on as hell."

She smiled. "Good."

"You're direct."

"It was just a kiss, Pace. And just a hug."

A hug that had involved having her strain up against him, all warm, sexy, curvy woman. "I know."

She cocked her head. "Do you? Because it seems like maybe you're having some trouble with it. Need me to back off? Am I scaring you?"

"No." He shook his head at her smile and had to let out one of his own. "Okay, yes. Yes, you're scaring me."

"Aw." She slung a friendly arm around his shoulders and squeezed. "I'll be gentle." She went back to her pizza with gusto. "I loved watching you play tonight. You looked good out there."

She was looking good, too, but he kept that to himself, as well as the fact that she was messing with his head without even trying. *Both* heads.

"So when you're out there on the field, can you hear us cheering you on?" she asked, catching a string of cheese off the tip of her pizza with her tongue.

"Yes," he said, staring at that tongue. "But it's more like white noise if I'm in the zone."

"Well, I made plenty of white noise today." She laughed at herself. "I really lost myself."

He was feeling a little lost himself, in both the sound of her laughter and the warmth of her eyes.

"What?" she asked.

"Ignoring you is going to be a hell of a lot harder than I thought."

She didn't point out the obvious, that he was a grown-up, that he could chose not to ignore anything, but she simply sat there and ate her pizza, easily becoming the most enigmatic, intriguing woman he'd ever met.

The next morning the news was buzzing about what had happened after the Atlanta game with those wild fans. The story had gotten exaggerated, with some of the papers reporting that Sam had been beaten and nearly raped. The Heat flew home, where they were met by Sam's entire family, all of them royally pissed off and ready to kick some ass.

While Sam cooled their jets and assured everyone she didn't have a scratch on her, the players got ready for their game. Pace wasn't pitching, but his shoulder felt good—okay, not good but not bad—so he still dressed out, as he'd be practicing in the bullpen while watching the game.

Which they lost.

As well as their next three games.

At the end of that week, the players chaired a 4 The Kids auction, raising $250,000 before facing another home game, this one against the Colorado Rockies.

This time Pace was on the schedule to pitch. He'd had to see the team doc every single day that week to get approval, but he got it, and two hours before the start, he stood in the Heat's luxurious clubhouse in front of his locker, looking down at the few vitamin packs he still had left. Most of the guys swore they noticed a difference in their energy and strength levels, but other than sleeping better, Pace hadn't noticed anything. Still, for Tucker, he kept taking the stuff. He was pulling on his jersey when Henry, Ty, and Johnny joined him. He glanced over, but they said nothing, just stood there staring at him like Curly, Mo, and Larry.

Ty shoved Johnny, who shoved Henry. Who then looked at Pace. "You've got to kiss her, man."

"What?"

"Holly," Ty clarified. "You have to kiss her the same way you did in Atlanta, or we'll lose again."

Henry nodded.

Johnny nodded.

And Pace just stared at them. No one knew he'd kissed Holly, no one but him and Holly. And . . . Red. *Dammit.* "I don't know what you're talking about," he said, sliding Red a long death stare across the clubhouse.

From twenty feet, Red lifted a shoulder, then ambled over. "They guessed."

"They did not."

"Okay, they didn't." Red jerked his head toward Holly, who was taking pictures of Mason and Kyle goofing off at the food table. "But the last time we won was the last time you kissed her."

Jesus. Normally Pace had a healthy respect for the superstitions of his sport, but this one . . . This one just might kill him.

"Just do it," Henry said. "Kiss her."

Yeah. Hardly that easy.

"If you want," Ty offered. "I can do it for you."

Over his dead body. Pace looked at Holly. She'd written two more intriguing, fascinating articles without more than a mention of him, and though the writing had been insightful and quite hard-hitting, she hadn't exposed any big secrets or been negative on the sport in any way. He kept waiting for the other shoe to drop, but it never did.

"Don't mess this up," Red said.

Pace tried to figure a way around this, but as he knew all too well, it was immaterial whether or not *he* believed that they'd lose if he didn't kiss Holly again.

The guys believed it.

Shit.

"Here," Henry said, offering up a Dr Pepper. "For forti-fication."

"No, dude, he quit." Ty offered his Nalgene bottle in-stead.

Pace downed the water in it, but his mouth was still dry.

"You ready?" Henry asked.

Wade had joined them, soaking up the conversation with interest. He slapped Pace's back. "Go take one for the team, big guy."

"Goddammit." He headed toward the woman he'd been doing his best to avoid for days and found her in the middle of an off-color joke that was actually pretty funny.

He waited until she turned and looked at him. "Hey, you," she said, a warm smile curving her mouth.

"Hey." He shifted on his feet, trying to figure out a way to ease into this. "Uh, can I see you a minute?"

"Sure," she said easily, because she had no idea how *not* easy this was going to be.

"In there?" He gestured to the shower room, following her there, until Gage caught his arm and whispered, "Kiss only."

Pace looked at him. "What?"

"Yeah, no sleeping with her or we'll lose."

"Okay," Pace said on a long exhale. "What the hell have you been smoking? What have you all been smoking?"

Gage hesitated. "Listen, certain people think it's the sex-ual tension between the two of you that gave us that win."

Certain people. Pace craned his neck and slid Red a look of disbelief.

Red pulled out his inhaler.

Dammit. Low blow.

"So kiss her," Gage said quietly. "But don't f—"

"Whoa." Pace shook his head and pulled free. "You're all a bunch of fucking nuts."

Holly was waiting for him at the door to the shower room, which he opened for her. She was carefully put to-gether today, surprise, wearing a white shirt opened over a red tee and snug, hip-hugging jean capris. Her hair had been contained in a ponytail, with long sweeping bangs outlining the face that continued to tease him in his dreams all damn night, every night, where he'd done a whole hell of a lot more than kiss her.

The shower room was humid from the team's recent showers, and as she turned to face him, her careful hair began to frizz adorably. "I didn't think women were allowed back here," she said.

"They're not, usually. This is a . . . special circumstance, approved by management."

"Really? What're the special circumstances?"

Stepping forward, he put his hands on her hips and pulled her up against him.

"Oh." Her hands went to his chest as she tilted her face up, her lips parting in a little breath of surprise that he leaned in and swallowed whole with his mouth, and God, just like that he died and went to heaven.

With her own soft little murmur of pleasure, she sank her fingers into his hair, pressing her soft, warm body up against his, completely surrendering to him and completely snagging his heart in the process.

Pulling back with reluctance, he stared down into her glazed-over eyes and nearly drowned.

She licked her lips, just a little dart of her tongue as if she needed that one last taste of him and gave a sweet, pleasure-filled sigh that went straight through him. "Not that I'm complaining, but what was that for?"

"Luck."

"Really?"

"Yeah." He grimaced. "Listen, you should know, the guys think you're a good-luck charm." He paused, expecting her to get mad, which she'd certainly be within her rights.

But once again, she surprised him.

"Well, then," she murmured, her voice still a little husky. "Best of luck to you."

* * *

The Heat won, then went on to take the series two out of three games. Back at home, Pace coached Chipper and the others through a pickup game and then worked another 4 The Kids charity event with his teammates, this one a big, fancy dinner where they served up the food to the rich and famous. He had a surprisingly good time, especially watching Holly, who'd volunteered to serve drinks, easily and sweetly helping warm up both the guests and their wallets.

They made a cool $150,000 that night for the charity's pockets, then flew to Houston. At two in the morning, with Pace scheduled to pitch to the Astros in less than twelve hours, his cell phone rang.

"Bad news," the Skip said without preamble. "Ty and Henry were just pulled over outside of some bar. Henry's been arrested for DUI, and Ty was hauled in along with him for disorderly conduct."

Pace's gut tightened. "Oh Christ."

"Sam is working on getting the disorderly charge dropped, but brace yourself for a media frenzy with the DUI."

He wasn't kidding. By the next morning, the papers and blogs had gotten a hold of the story, claiming Ty had been held for suspected drug possession. One paper even suggested that the relief pitcher had been taking a new highly controversial stimulant, controversial because it wasn't easily detected during drug testing. The rumor went that it worked better, faster, and with fewer side affects.

The rumors couldn't be traced, but they were persistent and spread like wildfire.

Henry admitted only to having two beers in his system when he got behind the wheel, stupidly attempting to drive himself and Ty back to their hotel, but that was it. He continuously and adamantly denied drug use, while humbly admitting that the DUI was bad enough, as it was going to cost him both personally and in the eyes of the fans.

In Ty's case, however, he refused to apologize, saying

the papers were not only wrong but slandering him, because the so-called drugs they'd found on him were nothing more than vitamins.

None of it mattered. Hell, the truth didn't seem to matter as the press continued to slaughter the Heat the whole time they were in Houston, proclaiming that they were young and wild and far too cocky, that they thought they could do anything and get away with it. The MLB commissioner came under pressure to do more random drug testing, and promised to respond.

Before the next day's game, Pace was in the clubhouse when things went from bad to worse: his father called. "You forget my number?" the old man asked.

Just what Pace needed, that disapproving tone right before a game. "Hi, Dad."

"I'm in Houston. You going to win or lose today? Because if you're planning on winning, I thought I'd come watch."

Edward Martin didn't make it to many games because of his busy schedule. And in truth, their relationship was far better for it. They had one of those things-are-fine-if-we-don't-spend-too-much-time-together relationships. "I'll get you a seat." Pace hung up knowing he'd either disappoint his father or not, but to stack the deck in his favor, he searched the clubhouse because he had a girl to kiss.

"She's not here," Wade told him. "No extras in the clubhouse today. Given our press problems, management thought it best."

Hell. He reminded himself that he wasn't superstitious, that of course he could win without kissing Holly.

"I'll go pull her from the stands," Red offered.

"Not necessary."

"Yeah, it is," he said, and headed out the clubhouse door, only to come back a few minutes later, flushed and wheezing—and alone. "Not in her seat," he said, calling Gage, who was just about to use the PA system to comb through the entire stadium looking for her when Pace stopped them both. "This is ridiculous. We are not hauling her in here for some stupid superstition."

But then he went out and pitched like crap and was yanked at the bottom of the third.

They lost.

The guys gave him shit on shit. Hell, Red didn't even speak to him the whole flight back. The only one who did was the sole flight attendant, who somewhere over Arizona pulled up her skirt and asked him to sign her inner thigh.

He sat alone on the plane, head back, eyes closed, until he felt a set of legs brush his.

Her scent teased his nostrils, some complicated mix of exotic fruit, maybe flowers—all he knew was that it was amazing. She was amazing.

He opened his eyes as Holly squeezed in past him and sat. Around them, the plane was silent. The lights were dimmed; most everyone was sleeping.

"You okay?" she asked after a minute.

"Been better."

"Is it your shoulder?"

"No." Nope, he'd stunk up the diamond all on his own today.

"You know what they all think," she murmured. "That we should have—"

"Yeah."

She stared at his mouth. "I wouldn't have minded kissing you." A smile curved her lips. "For the cause and all."

He felt a stupid, helpless smile hit him. "No?"

She shook her head, and she leaned in. "Maybe we should . . . I don't know . . ."

His heart leapt hard against his ribs. "Practice?"

"Great minds," she said, repeating his own words from Atlanta back at him.

Yeah, now see that's what he liked about her, he thought, sliding a hand to the nape of her neck. Always game. The leather seats crinkled comfortably as he shifted closer, and he watched as her lips parted in anticipation.

Oh yeah. His parted, too, and he let his eyes drift shut as he kissed—

Gage's hand. Because Gage had shot it between them from the seat behind them.

"You couldn't be bothered to kiss her earlier, but you'll do it now?" came the Skip's pissed-off whisper, the one that could skin alive. "Fuck, no. Not on my fucking plane."

"No disrespect, Skip," Pace said, eyes still on Holly, "but I can kiss whoever I want."

"Get off my plane."

Holly laughed, but Pace knew Gage was only half kidding. Maybe only one-quarter kidding.

"No kissing," Gage instructed. "And absolutely no fu—"

"Okay," Pace said quickly. "Somebody needs a nap."

"No," Gage grounded out. "Somebody needs a *win*."

That night, back at home in his own house, Pace retrieved his e-mail, which included a link to Holly's latest blog, sent by Sam. This time Holly had tackled America's fascination/obsession with the players—the good, the bad, and the ugly, from the little kids just wanting an autograph, to the drunk fans wanting a piece of action after the game, to women wanting body parts signed.

Pace shook his head. "Had a good time writing this one, didn't you?" he murmured, reading on to where she'd outlined the innate problems with the players being treated like royalty, how the fast celebrity status could lead to a false sense of reality, an inflated ego, and even a distance from the game and fans that paid them their millions.

False sense of reality? Not so much, not in Pace's case anyway.

Inflated ego? Maybe, and yet hopefully not.

But distance? Check. And it was that, he figured, that finger right on the pulse of his own personal problem, that bothered him the most.

He absolutely felt distanced from his own damn life.

The next day, he pitched in the bullpen for practice, badly, and in spite of Red making him stop early, his shoulder hurt like hell.

Gage blew his equivalent of a gasket and hauled Pace's ass to medical, where he was assessed.

Severely strained rotator cuff.

Red pulled out his hanky for the diagnosis, and Pace felt like shit. Management called a meeting to make the decision—either put him on the DL for a fifteen day stay, or listing him as day-to-day until he recovered.

With Red's help, Pace fought long and hard for day-to-day status, convincing the Skip that he'd do fine with physical therapy. It put a lot of pressure on him to recover quickly, but hell, he was used to pressure.

That night, Wade brought him pizza and they had a pity party, but it didn't help.

Without Pace, the Heat pulled Ty up to a starter. He was good, but not good enough to take the Dodgers, and they lost their next two games. The press continued their massacre of the entire team, and the uneasiness in Pace's chest swelled, tightening against his rib cage.

Because no matter how he tried to spin it, things had gone straight to hell.

Chapter 11

Baseball, it is said, is only a game. True. And the Grand Canyon is only a hole in Arizona.

—George F. Will

Sam was extremely careful with the press release regarding Pace's injury. Careful and optimistic, stating only that Pace had a strained his rotator cuff, to be treated with PT. Then Gage made him go into seclusion—no cell calls, no computer, nothing but PT and rest for three days.

He was kept busy with that and icing, along with lower-body workouts.

On the forth day, feeling caged in, he used Wade's cell phone and called Holly. He didn't know why, other than he just wanted to hear her or better yet, see her. "How about dinner?" he asked when she answered.

"Why, Wade," she murmured in his ear. "I thought you'd never ask."

"Funny," he said dryly, nearly laughing for the first time in days. "Say yes."

"Yes to dinner, and yes to news on you."

"I didn't offer news on me."

She sighed in his ear, a soft, anxious sound that made him feel like a jerk. "Just tell me this," she murmured. "Are you okay?"

"Fantastic."

"The truth, Pace."

"I'm working on being okay."

"Fair enough. Dinner would be great. So would an interview."

Hell. "I was thinking steak and a drink, and no interview."

"Fine, be mysterious. Name the place and I'll meet you. I'm in Los Angeles at a meeting with my publisher, but I'll be back in a few hours."

They arranged a time and place, but when Pace showed up at the restaurant, Wade and Henry were already there. He stared at them, knowing he wasn't going to like this. "What are you doing?"

"Gage sent us." Wade wisely handed Pace a drink to go with that news. "We're on babysitting duty."

"What?"

"Yeah, you can look, but you can't touch," Henry instructed in a perfect imitation of Gage, and when Pace scowled, he quickly added, "You know that was the Skip, right? Not me."

"You can tell Gage where to put his orders, and that's right up his—"

Holly came up to the table then, with a sweet, welcoming smile. "Hi, guys." She set a hand on Pace's arm and looked into his eyes and made him forget his own name. "How are you?"

"Fine."

Her hand ran lightly over his bandaged shoulder. "There's that fine again."

"Well I'm fine now," he clarified, knowing by her warm smile that she understood it was because of her presence.

Wade and Henry scooted in and made room, and that was that. A foursome. Terrific. With a sigh, Pace held out a chair for her and gave in, after which his two teammates spent the evening telling her stories, like the time they'd hidden all of Pace's luggage when he'd been in the shower at Houston.

"He was forced to come through the clubhouse butt na-ked in front of a pack of reporters," Henry told her with glee. "Fun times."

Yeah. Fun times. He looked over at a laughing Holly and found himself smiling. "You think that's funny?"

"I do."

After dinner, the guys faithfully stuck around in the parking lot until Holly kissed them each on the cheek and drove off, leaving Pace with the urge to strangle each of them.

And then Gage.

"Think of it this way," Wade said, putting a hand on his good shoulder as they watched Holly's taillights vanish into the night. "She's the first woman you haven't been able to have at the snap of your fingers when you wanted. She's also the first woman to stick on your mind for more than a split second. That's a good thing, right?"

"What are you getting at?"

"That this is new for you, this slow dating-ritual dance. And different. And maybe, it's also something really great."

"Which I would know by now if I was allowed to be alone with her for even a second."

"Maybe she's worth the wait."

Yeah. Yeah, maybe she was. He went home alone to channel surf for a while, then gave in to temptation and called Holly to make sure she got home okay.

And to hear her voice.

When she didn't answer, he left her a voice message, a stupid, stuttering, rambling message that came from acting without thinking, which he was most definitely doing. After hanging up, he promptly fell off the wagon and drank two Dr Peppers.

The next morning, he woke up to find that the sports world was filled with rumors of the real nature of his injury, that it was far more serious than reported, that it wasn't just a strained rotator cuff but a severe tear that could be the end of his career.

Gage blew an even larger gasket and had Sam working night and day trying to figure out where the hell the rumors were originating from, along with all the other rumors they'd been battling for weeks, needing to know who the hell was always one step ahead of them.

Pace lay in bed that night and knew who it could have been.

Holly.

Except for one thing—he didn't believe it. Refused to believe it.

The next morning, he drove to the park. Chipper and River were ecstatic and couldn't wait to tell him how great Holly was. Seemed she'd taken them to lunch, and now they thought the sun rose and set in her eyes.

Pace thought something else, and he didn't like it. "What did she want to know about me?"

"Nothing," River said. "We didn't even talk about you."

"Uh-huh." Could he really have been that fooled? "Come on, tell me."

"Jeez," Chipper said. "She came for us. Get your own girl."

He sighed, and spent some time working on their field work. Later he had a meeting with Sam, where he signed boxes of merchandise for the 4 The Kids website.

"Pace," she said quietly, helping him sort through the stuff. "About these press leaks." She paused. "Do you think Holly . . . ?"

He met her gaze, his even, and spoke what he wanted to believe with his whole heart. "I don't."

"Good." She let out a breath and shook her head. "I don't either, I just had to ask."

"Yeah." When he finished signing, he headed straight into physical therapy, and from there into the Heat's weekly team meeting.

In the middle of one of Gage's rants, Pace's cell phone rang. Never good, as Gage hated to be interrupted. Even worse, it wasn't Pace's usual standard-issued ring tone. Instead, his phone burst out with the theme song to the *Courtship of Eddie's Father.* As the chorus of "People, let me tell you 'bout my best friend . . ." started playing, Pace's eyes cut straight to Wade, who was doing his best to hold back his grin. Paced looked down at the screen and sighed.

Holly. "Are you kidding me?" he asked Wade. "You programmed her a ring tone on my phone?"

"No phones in team meetings!" Gage yelled.

"It's Holly, Skip," Henry said urgently. "If he ignores her, maybe she won't kiss him at the next game."

Gage ground his back teeth together. "Go ahead," he said tightly. "Answer the damn thing. Tell her you still can't sleep with her until October . . . politely."

As everyone laughed, Pace thought about killing Wade, but that was all he needed, a suspension for fighting, as satisfying as that might be. So with the whole team watching, he opened his phone. "Hey."

"Hey," she said, sounding sweet and open and warm. "Sorry I missed you last night. I was in the shower."

Ah, man. And now he had that image in his head, her in the wet, hot shower.

Naked.

And it was a damn good image, too.

"I saw the papers," she said softly. "I'm sorry it's so serious."

"It's not."

"It's . . . not?"

He turned away from Gage's questioning expression. "No."

She paused as if waiting for him to say something else, which he couldn't. Not with his fascinated audience.

"Are you busy?" she finally asked.

He felt twenty pairs of eyes staring at him. "I'm in a team meeting."

"Oh! I'm sorry. I'll talk to you another time."

"Yeah. Okay." Smooth. Jesus, wasn't he smooth. He hung up and slid his phone back into his pocket, feeling like a clueless teenager.

As soon as the meeting ended, Wade hightailed it out of there, probably to save his own ass, and Pace stood up to go after him. Red caught him by the back of the shirt. "You need to wait until the end of the season to kill him."

"No."

"Yes," Gage said in a voice of steel. "And as a bonus, I promise that if you wait, I'll even hold him down for you."

Good enough.

After two hours of only eking out half a page, Holly gave up on her article, shut her laptop, and called Allie. "I'm in over my head."

"I've seen the papers. The Heat's taking it up the ass."

"I know. The reports are brutal, and even worse, it's stuff no one's supposed to know. They can't figure out who's leaking the info."

"Does anyone think it's you?"

"I don't know." Holly leaned back in her chair, holding the phone in the crook of her shoulder as she flipped through the papers. "I think Sam believes I wouldn't do such a thing. But the guys? Who knows."

"What about the guy, the one who matters?"

"I haven't seen him," she admitted. "The clubhouse's closed to everyone except the team. If he's not locked in a private training session or being evaluated by management's medical team, or holed up with Wade and the others where the press can't get to them, then he's nowhere to be found."

"When is his surgery?"

"That's the thing. His injury was blown up in the rumors."

"Good. I think you should find him, kiss him so they win again, and then, after the game, sleep with him."

Holly choked out a laugh. "And how will that help?"

"Well, you'll feel much more relaxed, for starters. Especially if he's any good. But more importantly, the Heat will win because they're talented, not because you didn't have sex, and then all those stupid superstitions are poof, gone."

"You're as crazy as they are, you know that? How's the screenplay going?"

"Steamy. I'm in the middle of a sex scene right now. The hero's nailing his heroine against the wall of his shower and they're—"

"Okay," Holly said with another laugh. "I'll just watch it when it comes out on the big screen."

"If it ever gets there."

"It will," Holly said firmly. "Believe in it."

"I will if you will," Allie said with irony and clicked off.

Knowing Allie was right, Holly made brownies and drove to Pace's house, which was huge and new and on the bluffs overlooking the beach. It was gorgeous.

And empty. Through the window next to his front door, she could see his entire foyer. There was a large pile of duffel bags and three bats leaning in one corner, and along a wide bench sat his glove and a batting helmet, beneath which was a dizzying array of athletic shoes—Adidas, Nike, spikes, cleats, running shoes . . .

No sign of movement, though.

She left the brownies on his porch with a note.

He didn't call. She didn't get anything but a silent message, loud and clear. Either he believed she was the media leak or . . .

She was the only one yearning and aching.

She had no idea which was worse.

The next day, Ty's and Henry's mandated drug tests came back inconclusive. With the lack of evidence, the two were cleared to play.

Holly was fascinated and horrified by the whole thing. Fascinated by the baseball drug culture in general. Over the history of the sport, much of it had been knowingly swept under the rug by the very people who governed it. But in the past few years, fan pressure and bad press had forced a change. A change not everyone had been happy to make.

Her articles were supposed to be about the guys and their popularity, what made them so beloved, but she found herself shifting gears, wondering if maybe the secret she'd been looking for had been right under her nose the whole time.

At the next game, she went early to take pictures of the pregame practice.

There was no sign of Pace.

Not that it mattered. She had a job to do. Period.

She sat in the stands with Sam and her brother, Jeremy, who was as tall and elegant and well dressed as his sister, with a smooth smile that could sell flint to the devil. The three of them made small talk until, with thirty minutes before the start, Holly got a call.

"Can you get to the clubhouse?" Gage asked. "Now?"

"Sure." She went running, heart in her throat, picturing . . . Hell, she didn't know exactly. "What?" she gasped when Gage pulled her inside the moment she arrived, tugging her through the luxurious front room to the Heat's shower room. "What is it?"

"Wait here."

She blinked when he slammed the door, and then again when less than twenty seconds later it whipped open.

Gage pushed Pace inside. Pace turned back to the door only to have Gage slam it in his face. He was in warm-up sweats and a shoulder brace, his face dark and edgy and quite pissed off.

Which was interesting, as she should be the pissed off one. She'd tried to contact him. She'd even stopped by with her amazing brownies—and they were amazing.

And he'd ignored her.

So it was with no little amount of annoyance and hurt that she crossed her arms and tried to remain unmoved by the sight of him in that damn brace and failed. "Are you okay?"

"Working on that."

Okaaaay. "So what's going on?"

"The Skip's lost it."

"Meaning?"

"His elevator isn't going to the top floor. He's playing a couple of cards short of a full deck." He turned to face her and swirled his finger near his ear, whistling like a cuckoo clock. "He's crazy."

Which didn't answer the question. "Talk to me, Pace."

"Yeah. See that's not what we're supposed to be doing. We're supposed to—"

The door whipped open and Gage poked his head in. "Hurry the hell up!"

The door slammed again.

"Jesus." Pace shook his head. "Okay, listen. You're not going to like this, but we have to kiss again."

She narrowed her eyes. "But you're not even pitching."

A ghost of a smile twisted his lips. "Apparently winning has nothing to do my pitching and everything to do with your kiss."

She laughed, but when he didn't, she stared at him. "You're serious."

The door opened again. Gage's head reappeared. "Serious." The door shut.

Holly shook her head. "So I am supposed to just willingly kiss you even though you haven't returned my calls?"

Pace closed his eyes and shook his head. He looked miserable and incredibly hot under the collar, and suddenly she got it. He was pissed for her.

He swiped a hand down his face. "Gage is convinced that we can't sleep together until October, so he's pretty much got me in lockdown."

"From me."

"Yes."

"Are you telling me that a thirty-five-year-old man, a team manager of a major league baseball team, would actually believe that my kiss will win him a game?"

"I told you that you weren't going to like this."

"Ah." She nodded as if she understood, but then shook her head because she didn't. "Which part of kissing you again aren't I going to like?"

"The part where you have to." He grimaced and shoved the fingers of his left hand into his hair. "And then there are those press leaks."

Her stomach went cold. "They think it's me."

"They don't know. But *I* know, Holly, and I can't—I won't ask you to do this."

Yeah, he really was mad for her, and damn if that didn't drain the rest of her temper, and also do something else entirely—turn her on just a little bit. "Oh, gee, Pace." She stepped close enough to put her hands on his chest. Yeah, suddenly she was feeling a whole lot better. "I feel so put out, having to kiss a man who kisses like heaven on earth." She pushed him back to the shower wall then turned so that it was she who was trapped as she brushed her mouth over his jaw. "I really do . . ."

With a rough exhale, he turned his head and met her lips with his own, soft and gentle at first, then hungry and fierce, and the amusement faded right out of her lungs, replaced by an instant, staggering, brain-cell destroying heat—

"Okay, that's it," Gage said after letting himself in. "That's great, thanks." He wedged himself in between them. "That's all we have time for." And he unceremoniously pushed her out the door.

She turned back. "But—"

"We have another home game tomorrow," Gage said. "Same time, same place." And then he shut the door in her face.

* * *

Pace watched the Heat play while warming up the bench with his own sorry ass. They won, which helped some. Afterward he was checked again by the team docs, the news not good.

He wasn't improving on PT. But another MRI didn't reveal anything new. He went straight from testing to the big bash in the clubhouse, thrown by management with the sole purpose of bringing their popularity rating back up. It was a massive affair, heavy on the celebrities, press, and booze, cleverly designed to put on a good show.

Pace hated that kind of a show, and he went straight to the bar and ordered two Dr Peppers, full caffeine, full sugar. While he waited, he turned and surveyed the crowd, pretending he wasn't searching for Holly.

Tucker came up to him, clasped a hand on his good shoulder, and smiled with genuine empathy. "Sucks being on the sidelines."

For days people had been tiptoeing around him and his injury. Tucker was the first person to acknowledge to his face that he was screwed, a fact which Pace greatly appreciated. He was damn tired of empty platitudes. "Yeah."

"Look, man, just take the time to heal." Tucker nodded at Pace's surprise. "Yeah, I know. No one else is going to tell you that, not during the season—hello, you're their moneymaker. But you have to do whatever you have to do to get healthy, or you'll end up selling fucking vitamins."

With a heavy weight on his chest, Pace watched him limp away, then searched the crowd.

"She's not here yet," Wade said, coming up to his side, nodding to the bartender as he handed Pace the two tall Dr Peppers.

"Who's not here yet?" Pace asked.

"The woman you're craning your neck looking for who. Your sexy rabbit's foot. And what the hell, man. Double fisting this early in the night? I thought you gave those suckers up."

"Past tense." The twin Dr Peppers were cool and icy against his palms and calling to him like a pair of long-lost lovers. "And Holly's not mine. We're not . . . we're not." Dammit.

"Yeah. I bet all that kissing is a real drag then." Wade accepted his drink from the bartender and leaned against the bar. "I think you're making a mistake with her."

His gut tightened. "She's not the leak."

"I meant you're making a mistake waiting to go for it."

"Yeah, well." Pace downed one of the drinks. "I have strict instructions."

"Bullshit. You're only obeying Gage because it suits you to ignore this thing between the two of you, and there is a thing," he said when Pace opened his mouth. "And honestly? I don't get it. You stand on a mound directly in the path of baseballs flying at you at the speed of light, and yet you're afraid of her. One woman. I get that there's a reason you're afraid. Love can suck golf balls, and we both know it. But taking the walk instead of the hit? That's just stupid."

Holly appeared in the doorway, and as she seemed to be able to do, laid her eyes right on Pace.

And damn if something didn't shift inside of him. "I know," he said to Wade. "I know it's stupid to take the walk."

"Then go for it already. Go get her and take her home. Get some fun of the naked variety. It does a body good."

Someone handed Holly a cocktail. Her hair was down, loose to her shoulders, which was new. She wore a crisp business jacket over a matching skirt, which was not new.

And she was quite beautiful.

God, he'd missed her. "What if it's not just naked fun? What if it's more?"

"Then I'll get to watch the mighty Pace Martin fall on his face for once." Wade clasped Pace's good shoulder, a wide grin on his face. "Hell, man, everyone should get something out of this."

Holly saw Pace right away. It was that weird chemical vibe they had between them, and her own personal curse to be so hyperaware of him. She liked to think he was cursed with the same affliction when it came to her. He was at the bar with Wade, the two of them watching her intently, but only one of them stopping her heart in faded Levi's and a button-down and with a day's worth of stubble. With a careful breath, she headed over there, but was quickly sidelined by Samantha, who pulled her aside to stand with her and Jeremy.

"I don't know how or why," Sam said, "but per Gage, you've got yourself an unlimited pass to the clubhouse, with instructions to be there exactly one hour before the start of every game."

Jeremy raised a brow. "Impressive, as Gage's usually so tight-assed with those things that he squeaks when he walks. I had to beg for mine, and my own sister runs the PR department."

Knowing exactly why she'd gotten the pass, Holly took it and slipped it into her purse. "Thanks."

"What makes it the most interesting," Sam said slowly, watching her face, "is that we have obvious press problems. They've revoked the other press passes."

"Maybe it's my articles," Holly murmured, trying to deflect.

"Or maybe it's how the saying goes," Jeremy said. "Keep your friends close, and your enemies closer . . ."

When he moved on to talk to someone else, Sam arched a brow. "Ignore my ass of a brother, he's pissed because I wouldn't give him some Heat privileged information he asked for. So what's going on, Holly?"

"I'm not your leak."

"Good. Can you explain the pass?"

"Turns out you were right about that whole superstitious thing."

"Okay. More."

"Pace has to kiss me before each game."

The usually unflappable Sam blinked.

"The guys didn't tell you?"

"No, they didn't."

Interesting that that hadn't leaked like everything else. "Yeah. We have to kiss in the shower room." She paused. Blushed. "Up against the tile wall."

Sam choked out a shocked laugh. "Wow. Such a horrible sacrifice, having to kiss Pace Martin." She stared at Holly. "So that's it. The reason you've let your hair down, why you're smiling more. You've been ferreting out secrets, while holding one of your own."

"Hey, I smile."

"Yeah, but this is more of a goofy I've-kissed-a-hottie smile. It looks good on you. So . . . where's Pace on the kissing scale?"

Holly's eyes locked on Pace. He was still watching her. "Off the chart."

Sam laughed. "I knew it. Did he ever give you your interview? He certainly owes you now, doesn't he?"

"Yes," she murmured, still looking at him. "He most certainly does owe me."

Sam pulled out her phone, punched in a number, and from across the room Holly watched Pace pull out his cell phone and answer it.

Sam turned away so Holly couldn't hear how their conversation went, but when Sam closed her phone, she nodded. "He says—"

Holly's cell rang. She pulled it out of her purse and answered. "Hello?"

"Hey."

Her heart tripped. "Pace."

"Sam says you need the interview now."

"That would be great, if you have the"—she turned to

once again locate him in the crowd and nearly plowed right into him—"time."

Standing in front of her with his cell phone to his ear, he smiled, a mix of resigned and heated affection in his eyes. "I've got the time."

Chapter 12

You don't save a pitcher for tomorrow. Tomorrow it may rain.

—Leo Durocher

Holly took a deep breath as Pace slid his phone back into his pocket. He'd been hurting, he had a lot on his plate, and he'd clearly needed distance, whether imposed by Gage or not.

And in truth, she'd needed the distance, too, needed it to do the job she'd come here to do. But all that went out the window when he gestured toward the door to the shower room, a door she was very, very familiar with.

He held it open for her, and as she walked through, she brushed up against him, incredibly aware of the air molecules that seemed to sizzle between them.

His clothes were simple tonight but there was nothing simple about the dark gaze that met hers. "You okay?" she asked, realizing he wasn't wearing his shoulder brace.

He smiled a little tightly, but when he spoke, his voice was classic Pace, low throttled and sexy as hell. "Is that the woman or the reporter asking?"

"Let's start with the woman."

He let out a low laugh, scrubbed a hand over his day old stubble. "Not sure what the hell to do about this, Holly."

"This."

"Us."

She looked at the tile wall of the showers, which several times now he'd pressed her up against to kiss her. "We could do whatever comes to mind."

"I'm not sure you'd say that if you could see what keeps coming to my mind."

Her knees wobbled and she let out a shaky breath. "I'd like to see," she whispered.

"I thought this was going to be an interview," he said, sounding just as unraveled as she. "Sam insisted."

Right. "Okay, that first." She struggled to push aside the aroused woman and find her professionalism. "I'll try to make it painless."

He let out a soft laugh, suggesting he didn't figure that to be possible. "You do that. Come on."

"Where to?"

"I figure it should be up on the hill where you watched me practice in the beginning, where you weren't supposed to be. Remember?"

Where she had gotten her first look at him, where a part of her had begun to fall for him . . . "I remember."

"The diamond looks good from there, especially lit up at night, like now. If you want pictures."

"Wow, you really are going to behave."

"I didn't say that. This way." He took her through the equipment room, where he grabbed two flashlights, then led her out a door that opened directly outside, along the backside of the parking lot.

It was a very dark night, and quite a hike from here to the top of the hill, but he didn't say a word about either. Instead, he said, "Thanks for the brownies, by the way. They were the best I've ever had. You've got all these . . . pieces, Holly. So many pieces of you."

Yes. She'd flitted from one to another her entire life, never quite landing . . .

He was quiet a long moment as they climbed, as he began

to struggle for breath. "I think that's what's so attractive about you," he said. "You're whole. With a bunch of different pieces making that whole. Not me. I'm just the one piece—baseball."

And at the moment, he didn't even have that, which she knew had to be killing him. But there was much more to him than baseball, or there could be. "Wade introduced me to your father when he came to watch you play." Drill Sergeant Edward Martin had been tall, dark, and handsome. Like father, like son. He'd also been formidable and quite intimidating. "He seemed proud of you."

"He's confused by me is what he is."

"He was at your game. That says a lot."

He looked at her. "Your father miss your stuff?"

"He missed my life." She shrugged at his questioning gaze. "He walked."

"My mother did the same." He was quiet a moment, then when the trail got rocky, or maybe just because, he reached for her hand. "My dad's a busy guy. Not into kid stuff."

"And he considers baseball kid stuff?"

"He did. And maybe that's why I went for it. I couldn't please him to save my life, so why not royally piss him off." He shook his head. "I was a shitty kid. Bad attitude. You?"

"I don't know. I pretty much had the opposite thing going. My mom was the shitty kid. She had both a bad man habit and a bad shopping habit, each constantly landing us in trouble until I was old enough to take over. And even then, she was still sneaking around, spending what we didn't have, trying to fool me . . ."

"Ah."

"What?"

He squeezed her hand. "Explains your love of furrowing out secrets."

"Yeah. I guess it does."

He smiled and nodded, and they fell into a surprisingly

comfortable silence as they walked. At the top, he stepped to the edge and she pulled out her camera.

He looked down onto the field far below. "Looks different from up here."

"You miss it."

He glanced back at her, the affirmation in his dark gaze, a tough, edgy, beautiful study in the night, backlit by the lights over the stadium. A tough, edgy, beautiful, unhappy study.

"You don't have to be all baseball, Pace."

"Let's just get the interview part over with. Ask what you want to know. I'll answer."

"Not that I'm complaining, but I can't believe we're finally doing this."

There was a light breeze ruffling his hair, lit by the moon high above. He was definitely revealing more to her than he usually did, and she couldn't tear her gaze off him. His eyes were serious, so very serious as he said nothing, and slowly she lowered her camera.

Because she got it. A little slow but she finally got it. "You're not letting me do this, at least not willingly."

More of his famed nothing, and she let out a low laugh. "So what did they threaten you with?"

"Another game on the bench added onto my medical time off."

"Ouch."

"They wouldn't really do it, but they're pretty desperate for good publicity."

"It's not a death sentence, talking to me."

"That's not what I was worried about."

"What are you worried about?"

"How about the fact that I'm not too upset that Gage is going to make us kiss before every game for the rest of the season."

Yeah. That didn't seem to upset her either. "Is that a problem?"

An indefinable sound escaped him, a breath that cut

through the thick, steamy hot August night and stirred up all sorts of memories. "I'd have thought you'd have a thing against sleeping with one of your subjects."

"Sleeping with?"

His eyes were very clear and very direct. "That's the rational next step for this thing, don't you think?"

Her tummy quivered. "I thought you were ignoring it."

"No can do, apparently."

She let out a breath. "So we what, un-ignore it in the name of getting past it? Is that what you're thinking?"

"Sleeping with someone tends to do that."

More than her tummy quivered now. "Always?"

"Well . . . have you ever ended up keeping a lover forever?"

"No," she admitted, and he gave her an I-rest-my-case look. "Okay," she said shakily. "Maybe we'd better finish the interview first because I'm losing brain capacity quick."

"Fine."

She cleared her throat, slipped her camera in her bag, and pulled out her pad. Tried to switch gears from hot and bothered to professional. "Everyone knows your shoulder is in question. A strained rotator cuff, right?"

"Yes."

"Rumors are that it's torn."

"If it was, I'd be in big trouble. It's strained, that's all. Physical therapy ought to do the trick."

"And if it doesn't?"

He paused very briefly. "We'll worry about it then."

"How does that make you feel knowing it could all be taken away due to an injury?"

His fathomless eyes locked on hers. "How would it make you feel to give up writing for an unforeseen amount of time?"

"Terrified."

He said nothing to that, just turned his head and looked out at the field again. "I'll be fine."

She stared at his broad shoulders and ached for him,

hoping with all her heart what he said was true. "The press and blogs have been tough on you guys lately. Does that affect your game?"

"No."

"Why not?"

"Because press, good or bad, is intangible. It's about the game for me, not about what people think."

"But people are fascinated by you. You know that, right?"

He shook his head. "A fact I've never really wrapped my brain around."

"Your bio says you moved twenty-seven times before you graduated high school and headed off to San Diego State. After that, your record speaks for itself, but very little is known about your private life."

"It's not about my private life."

"Come on, Pace. You know people want to know about you, what makes you tick."

"What makes me tick . . ." He let out a long, exasperated breath. "You know my father, career military all the way. Hardcore. He expects the best of the best. The only thing I had a shot at being the best at was baseball. I just got lucky it panned out."

She suspected luck had nothing to do with it. It was most likely a product of growing up under the thumb of a man who'd been hard-nosed, hard-assed, and not exactly nurturing. "Actually, your life isn't so different from a military lifestyle. You're focused, disciplined, hard-working. You train daily, you're single-minded—"

"I play ball for a living, Holly. Fun and games, all the time."

"I don't believe that, and I don't think you do either. You take this profession incredibly seriously." He was silent so she went for anther angle. "What do you see yourself doing after?"

"I'm not retiring."

"Eventually you will. You going to enjoy your millions

or move on to something else? Coaching maybe, like Red? Managing, like Gage? Or maybe golf. You could play charity golf tournaments—"

"I thought you were going to make this painless." He turned his back to her and stood there, his broad shoulders blocking the moonlight, creating a sort of halo around him.

But he was no angel, and she knew it.

Not even close.

And she ached for him anyway. Maybe because of it. She wanted him, flaws and all. But this wasn't about her and her wants. "Back to the drugs," she said quietly. "Under the new rules, everyone gets tested annually. An invasion of privacy or a necessity?"

"Hell," he muttered under his breath and swiped a hand over his face. "A necessity."

"You've never had a whisper about you being on any stimulants, and yet you throw like a machine."

"Because I know how to throw like a machine. I don't do drugs, Holly."

She felt his temper, and his control, and could appreciate both. "What about the other players on the Heat?"

"You can't ask me a question like that."

True, it wasn't very fair of her. But her job was rarely fair. "Ty's been suspected."

"He tested clean."

"No, he tested inconclusive. There're new drugs out there, performance-enhancing drugs that are slipping past the testing."

"Shit."

"You and I both know, many athletes do drugs."

"Not me," he said. "And this is supposedly about me. What else does your pad want to know?" he asked, sounding quite over this whole thing.

Couldn't blame him. She was over it, too. She slipped the pad into her purse and took the leap. "It wants to know if you'd like to stop the interview and get back to that other thing."

"The other thing?"

"The whole getting-each-other-out-of-our-system thing."

His eyes were steady.

Calm.

Hot.

"Very much," he said.

She set down her purse and camera.

He put his hands on her hips.

Hers slid up his chest.

And then they both stepped into each other and his mouth covered hers, hot and hungry, and all their differences, disagreements, frustrations, and arguments went out the proverbial window.

Chapter 13

Baseball is the only field of endeavor where a man can succeed three times out of ten and be considered a good performer.

—Ted Williams

Holly's soft sigh of pleasure echoed in Pace's head as they dived into the kiss with reckless abandon. God, the way she fisted her fingers in his hair, the arch of her hips to his . . . it rocked his world. She rocked his world. "Holly—"

"Mmmm," she murmured, and just like that, the tension that had been dogging him finally began to drain away, replaced by a different sort of tension altogether.

There was only this, the feel of her soft, curvy body, the taste of her . . . Cupping the back of her head with his hand, he slid his tongue to hers, loving her moan of pleasure, the way she lost some of her carefulness, which was just as sexy as her being careful in the first place. She had the best mouth, warm and giving, and so damn sweet he could kiss her forever. And if kissing her was this good, his brain went hog wild fantasizing about what else would be good. All of it. That much he could pretty well guarantee, and his hands made themselves at home on her body, everywhere he could reach, feeling her response in every quiver she made. His hands slipped beneath her shirt, touching that creamy, smooth skin, making her whisper his name in a shaky voice.

More. That was all he could think, and pressing her back to the tree, he filled his palms with her breasts.

And then went still at the crack of a branch behind them. Someone was here with them. He pulled back, but the dark was so complete he couldn't see.

"Pace?" Holly murmured, her hands going to his wrists.

He could hear footsteps running away from them now, down the path. He bent for the flashlights, handing her one. "Wait here."

Their surprise guest was quick, but he was quicker, and just around the next turn he overcame . . .

Tia.

His crazy fan whirled to face him, breathing like a lunatic, her hair falling into her flushed face. Wearing his away jersey, which fell to her knees, she carried both a flashlight and an autograph book, with a small camera strapped around her neck, lens open.

"Hi. I wasn't stalking you, I swear," she said quickly. "I was just watching you on the field, which is totally allowed because it's like six hundred million yards away, so you can't get mad. Please don't get mad."

"But I wasn't on the field, Tia. I was up here."

"Yes, but I didn't know that. Well, sort of I didn't. Okay, I knew, but I just wanted to look at you, that's all, honest to God." Tears shimmered in her eyes. "I'm your biggest fan, Pace. You know that. No one's a bigger fan than me."

"Tia—"

"So dammit, you should be kissing me, not her. You should be getting me out of your system!"

"Tia, listen to me. You could go to jail." He didn't want her to, but the last time she'd been hauled down to the station, they'd found a huge Swiss Army knife in her purse, a fact that had made him more than a little uncomfortable given her habit of showing up wherever he was. "Remember what the police said would happen if they found out you'd ignored their warnings?"

"I'm not going to tell them. And . . . and you wouldn't, right? Because I'm yours, Pace. Forever yours."

"Tia—" He stared regretfully, slipping his hand into his pocket for his cell phone. He felt like a jerk, but there was something seriously off about her, and he had Holly with him—

"If you would only try me, you'd like me," she whispered, also reaching into her purse. "I swear. I'll do anything you want, anything—"

"Problem?" Holly asked, coming around the corner.

Pace reached for her hand and tried to pull her to his side, but she resisted, instead turning to Tia. "Hi there," she said to his crazy stalker. "Tia, right?"

Tia blinked, and a huge tear rolled down her cheek as she kept her hand in her purse. "He's mine. You can't have him."

"Have him? Pace isn't a piece of property, Tia."

"You know what I mean."

"Yes, I do. And stalking is a crime."

Tia clutched her heart. "I'm not stalking him. I love him."

"But if you get caught here, they'll likely take you to jail. And then Pace will get more bad press. If you love him like you say, you don't want that."

Tia opened her mouth, then shut it. With a pensive, petulant glare in Pace's direction, she whirled and stalked off.

"Interesting night," Holly said into the silence. "I got both to interview you and to save you—not that you needed saving," she added kindly.

He stared down at her with the oddest desire to say, Yeah, I do. I need saving. Save me. "You seem to have experience with stalkers."

"What I have experience with is pissing people off."

She turned to head back down the trail as well. "I'm trying to learn how to defuse instead of ignite."

He followed after her. "Who did you ignite?

"An ex."

He took her hand and slowed her down. He wanted to see her face for this. "What happened?"

"I wrote a blog series about his industry, specifically the space industry."

"I read that series recently," he said. He ran a finger over her forehead, where her bruise had been. "I was impressed."

"My ex wasn't. I exposed his team for cutting corners where they shouldn't have, linking an accident to their neglect, an accident where three astronauts died." She sighed. "The program lost its tenuous funding, NASA pulled out, and Alex was fired and went to civil court, where he was sued for millions." She paused. "And the truth is, though I hate that I got people I cared about in trouble with the law, I'd do it again because people got hurt directly due to the neglect. I have no tolerance for that."

"You did the right thing."

"Yeah." She paused. "But he said if I'd loved him, I'd never have written about him."

"Did you love him?"

She shrugged. "I liked him. A whole lot, actually. And when it was over, I hurt a whole lot. But love?" Something came and went in her eyes, a sorrow, a regret, but in a flash it was gone. "I don't think I'm really cut out for that particular emotion. I question everything too much."

"Because you don't trust anyone who hides things, and we all do," he said, watching her absorb that, and think about it.

"I guess that's true enough."

She'd done a hell of a job raising herself in spite of being very alone and undeniably neglected to boot. But she'd made something of herself, and he loved the inner strength in her. "Thing is, Holly, I know that secrets make you feel unsafe, but the plain fact is that not everyone is hiding something bad or out to hurt someone."

"I'm getting to that realization. It's a balance thing for me, between the Holly of old and the new me."

She was the first woman he'd met since his career had taken off who looked at him without diamonds and money signs in her eyes. "So this new Holly, is she going to believe in love?"

"Probably not for myself." Pulling free, she headed down the hill.

"Wait," he said to that sweet ass. "So you're saying you don't want a happily ever after? I thought all women wanted that."

"Fairy tales don't exist in real life," she said over her shoulder.

He had pretty much seen and done it all. Sure, he was a little cynical, a little jaded, but in that moment, he realized he'd met his match. "Wow."

She sent him a questioning look over her shoulder.

"You mean it. You really don't believe in love."

"And you do? Have you ever been in love?"

"With baseball, just about all my life."

"With something that loved you back," she said dryly.

"I don't know, baseball's showed me the love."

"Women, Pace," she said with a shake of her head. "You ever loved a woman?"

"Maybe," he allowed. "Maybe a couple of times. I was even engaged once when I was very young and stupid. But if we're being honest, that wasn't the forever kind of love either."

"Are there two kinds of love then?"

"There are lots of kinds."

At that, she stopped walking to face him, hands on her hips, expression amused. "Okay, Mr. Expert, like what?"

"Well, there's the love that hits you after a few drinks and laughs, the one that says take this woman to bed for the rest of the night."

Her mouth curved. "That's lust."

True. "Then there's the kind after you've already slept together and you're still not over it. That kind of love takes several dates to get over."

"Again. Lust."

"Man, you really are a cynic," he murmured. "How about when you're with the same person for a while, a long while, and you still want to be with them naked? What's that?"

"A rut."

He laughed. "Okay, smarty pants, what constitutes love then?"

She lifted her nose in the air and started walking again, somehow in spite of the game, the kissing, the hike, the stalker, still looking completely, carefully put together. "I'll have to let you know," she finally said.

"Maybe you should write a series on that."

She smiled at him as they came to the now nearly empty parking lot. "Interesting idea." She looked around. They'd missed the mass exodus. "Do you think she's gone?"

"Tia? Hard to tell." His car was in the front row, in one of the reserved spots in all its apple red glory, but he passed by it, intending to walk Holly to her car. "Where did you park?"

"All the way in the back."

They hoofed it out there, and she came to a stop in front of her beat-up Subaru.

"You need a better-paying job," he said.

"Hey, this baby explored the ghost towns of California and lived to tell the tale. I can't dump her now just because she's not pretty."

"What about dumping her because she's looking as un-reliable as hell?"

She pulled out her keys. "Thanks for the interview." She cocked her head and looked at him. "I'm going to be honest with you here, Pace."

Uh-oh. "Is it going to hurt?"

"Maybe." She paused. "I'm interested in pursuing the drug angle."

"Ah, hell." He sighed. "It is. It's going to hurt."

"I want to write about what happened to Jim and Slam, and what happened to Henry and Ty."

"You've got apples and oranges. Jim and Slam tested positive for drugs. Henry and Ty didn't."

"The pills—"

"Vitamins. Tucker's, actually."

"You take them, too, right?"

"Sometimes. When I remember. You're not going to find anyone using on the Heat."

She looked at him a long moment, then nodded. "Thanks for tonight."

"But . . . ? Because I definitely sense a but at the end of that sentence."

"But," she agreed. "I'm going to write about what I want to write about."

He thought about what she'd told him about her last boyfriend and how that had ended, and understood that this was the same sort of situation—her work came first, always, a fact he reluctantly understood, even respected, though he didn't necessarily like it.

She tossed her purse and her keys into the passenger seat of her car and turned back to him. "I should tell you, I have a secret of my own."

"You do?"

"I seem to have this little crush." Her gaze warmed. "Three guesses."

There she went, being direct again. If she was angry or hurt or mad, or whatever emotion she was feeling, she put it out there for the whole world to see. No games. No subterfuge. No guesswork. She was open and honest and blissfully candid. And though it was crazy, he was crazy, he put his hands on her hips and pulled her in. Needing to assuage the ache low in his gut, the ache that said that the one thing that had been his entire life was no longer enough, that he needed more, he stepped into the only person he wanted to give it to him. Heat coiled low in his belly as he said, "I have a crush, too, along with my own secret."

"Which is?"

"You, Holly Hutchins, scare the hell out of me."

"Ditto," she whispered, not looking scared at all as she slid her fingers into his hair, tugging him down to put her mouth to his in a hard, smoldering kiss that managed to convey frustration, affection, and a mind-staggering heat. Far before he was ready, she let him go, and with a little smile, got into her car and drove off.

Chapter 14

Baseball is a fun game. It beats working for a living.

—Phil Linz

The Heat flew to Florida for a two-game series against the Marlins. When the private plane they usually chartered was grounded for maintenance at the last minute, they had to fly commercial, which meant much of management was left behind in order to get the entire team and the coaches there in time.

Everyone grumbled nervously without Holly there to kiss Pace, who felt good enough to start. He did okay, but Gage pulled him after three innings to save him for the Mets.

Pace sat on the bench and watched Ty struggle to keep their lead.

They lost seven to six.

The next day Holly's article came out, this one opening the door for the fans to the last mysterious frontier left in America—the Major League Baseball clubhouse.

She described it as a self-contained world where players lounged, bonded, ate, and occasionally fought, but she wrote that one undeniable thing about any clubhouse remained: the chemistry inside it made or broke a team.

Once again, she was right, and eloquent, and this time she landed a live interview on SportsCenter, which had been following her summer series with great interest. Pace and Wade sat in their hotel room and watched as on live TV she came off as sharp, funny, and—

"She's smoking hot," Wade noted.

Yeah. That. God, he missed her.

They flew from Florida to New York, where the rest of the support team finally met up with them for a three-game series against the Mets. Pace was up in the rotation for game two, and in the locker room, just before the start he felt Gage's beady eyes drilling a hole in the back of his head.

"Sorry," Pace said. "I have no idea where Holly is, but if you want, I'll kiss you instead."

The guys all laughed and Gage lifted his clipboard to throw it at them, but then the door opened and in walked Holly.

She wore a pristine white halter sundress and a Heat-orange belt, the definition of sweet and sexy all at the same time, and Pace wanted everyone to vanish so he could slide his hands all over her and ruffle her up. Ruffle her up and down . . .

Everyone smiled and greeted her, thanking her for showing up as if she was the second coming of Christ.

Or the woman who could seal the deal on a win for them.

With a small smile playing about her lips, she walked right up to him, her eyes lit up with warmth and affection, and as happened every single time he looked at her, something deep inside him split open.

"I'm not late, am I?" she asked.

"No."

They stared at each other, and everyone stared at them.

"It's nice to have everyone happy to see me," she murmured. "Are you happy to see me, Pace?"

If his hard-on was any indication, then yeah, he was

happy as hell to see her. He gestured toward the shower room, and she led the way.

As he followed her, the guys whistled and hollered and hooted, not that he paid attention to anything but how sweet her ass looked in that sundress.

He wanted to bite it.

Then the door shut, and they were alone in the damp, musky shower room. "This setup isn't nearly as luxurious as some of the others we've kissed in," she noted.

"Yeah." He turned away to look around. "Sorry about that—" He turned back and bumped right into her, sucking in a surprised breath as she pulled him in, slipping her arms around his neck. His hands went to her hips, squeezing gently before gliding up her back for the simple pleasure of touching her. "Holly—"

"I don't believe we're in here to talk," she said. And then she went up on her tiptoes, brushing her breasts to his chest as she did, and planted one on him, a kiss that meant business, instantly turning him into a snarling, rapturous beast, which he managed to hide by going very, very still instead of doing what he wanted to do—which was push up her dress and bury himself deep.

"This is more fun if you participate," she whispered against his mouth, her body doing a little wriggle that had his eyes crossing in sheer lust.

He tightened his hands on her. "Trying to keep us both clothed here."

Her eyes lit with fire and curiosity, and such excitement he had to close his and press his forehead to hers. "Okay, new tactic," he said. "Don't move. Just stand there."

She put a hand on his chest, the warmth of her palm spreading through him, joining the wildfire already in progress. Her other hand was on his neck and she slipped her fingers into his hair, playing with the strands, and twisting his gut with pleasure in the process. He could feel her soft breath against his mouth, and he let out a rough breath. "Holly."

"Maybe . . ." She ran her fingers over his chest from one side to the other, staring into his eyes as she very purposely pressed her body tighter to his, arching her hips to what had to be a very obvious erection. "Maybe if we kiss for longer," she said, "you'll win by even more."

"Yeah?" He let out a low breath and a laugh. "I like the way you think."

She lifted her face expectantly, and with a low groan he bent lower, once again covering her mouth with his.

She let out a soft, shuddery sigh of sheer pleasure and that was it. Goners. He yanked her up against him, she dropped her purse to the floor and flung her arms around his neck, and the kiss went as wild as his hammering heart. "Pace . . ."

Yeah. He knew. His stomach felt funny, his breathing was out of control, and all he could think about was that he could feel the two hardened tips of her nipples boring holes into his chest. It wasn't enough, not nearly enough. He covered them both with his palms as she slid her hands beneath his jersey, but that wasn't enough either.

It took him less than two seconds to untie her halter top and tug it down, baring her breasts, which were perfect, mouthwatering handfuls. Her fingers were fumbling with his pants as his thumbs grazed over those nipples he wanted in his mouth.

Wanted.

Needed.

So he bent and gently sucked one between his tongue and the roof of his mouth, loving the shocked, needy little gasp that tugged out of her. She got his button undone and his zipper down and her fingers danced over him, which had her letting out another gasp. Gratifying? Oh, hell yeah, and with a nipple in his mouth, he slid his hands up her thighs beneath her dress and found—

Ah, man.

A thong. God bless the thong.

He hooked his fingers in the silk sides and tugged, rolling

the silk down her legs until it hit the floor, his favorite place for panties. Palming her sweet ass, he slid his fingers lower, finding her wet and creamy. His ears rang with the hunger pounding through him as he slipped into that wet heat—

Wait. That wasn't the blood in his ears pounding.

But someone pounding at the door.

"Gage. It's Gage," Holly hissed and pushed him back a step, lifting shaking hands to adjust the dress he'd nearly torn off of her.

He concentrated on zipping his pants and dragging air into his lungs as he watched her cover her gorgeous breasts, the one still wet from his mouth—

Her thong was on the floor, but just as he took a step toward it, Gage stopped knocking and opened the door. "Showtime," he announced, coming right in. Oblivious.

Pace tore his gaze off the tiny white scrap of material and looked at Holly. Her eyes were wide as she stood there in the pretty halter dress, looking sweet and professional and just a little bit panicked.

Because she wasn't wearing panties.

"Showtime," Gage repeated to Pace. "You ready?"

Right. "Ready." His voice was low and husky and just a little bit hoarse. He tried not to look at the thong, but it was hard, he was hard, and his brain was suffering from severe blood deprivation. If he wasn't careful, he was going to bust another zipper, and this time it would be his fault.

The thong, the thong . . .

Gage looked at Holly and frowned. "You okay?"

"Fine." She flashed him a smile that worked because Gage didn't know her like Pace did. And he did know her. He knew she wanted her underwear. "Gage," he said. "What's that behind you?"

When Gage craned his neck to look, Pace scooped up the panties and slid them into his pocket.

"I don't see anything," Gage said.

"Sorry. It's nothing."

Holly shot Pace a slightly wide-eyed, sexy-as-hell look and held out her hand.

But what was he supposed to do, hand them over in front of Gage? He shook his head.

With a low, indistinguishable mutter, she headed for the door. He watched her go, his only coherent thought being that she was going to sit in the stands and watch him play.

Without panties.

Which meant he was going to be sporting a boner the entire game.

"Pace." Gage was looking at him, eyes sharp. "Shake it off. Get your head out of her pants and into the game."

Out of her pants. If he'd had even twenty more seconds, he'd have been out of his pants and buried deep inside her right here in the unlocked shower room, where anyone could have walked in on them.

He was such an idiot.

With huge effort, he managed a nod. He was ready to play. Or he would be, soon as he recovered from that kiss.

If that was even possible.

Chapter 15

I don't want to play golf. When I hit a ball, I want someone else to go chase it.

—Rogers Hornsby

It was hot and muggy in New York. Even more so sitting in the stands without panties. It was a ridiculous situation, one that Holly firmly blamed Pace for.

And how had things gotten so out of hand that she'd lost her underwear in the first place? One minute he'd been kissing her and the next she couldn't have even remembered her damn name to save her life, and before she'd known what had hit her, his long, talented, greedy fingers had hooked into the silk at her hips and slid it down her legs.

And then those fingers—

God.

Even thinking about it had her pressing her thighs together as need and heat swirled low in her gut. It was him, she decided. Pace. Those eyes, those fingers, that mouth . . .

If he hadn't been so damn sexy, none of this would have happened. This was all his fault, and she closed her eyes, trying not to think about how big and tanned his hand had looked holding her tiny white thong . . . and for the millionth time had to shift in her seat, which only served to make things worse.

So close.

She'd been so shockingly close to an orgasm. Even now, she could still feel the need grinding inside of her. Worse, she knew that if Gage hadn't knocked, they'd have gone at it right there against the wall, and anyone, anyone could have walked in and seen them.

Hard to believe she'd so lost her mind.

Disengaged? Ha!

Distanced? Ha!

Apparently she'd finally stepped inside the batter's box that was her own life and taken a swing at living. Hell of a time to figure that out.

She wanted her underwear.

Pace could have found a way to get them back to her before the game. He should have. But she'd known by the way he'd slipped them possessively into his pocket and sent her that heated look that she was going to have to fight for them.

Dammit.

She squirmed some more.

"What's the matter with you?" Samantha asked. She was on the phone with Jeremy. They'd been talking about some mutual charity events they had going. Actually, they'd been arguing, because Jeremy wanted top billing for the Bucks even though Sam had put the entire thing together. She pressed her phone to her chest as she regarded Holly. "You're acting like you've got ants in your pants."

Holly laughed tightly. "Yeah."

Sam put her phone back to her ear. "Jeremy, I've got to go. I'll yell at you some more later." She shut her phone and looked at Holly. "Spill."

Well, let's see. Her dress kept touching her like a damn caress. She could think of nothing else, and if Pace was here in the stands instead of in the dugout, he could probably

give her one look with those dark eyes and finish her off.
"Nothing's up. I'm good."

Sam narrowed her gaze. "Is it Pace? You just kissed him,
right?"

"Yeah." Among other things.

"Huh."

"Huh what? There's no huh."

Sam sent her a knowing look. "Just stay out of elevators.
All I'm saying."

Pace let himself fall into the zone, and played hard. He
pitched a solid two innings, giving up no runs, but during
the bottom of the third, he went into his rotation and did
something that sent a white-hot poker of pain through his
shoulder. Through his entire body. All he knew was that
oh holy shit, he couldn't breathe, could barely see past the
blinding, searing pain.

To add insult to injury, the batter got a piece of the ball
and whacked it, a fast line drive to left field that took him
to second while Pace stood there panting and seeing stars.
He had to force himself to breathe through it as the New
York home crowd roared with pleasure.

Wade signed, asking if he needed a minute.

No, he didn't need a minute, he needed a new goddamn
shoulder. He shook it off, then proceeded to throw out
eight piece-of-shit pitches in a row, walking two batters.

Bases loaded, the crowd went wild. *Fuck.*

Wade ignored Pace's next motion that he was fine and
walked to the mound. Pace kept his hat low over his face,
because out of anyone, Wade could read him like the back
of his hand.

At first, Wade said nothing. Nope, as if they had all the
time in the world, as if thousands and thousands of people
weren't watching and waiting, both in the stands and also
on television, he calmly stood there, taut and steadfast. He
adjusted his cap, then his mitt. Looked at the sky.

"You got something to say?" Pace finally asked.

"Yeah. It's fucking hot out here."

Pace let out a low laugh, which hurt like hell.

"So . . . Pizza after the game?"

Wade loved pizza, it was his comfort food. Pace's, too, but at the moment the thought of food made him want to hurl.

Wade eyed the crowd, then the batter waiting on them. "He likes the ball inside. Don't give it to him. Unless you'd like to give up another hit with bases loaded."

Pace said nothing.

Wade adjusted his cap again. "You going to tell me the real problem or not?"

Pace turned the ball in his fingers.

"Not." Wade sighed. "You want to get us through the inning?"

"Hell, yeah, I want to." Pace pushed up his hat and revealed his face.

Wade met his gaze, his own going very somber. "But you can't."

At his imperceptible nod, Wade closed his eyes a minute, then gestured for Gage.

The Skipper jogged out, took one look at Pace's face, and got a tick in his jaw. "You're green. Tell me you have the flu."

"No."

"The shoulder?"

"Yeah."

"Well, fuck me."

"I'd rather not."

Gage wasn't amused. They lost eight to one.

In the medical room afterward, Pace had some X-rays taken but he was too swollen to see anything. It didn't matter, in his gut he knew the truth. He'd likely torn his rotator cuff. That, or his arm was falling off, because that's what it felt like.

On the bus back to the hotel, he sat packed in ice, his

free hand in his pocket, his fingers wrapped around Holly's thong.

Gage dropped into the seat next to him. "You okay?"

"No."

"You want to talk?"

"No."

"Okay." Gage nodded. "Good. I'll talk. What the hell happened in that shower room?"

"What do you mean?"

"You do more than kiss her?"

"Are you really asking me that?"

"It was supposed to be just a damn kiss. Whatever you did, you screwed with the flow."

"Come on."

"I'm serious. Now look at you, hurt."

Pace let out a careful breath. "We did not lose because of whatever I did or didn't do with Holly in that shower room and I sure as hell didn't get hurt because of it."

Gage leaned in and lowered his voice. "Maybe that's true. Maybe you and I know it, but the rest of the team? They don't know it. So you're going to do this. Or not do this, in this case. No more hooking up with her." Gage took in Pace's expression and nodded. "Yeah, it's stupid and juvenile, but it's as good as fact that if they believe you've screwed with the routine and it's over, then it's as good as over." With that, he got up and left him alone.

And he stayed alone for about two seconds before Wade slid into the spot. "Hey. Are you—"

"Don't ask me how I am."

Wade looked at him for a beat, his eyes sliding to Pace's shoulder, and then he nodded. "Fair enough. We got some interesting rumors going on."

Pace leaned back wearily. "I don't care."

"There're two camps," Wade said anyway. "One says you've already done the deed with the hot reporter and the lack of sexual tension between the two of you is the reason we lost."

Pace closed his eyes and shook his head.

"The other says that you haven't slept with her yet but that you took it too far in the shower room today, and that's why we lost."

Pace sighed.

"Personally, I have a different theory."

"That we lost because I pitched like shit?"

"That we lost because we sucked today. All of us." Wade smiled wryly when Pace opened his eyes. "Look, man, I'm going to make a suggestion."

"Do you have to?"

"Screw the team and our stupid superstitions. Sleep with her already."

"How do you know I haven't?"

"Because if you had, you'd be a helluva lot more relaxed. At least if you're doing it right." He lifted a brow. "Is that the problem? You forget how? You need some pointers?"

"Wade?"

"Yeah, yeah, I know. Shut the fuck up." Again he looked at Pace's shoulder, still packed in ice, and his eyes sobered. "I meant what I said before. You need to go for it with her. You need to get yourself something outside this game."

"Why her?"

"Because she's the first woman to drive you insane instead of the other way around. Because you're different with her. You're happy around her."

"What if I told you that she's decided to go after a drug story regarding the Heat?"

Wade was quiet a moment, then he blew out a low breath. "Shit."

"Yeah."

"What did you tell her?"

"That I had nothing to tell her." He closed his eyes again and rested his aching head against the headrest. "And I just hope to God it stays that way."

*   *   *

When they arrived at the hotel, Pace had to jump through hoops for the team doc before getting to go to his room. They would evaluate him in detail back at home, but the grim consensus was that he'd most likely torn his rotator cuff. Alone in his room, Pace stripped down to his shorts, stood in front of the blasting AC and breathed in the blissful silence until someone knocked on his door.

Hoping it was someone with a hammer to bash in his head and put him out of his misery, he pulled open the door and found Red. "I don't want to watch any tapes." He stood blocking the doorway. "I don't want to even think about baseball."

"What crazy talk is that? Baseball is all you think about."

"Yeah, well things change." His every movement was agony. Plus, he was feeling the need to beat something up.

Or sleep with someone.

Holly.

"You're hurting," Red said, gazing worriedly over Pace like a mother hen. "Let me call a masseuse in for you or get you something for the pain."

"They already offered me something for pain." He knew nothing would help, not the knee-weakening fire in his shoulder or the wrenching ache in his gut because he was afraid, so fucking afraid. "I don't need anything." Except maybe a lobotomy. Yeah, that would help. He could stop hurting and stop thinking. Thinking and wondering how it'd happened that he had no life, and that he'd never even noticed until now.

"You need something to sleep," Red said. "So you can heal better, faster. Whatever you want, just name it. Vicodin? Something strong? Have you been taking the vitamins Tucker gave you? I have some herbal shit from Tucker that's amazing. You should see what it did for Ty—"

"I'm good, Red."

"But—"

"I said I'm good. Jesus."

Red stared at him. "Fine. Stare at the ceiling all night, in pain when you don't have to be." Turning stiffly, he stalked off, hurt, and Pace sighed. "Don't do that. Dammit, Red."

But Red kept walking. The man was as stubborn as a damn ox. "Fine. I'll take the damn pills," Pace called after him, even stepping into the hallway, but Red didn't stop.

Shaking his head, Pace turned back to his door, nearly plowing over Holly. God, not her, not now. He didn't want her to see him like this, and he sure as hell couldn't take the way she looked at him, as if even in spite of not believing in happily-ever-afters, she secretly hoped he was hers.

He had no happily-ever-after in his future.

Her gaze tracked up his nearly naked body to meet his. "I'd ask you if you were okay," she said. "But I know the drill by now. You'd just say—"

"I'm fine."

"Yeah," she said softly. "That. Pace . . . are you okay?"

"Don't." He couldn't go there, not right now. "Please, just . . . don't."

"Okay." She held out her hand. "I believe you have something of mine."

Yes. Yes, he did, and images flashed in his brain; her pressed back against the tile wall, her halter dress untied and revealing her breasts, a perfect nipple hardening in his mouth . . . how wet she'd been. "Finders keepers."

"Aren't you funny. What 'damn pills' are you taking from Red?"

The question managed to do what nothing else had. It cleared the sexual haze. "What?"

"He's not a doctor. You know he can't prescribe. Is it painkillers or other stuff, like performance enhancers?"

Insulted and pissed, never a good combo, he let out a short, mirthless laugh. "Didn't realize we were on the record."

"Sorry." She shook her head at herself. "I'm researching that article, and—"

"And you're curious. You're also sure there's a dirty little secret to ferret out. Well, you caught me. I'm having a drug party tonight. Sorry, no reporters invited." Sick, hurting like hell, he turned and stalked into his room, half wishing he'd let Red give him something after all, anything to get rid of his pain, both physical and otherwise.

Holly caught Pace's hotel door just before it closed in her face. She let herself in and looked around. Nicer than hers, bigger, fancier, but she'd never needed big and fancy.

She needed the truth. And she really hoped she hadn't just accidentally found it. "Pace—"

"Look, I've had a fairly fucked-up evening, so I really don't want to go around and around with you on what you think you might have heard just now."

She'd come to see how he was. To talk about what had happened in the shower room.

And to retrieve her underwear.

And maybe . . . maybe to figure out what the hell they were doing with each other, if it was real or imagined on her part. "Fine enough, except I don't remember asking you to go around with me at all."

"Ah Christ. We're going to." He shoved his fingers through his hair and turned in a slow circle, coming back to face her, arms still up, eyes resigned and exhausted, body tense.

He wore only knit boxer shorts low on his hips and getting lower with his every movement, a fact that was hugely distracting, emphasis on the huge. "Your shoulder," she said softly, clearly her throat and trying to clear her mind as well. "You've got some mobility at least."

"I can lift it up until the cows come home," he said wearily. "It's lowering it again that kills me."

She looked at the taut strength in his arms and shoulders, at his hard chest, the ripped abs. At the way his shorts gaped away from those abs with every breath.

Concentrate.

Noting the pain he was clearly in made it easy. "Pace," she murmured softly.

He turned away, carefully lowering his right arm. She couldn't see his face, but she heard his low breath of pain, which shot straight to her heart.

"How bad?"

Not answering, he strode to the duffel bag open on his bed and pulled out a foil pack. Ripping it open with his teeth, he poured what looked like at least five different pills into his hand and then tossed them into his mouth, dry swallowing them whole. "Better call the DEA," he said when he noted her watching him.

"Those were just vitamins, right?"

Without answering, he turned and headed straight for the minibar, grabbing a small bottle of vodka.

"What are you doing?"

"Getting some good old-fashioned pain relief." He tipped his head back and drank it down.

"You shouldn't mix pain meds and alcohol."

"Jesus." He set the now-empty glass bottle on the night-stand, grabbed another, downed it, too, then strode to the door, which he whipped open.

A not-too-subtle invitation to leave.

Well, it wasn't the first time she'd irritated a man beyond repair, that was for certain. And if she was being honest, she could admit that maybe, just maybe, she'd pushed his buttons to see how easily he'd cut their tenuous relationship.

Pretty darn easily, apparently.

She moved toward the door, then stopped only a breath away from his tall, built, hurting body. Lifting her head, she looked into his eyes, searching for the truth, or a flicker of regret, some knowledge that he was sorry it had come to this.

Nothing.

"You can be pissed at me all you want for asking about drugs," she said. "But why would Red so easily offer you some if you never use them?"

He stared down into her eyes and then at her mouth. And then the next thing she knew, he'd slipped his good arm around her back and tugged her up until her toes were dangling off the floor. His eyes were sleepy and at half-mast as he licked his lower lip, then kissed her—a deep, wet, hot kiss that came out of nowhere and stole her breath, her reasoning, and more than half of her brain cells.

She heard her purse hit the floor. One of her shoes joined it. He groaned into her mouth as her arms entwined around his neck, ripping a shockingly needy little sigh of pleasure from her as she gave him everything she had.

Until he pulled back.

Her eyes slowly opened as he let her slide down his body so that her feet were back on the floor.

"Sometimes," he said, his voice hoarse, "Sometimes, Holly, people do crazy odd things in the name of caring and love. Things they normally wouldn't do. Things that might look wrong in a black-and-white world. But see, in this world, my world, not everything is black-and-white."

She was so turned on, so revved up, it was nearly impossible to put words together. "You're talking about what you might put into your body in the name of your love for baseball."

He stared at her, then let out a low breath. "No. I'm talking about what Red would do for me. Which is anything, by the way. The very definition of love." Seeming weary to his very core, he shook his head. "You know what, forget it. You wouldn't understand."

She felt like she couldn't breathe. "Because I told you I don't believe in love? Or because I turned my last boyfriend in for his unscrupulous actions?"

When he didn't say anything, she took a step back, pressing a hand to her chest because her heart hurt. "You know what I think?"

"That I'm right?"

She'd been about to say that his fear of her was showing, but the same was true in reverse as well, which felt too revealing, so she swallowed hard. "I'm thinking that you, Pace Martin, are a very stupid male." She bent for her shoe and purse. "And I want my panties back."

"No."

"Oh, for God's sake." She had to brush against his body to get out, that warm, hard, amazing body she'd been hoping to have pinning her down on the bed right about now. Ha! Turned out he was no better than any of the other men she'd known.

Actually, he was worse.

Because he, unlike the others, had sneaked in past her defenses when she wasn't looking. He'd made himself at home in her heart and was right this very minute power blasting his way back out again, destroying the organ in the process. "Excuse me," she said stiffly.

Stepping back, he let her go.

She walked down the hotel hallway, her face hot, body hot, everything damn hot, and stopped at the ice machine. Grabbing a spare bucket, she filled it, then lifted the thing and pressed it to her cheek. When that wasn't enough to cool her jets, she took a piece of ice and ran it over her forehead and then down her neck.

Temper and arousal did not mix well, not with her, and with a sigh, she turned and then went still. Pace stood in the opened doorway of his room, arms crossed, that big body leaning causally against the doorjamb, his eyes calm and steady for someone who'd just had two shots of vodka straight up.

And cynically amused.

"I have a better way of cooling down," he said.

Yeah. But she didn't think she could take it. She certainly couldn't survive it. So she lifted her chin and continued down the hallway, stopping only to reach back for the bucket of ice, which was definitely going with her.

His soft, mocking laugh followed her all the way to the elevator.

Chapter 16

Three words that describe baseball: You never know.

—Joaquin Andujar

Holly went back to her room and, pressing the ice to her hot face, called Allie. "Heading to LA seems more and more appealing every day."

"Yay for me. To whom do I send a thank-you?"

"No one in particular."

"Baseball stud," she guessed. "Ah, honey, is he an ass then?"

"Yes. No. I don't know." She blew out a breath. "Truthfully, I think I might be the ass."

"Well, admitting it is half the battle."

Holly sank to her hotel bed and laughed. "My damn head isn't on straight and I can't find my usual happy place, and you have me laughing."

"You can't find your cool, calm happy place because your heart's involved. It's about damn time, chica. If I was there, I'd hug him myself for that alone."

"You'd hug him? He's driving me crazy and you'd hug him?"

"Yes. Call me when you can admit I'm right."

Holly closed her phone thinking that would be a cold

day in hell. But knowing she needed to, she put on gloss, combed her hair, and went to the one place she'd discovered over the years that she could get an answer to any question she had.

The bar.

Wade was nursing a drink and staring off into space. Except that when she got closer, she could see he wasn't staring into space at all but onto the dance floor, where Sam was doing some country swing thing with Henry, the both of them handling themselves with surprisingly good moves. "Hey." Holly smiled at Wade. "You okay?"

Wade tossed back his drink. "Never better." He gave one last long look at the hands Henry had all over Sam, shook his head, and stood. "I'm hitting the sack. You need anything before I go?"

She'd never seen him anything less than easygoing and laid-back, but what she saw in his eyes now was anything but. There was solemnness that might have stemmed from the Heat's earlier loss, Pace's injury, or, as she suspected, Sam doing her damnedest out there to drive him crazy. "I'm good. Wade?" she said as he began to move away. "Get some good sleep."

With a smile that didn't quite meet his gaze, he leaned down and kissed her cheek, giving her arm a gentle squeeze. And with one last look to the dance floor, was gone.

Holly sat next to Ty and bought them each a round. Sam stopped dancing long enough to talk Holly into helping her run the next big charity event for 4 The Kids, their upcoming Third Annual Poker Night, before hitting the dance floor again.

Ty eyed Holly over his beer, a good-looking guy with sweet eyes and a sweeter smile, and the best stats in the relief bullpen. A miracle, when she thought about the childhood leukemia he'd overcome.

"Hope you were gentle on him tonight," he said, raising his drink to his lips.

"On who?"

"You sleeping with more than one of us then?"

"I'm not sleeping with Pace."

But she'd wanted to be. Damn stubborn man. So she had a mind of her own and liked to use it. So she'd seen something between him and Red and had dared question him. So she'd . . .

Assumed the worst.

Okay, she'd been wrong there, very wrong, but she'd seen and heard it all in her life, and often from those she'd thought she'd trusted.

But Pace had overreacted. Seriously overreacted. It'd startled her and had also made her wonder . . . why? Why overreact if nothing was going on?

A little smiled curved Ty's lips. "If you're not with Pace, maybe there's another ballplayer on the Heat who can float your boat."

She cocked her head and studied him with a little smile of her own. "Does that line ever work for you?"

He laughed ruefully. "You'd be surprised."

She just shook her head.

"Maybe you'd go out with me if I asked."

"Are you asking, Ty?"

"Would you say yes?"

She laughed. "I think I just discovered why you're sitting at the bar and the other guys are with women."

He tossed his head back and laughed. "Maybe I'm gay. You ever think of that?"

He was built and warm and funny, and looking at her as if he'd like to butter her up and nibble on her all night. He wasn't gay, but she played along. "Are you?"

He touched her jaw, gently stroking a strand of hair behind her ear, his eyes going sleepy and sexy. "No. But I have a feeling if Pace walked into this bar right this minute, he'd want me to be. He'd probably make me a eunuch."

"I make up my own mind about who I see."

"And it's not going to be me," he said, good-naturedly resigned. "Or you'd have let me know by now." He leaned back and settled in. "Okay, so what is it you need to know?"

"What makes you think I need to know something?"

"Well, to my eternal disappointment, you're not here for my fine body."

She laughed again. "Okay, so I wanted to talk about Jim and Slam."

"We've done that."

"Yes, but I've been thinking."

"Uh-oh." He reached for his beer.

"From everything I've read and been told," she said carefully, "Jim never admitted guilt and Slam claimed innocence, in spite of both of their toxicology reports coming back positive."

"True. Jim has never talked about it, and Slam is still claiming he never knowingly took any steroids or enhancers."

"So what does that mean, that someone fed them to him without his knowledge?"

Ty lifted his shoulder. "He's not the first to claim such a thing."

True enough, but the thought of a trainer or someone doing such a thing without a player's permission was galling.

"Ask me what you really want to know, Holly."

"Could it happen? Honestly?"

"Honestly? In a billion-dollar sport, where more than just bank accounts are on the line? When it's also reputations and traditions and egos? Anything could happen."

"I've read that something like one out of ten professional athletes use steroids or stimulants."

"Right, but that's all sports combined—wrestling, football, track and field . . . Look," he said. "Athletes, both professional and amateur, have an incredible amount of pressure put on them to perform, and perform well. Add to that the fact that there's a limited amount of time for them to do their best work and gain success before ego or injury sets in. So if there's a shortcut to that success, someone's always going to be willing to take it."

"Even if it's risking their career."

"But," he said, "you have to take into account that historically speaking, it's only been recently that enhancers and the like have come into play as the bad guy."

"So what are you saying? That it's okay for the public and the industry to put this kind of pressure on the athletes, that it's okay for the athletes to respond by using drugs to enhance their bodies and performances?"

"Actually," he said calmly, "I'm just saying you can't believe everything you read."

"One out of ten . . ." she murmured, brain whirling. "That would mean that statistically speaking, at least two members of the Heat are using."

At that, some of the affection and amusement went out of his eyes. "It doesn't work like that, Holly."

"No?"

He sighed, set down his beer, and stood up, pulling some cash from his wallet and dropping it on the bar.

"Well." She sighed. "I've certainly got the knack of pissing people off tonight."

"We've got an early flight, that's all. Time to hit the sack."

When he was gone, she stood up, too. And ran smack into Gage.

"Where are you off to?" he asked. As tall and built as his players, he could be charming as hell when he chose. Though he was smiling, this wasn't one of those times. His eyes were troubled.

"As Ty just pointed out to me," she said, "we have an early flight. I'm going to bed."

"Alone?"

"Excuse me?"

He appeared to wrestle with himself, then grimaced and muttered, "What the hell," before swiping a hand down his face and meeting her gaze once again. "Let me walk you to your room."

"Are you coming onto me, Gage?"

"What?" He looked so horrified she almost felt sorry for him. "No!"

"Okay, that leaves babysitting. I don't need babysitting."

"Just tell me that you're not going to Pace's room."

"Oh, for the love of God." She tried a deep, calming breath, but it didn't work. "You know what, Gage, I don't even know where to start with you. But I'm thinking of wrapping my fingers around your neck and squeezing. Fair warning."

"Warning taken."

"And I'm not sleeping with your precious pitcher."

"Okay. If you could keep it that way . . . ?"

"Oh my God." She stared at him, slowly shaking her head. "You know what? All of you are—"

"Crazy. I know." He gently took a hold of her arm when she turned away. "Listen, I'm sorry. But honestly, given the sparks coming off of you two, I'm afraid if you . . . investigate that, then—"

"What? You'll lose? In case you haven't noticed, that's what you've been doing anyway."

"It's not for me. It's everyone else. They're unbelievably superstitious, and now we're facing Pace's injury and possible surgery—"

"Surgery?"

"—and all that bad press, it's just blown out of proportion."

"Surgery?" she repeated so that Gage finally shut up and just looked at her.

"He didn't tell you. Fuck." He took a deep breath. "Okay, listen, this is between you and him. Just . . . just don't go try to talk to him tonight—"

"Oh, I'm going." She pointed a finger at him. "But I can promise you this: there will be no sleeping involved."

"Uh . . ." Gage was clearly trying to evaluate her intention. "If you could not kill him, that would be really great, too."

"Now there's a promise I can't make." She headed to the elevators and pounded the button for Pace's floor. Possible surgery. Which meant he'd probably torn that rotator cuff. How ironic that the press had been claiming that very thing for weeks.

Of course he hadn't mentioned how bad it was earlier, which left her to wonder if that was because he didn't trust her not to put it out to the public, or because he didn't want her sympathy.

Or maybe it was far simpler than that. Maybe he just didn't care enough about her to bring it up.

No. No, she refused to believe that, and got onto the elevator. The man who'd kissed her tonight hadn't been a man who didn't care. Which left her to believe something else. He'd picked a fight so she'd go away and leave him to his own misery. Yeah. It was entirely likely that he'd do exactly that rather than talk to her about his fears and pain. "Damn idiot."

The man with her in the elevator shot her a startled look.

"Not you," she said quickly. "I—"

He hit the button for the next floor and got off as quickly as possible, without a backward look.

With a sigh, she leaned back against the wall. Yeah, she certainly had a way with men tonight.

When the elevator opened on Pace's floor, she went straight to his room and knocked. But either she was wrong and he'd gone off for his own fun for the night, or she was right and he was ignoring her, because he didn't answer.

And she slept alone, granting Gage his wish.

The Heat flew home, and Holly's next article came out. This time she'd written about the pitfalls of the sport, the number one thing being injuries—the ugly side of an industry that required so much from a person's body. She'd blamed the owners, trainers, and managers for pushing the players. She'd blamed the players for caving to the pressure and not knowing their own limits well enough to back off when necessary.

Up until now, the articles had been extremely popular with her readers and the industry. But today, the industry wasn't sending the love; they were sending hate mail.

Tommy was in heaven, loving the increase of traffic to the site, negative or otherwise. "That's what you're there for, doll. To air the laundry and stir things up."

And to raise his ad rates.

"But I still need a secret," he reminded her. "The readers keep asking for the big one."

"Maybe there isn't one this time."

"There's always a secret. Now go find it."

Sure. She'd just go find it.

The next day, she still hadn't heard any news from Pace, or about Pace, and she wondered what the final outcome on his shoulder injury was. She wondered how he was.

If he was doing okay . . .

Going stir-crazy, she grabbed her camera and headed to the Heat's facilities. She told herself that she needed some pictures of the team, but if she ran into Pace, so much the better. They had a few things to discuss.

Okay, maybe it was just her. She had a few things to discuss.

And she wanted her underwear back.

His fancy car was in the lot. There were plenty of other cars, too, including a few police units, who were probably watching practice on their lunch break again. That was good; she and Pace wouldn't be alone. If they weren't, she had a fighting chance of not losing today's underwear as well.

Not that having people around had stopped her before . . .

That she was even thinking that way had her rolling her

eyes at herself. She was not letting him anywhere near her underwear! She'd just reached for the door of the facility when someone behind her yelled, "Hey!"

Turning, she came face to face with Tia, who wore Pace's jersey again—or still—and a tight smile. "You," Tia said stiffly.

"Hello."

Tia didn't crack a smile. "I told you he was mine."

Oh boy. "Are you supposed to be here?"

Tia ignored that and gestured to Holly's camera. "Pace doesn't like pictures taken of him when he's not aware of it. He'll be upset, and he doesn't need that right now." She held out her hand. "You'll have to give that to me."

Holly slipped her Canon into her big bag. "I don't think so."

"If you don't, I'll be forced to confiscate it personally and turn both it and you over to the authorities."

"Tia, I'm not giving you my camera."

"Hey, I'm an official here, and—"

"You are not. You're a stalker—"

"Okay, that's it. I've asked politely. Now you'll have to pay the consequences." With that, Tia took a diving leap toward her.

Holly was so shocked, she hit the concrete before she knew what had happened, with Tia on top of her. "Are you crazy—" But she was stunned into disbelief when Tia took a swing at her.

"Hey!" Holly tried to roll away, but though Tia was bad with the aim, she could hold on like a monkey, and they both fell off the curb, knocking the air out of Holly.

Tia lifted her head, and hair wild, eyes wild, everything wild, she gritted her teeth. "I just broke a nail!"

Holly might have laughed, but she was on the ground in white jeans and a pale pink T-shirt she'd just gotten on sale, and that pissed her off. So did Tia grabbing her hair. In retaliation, Holly took a fistful of Tia's hair and a big chunk came off in her hands.

"Oh no, you didn't!" Tia shrieked and took her hands off Holly to hold her head. "My weave! My expensive weave!"

"That's not a weave, it's a damn wig." Holly took a look at the thing in her hand. "And a cheap one."

"You bitch!" She slapped Holly right across the face. "Now I'm going to kick your ass—"

Holly rolled Tia to her back and held her down, cheek and jaw stinging. "If there's any ass kicking, it'll be me, and—"

And nothing. Because suddenly she was hauled off Tia, her arms yanked behind her back. "Ma'am," an unfamiliar male voice said in her ear. "You have the right to remain silent."

Pace stood outside the police station, leaning back against his car, soaking up the sun, sipping a Dr Pepper he held in his left hand. Fuck quitting. His right hand was in his front pocket, the only position his arm felt comfortable.

When Holly emerged half an hour later, she winced at the bright sunlight and slipped on a pair of sunglasses from her purse.

He straightened from the car. "Hey."

With a deep breath, she walked down the path, right by him.

"Holly."

She kept walking.

With a grim smile, he caught up with her, touching her arm.

"You," she said as if speaking to a piece of shit on her shoe.

"Me? What did I do?"

She sent him a glacial look. "You're breathing, aren't you?" She shoved him away, careful, he noted, not to touch his bad shoulder, and kept walking.

She didn't live anywhere near here, and he knew damn

well her car was still at the stadium, so he had no idea where she thought she was going. "Not even a thank-you?" he asked, easily keeping pace with her, his eyes narrowing in on the bruise forming on her cheekbone.

"You're right," she said with mock politeness. "Thank you for getting me arrested."

"I meant for bailing you out." He took her arm and pulled her resisting body around, lifting a hand to gently touch her face. "She got you good."

She lifted a shoulder and relented slightly. "I got a few licks of my own in."

"Atta girl." He looked her over but saw no other injury. "You okay?"

"Yes. Thanks for posting bail." She said this begrudgingly, barely allowing him to redirect her toward his car.

"Tia's still in lockup." He figured that piece of news would cheer her up.

"I hope she rots in there. Can I drive?"

"She's in a 5150 hold. And no, I'd have to be on a 5150 hold to let you drive this baby in your current mood." He opened the passenger-side door for her.

"They're going to let her go in three days?" she asked indignantly. "The woman is completely insane."

"Yeah, well the police think the both of you are. I talked them out of holding you." He went around to the back of his car, opened the trunk, and pulled out his first aid kit. He grabbed the portable ice pack, slapped it against his thigh a few times to activate it, and then got in the driver's side, gently pressing it to her face. "Hold that."

"I really want to be pissed off at you."

"You'll have to stand in line." He pulled away from the curb, letting her be for a few minutes.

"Jail sucks," she finally said. "So do you."

"I vouched for your sanity, you know. And believe me, that took some doing. I should get some points for that."

"It did not take some doing."

"It did." He shot her a glance, satisfied that she was

holding the ice to her jaw. Her clothes were filthy, but her hair had been tamed. That was his careful Holly. "So what the hell happened anyway?"

"She was going to take my camera."

"So you beat the shit out of her?"

"Is that what she said?" She sounded pleased as she leaned back, resting her head. "Good." She was quiet for another few minutes. "I really wish I'd started a series about the beauty and serenity of some island in the South Pacific instead of doing it on baseball. I'd be on the beach right now, my toes in the water, sipping something cool and refreshing while being served by a cute—and silent—cabana boy."

"It's not too late." He drove into the stadium and pulled up to her car.

"I want my panties back, Pace." She didn't get out. She didn't move a muscle actually, except to slowly turn her head and give him a pissed-off look. "Don't make me take your ass down like I did Tia's. I could do it, too."

Torn between laughter and the need to wrap his fingers around her pretty neck, he just looked at her. "Honest to God, I don't know what to do with you."

"Trust me, you're not the first one to face that problem." She got out of his car, shut the door, then gave him a long, indecipherable look. "But when you figure it out? Let me know."

Being taken down on the asphalt by a crazed baseball fanatic and then being arrested had discombobulated Holly for a few shocking hours, but she'd gathered herself now.

And gathered quite a temper as well.

She stood in her shower until she had no hot water left, then pulled on sundress as someone knocked on her door. Unless it was a loaded pizza or a chocolate cake, she was not interested. She looked through the peephole, saw Pace standing there and her heart leapt inexplicably into her throat. Dammit, she was mad at him, and yet there he stood, calm and steady.

It didn't escape her how carefully he was holding his right arm as he waggled the fingers of his left hand at her through the tiny glass.

She opened the door. "Go away."

He shook his head. "No can do," he said and gently nudged her aside so he could step in.

She slapped a hand to his chest, giving him a shove back.

His lips curved as he allowed her to roughhouse him, when they both knew if he used his strength and dug in his heels, she couldn't have budged him a single inch.

"I'd really like to come in," he said.

"If you do, I have questions."

"What a surprise." Making the decision for her, he kicked the door closed behind him and reached for her hand. He was in jeans and battered Adidas, his shirt stretching taut across those yum shoulders, and suddenly all she wanted to do was hold onto him, and maybe kiss him, and maybe also get his clothes off.

He'd once said people do crazy things in the name of caring. Getting a real feel for that, she stepped into him and wrapped her arms around his neck.

Chapter 17

Baseball players are smarter than football players. How often do you see a baseball team penalized for too many men on the field?

—Jim Bouton

As Holly wrapped Pace up in a hug, loving the feel of his warm, hard body, she whispered his name. At the contact, he murmured with pleasure, his arms coming hard around her.

This, she thought. This was what she needed. Not talking. Not more of that odd and disconcerting dance/flirt thing they had going on.

This.

Pulling back, she tossed aside her wet hair as she unbuttoned his shirt, nudging it off his broad shoulders, leaning in to kiss the one that was swollen. God, he was so beautifully made.

He made a low sound as she touched him with her mouth, his hand coming up to cup her head as she soaked in the sight of his taut, tanned torso.

He was busy soaking in her sundress. The one with no straps, just a zipper up the back.

"What's beneath it?" he asked hoarsely.

"Maybe a little leftover tan, but I think it's mostly faded by now."

He let out a shaky breath.

Fully aware that he was watching her intently, she reached behind her to unzip herself.

His eyes went dark. "What happened to your questions?"

"I've decided to help you get me out of your system instead."

"Holly—"

"I'm trying to get out of my dress, Pace. Do you really want to talk right now?"

"No." His jeans were no longer so loose, and at the sight of the intriguing bulge behind his button fly, she had to swallow hard. Suddenly she knew how he felt because her skin seemed too tight for her body and she was breathing as though she'd been running uphill a good long time rather than just fighting with her zipper.

He lent his hands to the cause, putting his hands on her hips, turning her away from him so he could see. Then she heard the zip and felt a rush of cool air hit her back. "Thank—" The word backed up in her throat when he put his mouth to the sweet spot just beneath her ear as his hands slid inside the loosened bodice of her dress to cup her breasts.

"Problem," he said, his voice low and husky in her ear. "This is pretty much the only move my right arm makes."

"That's okay," she panted as his very talented fingers teased her nipples and turned her knees into overcooked noodles. "I can work with that."

"Good." He opened his mouth on the spot just beneath her ear, nuzzling as he maneuvered her down the hallway. "Bedroom?"

"Here." Her room was small and neat. He'd probably call it careful. Her bed was made. The furniture was cherry, including a dresser with a mirror over it, reflecting her own flushed, aroused expression and the man behind her causing it.

"Since that first day I met you," he murmured, his mouth

on her shoulder, "when you were so carefully buttoned up you drove me crazy, I've wondered . . ."

She tried to turn to face him, but he held her still, dragging hot, openmouthed kisses up her neck. "Wondered if you like your sex careful, too."

She opened her mouth to answer just as he gently sank his teeth into her, lightly tugging, and her entire body erupted into goose bumps. Her toes curled, too, which had never, ever happened. "Um—"

He met her gaze in the mirror. "Because I'm going to tell you right now, Holly, there's going to be nothing careful about this." His left arm tugged her dress down to her hips. "It's going to be the opposite of careful. Which, in case you're wondering, is hot and messy, and a little bit dirty."

He tugged again, and her dress slipped to her ankles, leaving her in nothing, not even her temper, which had deserted her at his first touch. She stared at their erotic reflection, his sinewy tanned arm encircling her much paler, softer body, and felt her knees wobble.

"Holly," he murmured on a shaky exhale, sweeping his hand over her belly. "You're so beautiful." His mouth moved over her jaw. His right hand, so dark against her pale skin, cupped a breast, his left slipping down her belly. "Beautiful and . . . ah, yeah. Wet." His fingers slipped even lower, unerringly finding her. "So wet."

"Imagine if I wasn't mad at you," she managed, gasping when his thumb flicked over her. She couldn't take her eyes off their reflection, at his big hand between her thighs. "I'd probably go off like a firecracker."

"You're still going to," he promised, and slipped a finger inside her, flexing it as he played his thumb over her center in exactly the right rhythm.

Her knees buckled but he caught her, effortlessly holding her as he continued to drive her right out of her mind, and she thought he just might be right. He just might get her to go off like a firecracker before he even got inside her.

"Spread your legs," he commanded softly, and when she did, he added another finger and deepened the pressure of his thumb.

With a gasp, she rolled her head back against his chest, aware of the picture she made in the mirror—naked, legs wide, arms up, entwined around his neck while his hand cupped a breast, the other played between her thighs. "I can't keep standing," she gasped.

"I've got you." And he did. He had her completely under his control, his mouth on her neck, his hands possessively, erotically on her body, which was more than halfway to orgasm. Her response was uncharacteristically and inexplicably uninhibited, wildly so, and she didn't care as she arched under his hands, desperate for more.

He gave it, gave everything, as if he already knew her body, knew what she needed, working her over until she could hardly draw air into her lungs. "Come for me," he murmured in her ear, his fingers masterfully stroking her, keeping her poised on that very edge. "I want to feel you come."

"I can't," she gasped. "Not standing—"

But then his fingers twisted inside her, pressing against a spot she didn't even know she had, while still stroking his thumb over her, and that was it. She did as he'd asked and came.

Standing up.

When she was still shuddering, he turned her to face him, backing her up a few steps until the mattress hit the backs of her thighs. Urging her down, he followed, sprawling his big, hot, heavy body over hers, spreading her legs with one of his own, dropping his head low enough to give her a deep, long, carnal kiss that had her gasping and hungry and desperate all over again.

"Your pants." She tugged at them. "Off."

Rolling to his back, he popped open the buttons and kicked off his shoes but then shook his head, panting. "I can't get the jeans off. My shoulder—"

He was sprawled flat on his back, chest bare, pants low on his hips, looking hot and bothered and sexy as hell. She could have just looked at him like that forever, but he was struggling and she was afraid he'd hurt himself. Coming up to her knees, she worked to tug his jeans down his hips. When his very large erection sprang free, her mouth went dry. "You're commando, too," she managed, staring, unable to stop from wrapping her fingers around him.

A rough groan rumbled up from deep in his throat. "My damn shoulder—getting dressed sucks, so I— Jesus," he gasped when she stroked him from root to tip. They hadn't gotten his pants past his upper thighs, so his legs were pinned. He couldn't move his right arm. And damn if there wasn't something about the sight of him, huge and gorgeous, and just a little helpless. Feminine pleasure and power surged through her in unprecedented waves, and while he struggled to finish stripping, struggled to touch her from his position, she decided to take matters in her own hands.

Literally.

Opening her nightstand, she pulled out the unopened box of condoms she'd had forever, and struggled to roll one down his thick length. She took so long her thighs were quivering and his torso was damp with sweat, and with a laughing low groan, he took over the task.

"Sorry," she murmured, watching him. "Been a while."

He shook his head. "There's no hurry—" This sentence ended in a rush of breath as she straddled him, then kissed him. He nudged her closer, kissing her back hard and deep as he thrust into her.

Her own gasp of pleasure filled her ears, along with a rough groan from him, and suddenly she was on the edge all over again, quivering with it, and he hadn't even moved inside her yet.

Then he did, and oh good Lord. "Pace—"

"I know." His hand skimmed up her belly to a breast. "I want to—"

She rocked her hips, dragging another rough groan from him. His head was back now, the tendons in his neck standing out in bold relief as his fingers dug into her moving hips, guiding her, urging her into bold thrusts that he couldn't quite manage on his own because of his injury. He encouraged her with low, wordless murmurs and that was it for her. He was it for her, and she came again, flying high as he joined her with one last hard thrust, her name on his lips.

It took her a while to reacquaint herself with her muscles. When she managed to lift her head from where she'd pressed her face against his throat, she blinked and tried to focus.

He lay flat and utterly still. She could feel his heart still racing in tune with hers, but other than that, he wasn't moving. "Did I kill you?" she whispered.

Eyes still closed, his lips curved. "Very nearly."

Good. That made them even. With her body still quivering, she slipped off him to her side and sighed with a bone-deep pleasure. "That should be a required bedtime activity."

"Agreed. Every single night." He still didn't move, and she didn't mind because the sight of him sprawled there on his back, arms and legs wide, was like a vacation for her senses.

"Pace?"

"Hmm."

"Did that do it?"

He sighed and blindly reached out a hand for hers, stroking a finger over her palm. "Get you out of my system? No. Not even close."

She felt herself relax, as if she wasn't relaxed enough. "I have another question."

He lifted her hand to his mouth, kissed her palm. "Shock."

She smiled, but it faded readily enough. "You definitely need surgery?"

His hand went still in hers.

"I'm taking that as a yes. Why didn't you tell me?" She paused, and when he didn't speak, she did. "I figure it's one of two things. Either it slipped your mind, or you didn't trust me with it."

He opened his eyes, stared up at the ceiling, and sighed. "It was neither."

In all the time she'd spent with him, he always seemed so big, so utterly invincible. Lying next to his tough, built body now, suddenly, she saw something else.

A hollowness, and a vulnerability.

And right then and there, her heart melted. Not good, but apparently she couldn't control her own heart any more than she could control him. "I'm so sorry," she whispered. "So damn sorry—"

"Don't." His voice was low, rough. "I can't take the pity, I'll—" He shook his head. "Just don't. Please, don't."

She wanted to hug him. Wanted to make it better and couldn't. "When?"

"When did I find out? The minute I did it in New York. I knew."

"I meant the surgery."

"Day after tomorrow."

She let out a breath, some of the tension he'd just gotten rid of for her coming right back. "You didn't tell me because you think I'm the press leak. That, or you thought I'd blog about it." Either way, a shitty realization.

"It's bad enough that the rumors turned out to be true." Turning his head, he met her gaze with his own. "I didn't want to face it."

She opened her mouth to tell him that she wouldn't have repeated it, but nothing came out. Because the truth was, there'd been times in her life where little had been more important than the story she'd been telling, nothing more critical than dispensing the facts, without much concern for the aftermath.

Or people's feelings.

And that, she realized, made her cold, and maybe just a little bit hard.

With a low exhale, Pace turned on his side and settled a big hand on her hip. His hair was disheveled, his eyes dark and sleepy and damn sexy.

And he had a bite mark on his neck. She'd done that.

"I can hear the wheels spinning," he said softly.

"You don't trust me, but you slept with me."

"I'd like to point out the definite lack of sleeping."

"Pace."

He drew a deep breath, which filled his chest, which in turn brushed against her nipples, making them tight and achy all over again. Pace's gaze locked in on one of them, his hand drifted up her ribs, and he lightly ran the backs of his fingers over her nipple, watching it pucker up even more. "It's not a matter of trust."

"It most definitely is."

"Okay, it is." He lifted his gaze to her. "I like you, Holly. I like you a whole lot."

"But you still don't trust me."

He didn't say anything for several beats. "I don't trust easily. You might recognize that little issue." He looked at her, seeing that she did, and nodded. "Yeah. But I can tell you this. I want to be able to trust you."

"Did you pick a fight in that New York hotel just so I'd leave you alone with your misery?"

"Yes."

The easy, ready admission should have made her feel better, but it didn't.

"Look, Holly, I realize my work is public. I also realize I should be used to my life being the same, but I'm not."

That much she believed. "So what's going to happen?"

"I'm on the DL for fifteen days minimum, to be reassessed after surgery. That news will hit soon enough."

She settled her fingers on his chest, felt the warmth radiating through him, the stable and sure beat of his heart.

She met his steady gaze and let out a breath. "I meant what's going to happen between us."

He just looked at her, and suddenly feeling extremely naked, both physically and mentally, she rolled to her belly to get out of the bed. She nearly escaped before he caught her, wrapping his fingers around her hip. "What are you doing?" she asked with remarkable calm and a good amount of attitude as he easily kept her pinned, even without the use of his right arm.

"Wondering where you're going."

"To get dressed. And you're leaving, by the way. I no longer sleep with people who don't trust me. It's a new thing. Call it a self-improvement."

He merely shifted his body over the top of hers, his chest against her spine. "It's because I was honest with you and pissed you off."

"Okay, yes. That, too."

"You want me to trust you, but you don't have to trust me. That sucks, Holly."

She spit a strand of hair out of her mouth and shifted her head to the side so she didn't suffocate, which wasn't to say that she didn't like the way his weight felt holding her pinned to the mattress, because she did.

A lot.

And she especially liked the way he thrust a thigh between hers, using it to spread open her legs. She just didn't want to like it.

He nuzzled the back of her neck. "You, Holly Hutchins, are a conundrum."

Dammit, so was he. He was supposed to be just a big, sexy jock. What the hell was he doing using a word like conundrum, whispering to her in that soft, sexy voice, using a powerful thigh to hold hers open as his mouth found the sweet spot between her neck and shoulder that she loved, loved, when he kissed. "I'm really mad at you right now."

He slid a hand down her body, slipping it between her and the sheets, cupping her between her legs, feeling exactly how not mad she was. "Mmmm," he said in a voice thick with appreciation as he played in her slippery heat. "Tell me you still want me to leave."

She opened her mouth to do just that but his fingers—God. She moaned instead.

"Yes or no, Holly."

"Stay," she managed.

He pulled out another condom from the box, put it on, and then slid inside her from behind as he kissed his way along her shoulder to her neck.

She opened her mouth to tell him that they were doing this but she was still mad, but only moaned as he gave a slow thrust, filling her deeply, so deliciously that her hands fisted the sheets on either side of her head to hold on tight. She bit her lip to keep her next moan in, but she couldn't stop herself from arching for the next long, slow thrust. "Still mad," she gasped.

He covered one of her fists with his hand, entwining their fingers, while his other slipped beneath her, stroking her where they were joined, slowly driving her straight to heaven without a seat belt. "Then I should stop."

Her toes were already curling, her thighs quivering. She only needed one more thrust, maybe two . . .

"Don't even think about stopping, not until—"

"Not until," he promised, and pulling her up to her knees, set about making good on his promise.

Chapter 18

I've come to the conclusion that the two most important things in life are good friends and a good bullpen.

—Bob Lemon

The next day, Pace entered the Heat's facility for a lower-body workout before his team meeting, torn between terror over his impending surgery and feeling damn good about the night he'd just spent with Holly.

Red was in the bullpen barking orders at Ty, but brightened at the sight of Pace. "It's not the same without your ugly mug around here."

"Yeah." Pace stood next to him and watched Ty throw, wishing he was the one out there.

"You'll be back in no time," Red said.

They both knew that was likely an empty platitude. Ty was doing a good job, throwing tight and fast. "He's coming along."

Red nodded along with that, then kicked at the ground. "A month, tops." He coughed at the dirt he'd stirred up, and pulled out his inhaler.

"Are you—"

"Fine." He pushed away Pace's concern. "Get to your meeting."

Pace headed inside and found Wade on his laptop. He

was skimming the blogs, but he took one look at Pace's face and nodded. "Nice."

"What?"

"You finally stepped up to the plate. Was it good? Never mind, she's hot, so of course it was good."

Pace grabbed a Dr Pepper with an utter lack of guilt since he was done playing for a while—Christ—ignoring Wade's knowing grin as he popped it open.

"Want to talk about it?" Wade asked.

"No." He nodded to the laptop. "What's up?"

"Not you. It didn't get out yet."

"Yeah, well. Holly knows."

Wade leaned back in the chair. "So?"

"So . . . she's a reporter, in case you missed that."

"Maybe she's not wearing her reporter hat with you. You ever think of that?"

"I don't think the hat comes off just for me."

"Then she would have reported it in her blog by now, but she hasn't."

"Not yet."

Wade shook his head. "You know, I thought it was your shoulder that was fucked up, but really, it's your head."

"You're *that* sure she's not our leak?"

Wade was quiet a moment. "Actually, I thought you were that sure. Look . . . you keep waiting for her to screw up so you can be over her, but she isn't screwing up, at least not that we know of, so what's next? How will you push her away now?" Wade shook his head. "Hope you have a parachute for that fall, buddy."

"What fall?"

"The one you're taking for her. You're falling hard and fast."

Which was just true enough to scare the hell out of him. And suddenly, the cool clubhouse felt hot, way too hot. "I need a water." He set down the soda.

Wade handed over his Nalgene water bottle, which was only a quarter full but Pace took it. Downed it.

Sam came into the room, carrying her newly printed brochures for the upcoming Poker Night. "Pace? You okay? You look pale."

"I'm fine."

Gage came in next and also gave him a funny look, but didn't say anything. Pace managed to avoid sitting next to him, sitting instead next to Ty, who had returned from pitching practice with Red and was now leaning back in his chair, eyes closed, waiting for the rest of management to arrive. Ty could be counted on not to ask questions. And also to carry water. Spying Ty's water bottle, Pace picked it up and chugged it, and finally began to relax.

When Pace set the empty bottle back down, Ty opened his eyes, looked at what Pace had done, and said, "Hey."

"I'll get you more—"

Ty stopped him from getting up. "Don't worry about it. But I had a mix in it."

"Tucker's vitamin pack? Or did I just drug myself?" Pace joked.

Ty laughed. "Yeah, good thing we've already both had our testing for the season."

"Yeah." So he'd just doubled his vitamin intake today. Hell, maybe it would perform some miracle on his aching body. His shoulder was killing him, and he couldn't get comfortable no matter what position he did.

Well, that wasn't quite true. Flat on his back with Holly riding him had been a pretty great position. So had been being on his knees behind her . . .

Somehow he survived the team meeting, listening to Gage talk about the upcoming game he wouldn't be playing. Afterward, in the parking lot, Gage caught up with him and gave Pace a long look.

Ah, Christ. He braced himself. "What now?"

"You're looking a little loose."

Was he wearing a Just Been Laid sign? "Don't worry, Dad, I used protection."

"Goddammit."

"Oh, and I also doubled up on the vitamins today, so all is good."

Gage sighed.

"Don't start. I'm having surgery tomorrow."

Gage's face filled with sympathy. "I know."

Pace turned away, looking at the Santa Ynez Mountains, not seeing the peaks but his own bleak future. "I guess I just needed . . ." He shook his head and closed his eyes.

"Yeah." Gage sighed and shook his head. "Forget it. There's something else anyway."

At the serious tone, Pace turned back to him, a little surprised to see the somber light in Gage's eyes.

"You remember after Ty and Henry's thing, the commissioner said they were going to randomly test some of us."

"Yes."

"Well, you're up. When you go in for your pre-op workup later today, they're drug testing you as well."

Well, wasn't that a nice cap on his day. "Fine."

Gage lifted a brow. "Fine?"

"Well, it sucks, but I have nothing to hide."

Gage let out a breath. "Okay then."

"Did you think I did?"

"I know you're in considerable pain all the time. I wouldn't have blamed you if you'd been taking something to offset it."

"Something that would show up on a drug test? Jesus, Skip."

"Just checking."

Pace knew his sport, knew the reputation it had, but with the new rulings in place, with a first-time offense for steroids being a fifty-game suspension, and a twenty-five game suspension for stimulants, people weren't going to mess around with their careers.

At least he wasn't.

"You're not the only one being tested," Gage said. "If that helps."

At Gage's tone, Pace looked over. "You worried?"

"When are you going to learn?" Gage let out a breath. "I'm always worried."

Later that afternoon, the Heat headed to Baltimore, and for the first time, Pace was left behind. He was back at home gathering gear to go meet the kids at the park when his father called.

"Surgery tomorrow, right?"

Pace had e-mailed him last week to tell him the news, but that his father was actually calling to offer some sympathy was so far from the marine drill instructor's usual tactic—which was to say something along the lines of "Suck it up and take it like a man"—that Pace was stunned. "Yes," he said, surprised. He moved to his front window and looked out, frowning at the movement at the end of the driveway. Probably deer again, eating the wildflowers. He'd always wanted a big, dopey, happy mutt to chase them away, but he was gone too much for a dog. "I'll be fine."

"Of course you will. Just do what you have to and get back in the game. You don't want anyone calling you a pansy-ass for taking a break midseason."

Pace let out a low laugh. Okay, so he wasn't calling to offer sympathy. "Yeah. Thanks for the call."

"I'm your emergency contact, I assume. So I'll hear if anything goes wrong."

Actually, Wade and Red were his emergency contacts. "I'll make sure you hear. Bye, Dad."

But his father was already gone. "Pansy-ass," Pace muttered, and frowned at another movement on the driveway, and a flash of blue. Okay, that wasn't a deer. He headed outside, but when he got out there, he saw nothing.

Tia?

Since he had bigger worries, he shrugged it off and headed to the park. The grass hadn't been mowed. Another fence had fallen down. And once again the bases were gone.

There was no playground equipment or lights here either, just a group of good-at-heart, ragtag kids making the most of what they had, and at the sight of them waiting for him, some of his tension drained. All of them were here today—Chipper, River, Danny, and . . .

Holly.

She stood next to where home plate should have been, holding the bat with Chipper directing her. She wore a pair of shorts and a T-shirt with a Heat hat—*his*—low over her eyes. He had no idea how the hell she could see anything, but there was River, preparing to pitch to her. Jesus, she was either brave or stupid, and he had a feeling, given the way something in his chest expanded just looking at her, it was the former. He dropped the new bag of gear he'd brought and ran. "Wait!"

No one listened to him. River pitched, and Pace stopped short as Holly swung. It was a god-awful swing, too, so low she might as well have been golfing. She missed, and Chipper also missed the catch, which had the ball bouncing and rolling, landing at Pace's feet.

He scooped it up as everyone turned to look at him. "What are you doing here?" he asked Holly.

"We're teaching her how to play." Chipper grinned. "She's great at hitting."

Pace raised a brow as Holly flashed him a smile void of her usual wattage. He wondered what was going on inside her head. He knew what was going on in his head, which was a running motion picture of how she'd looked when he'd last seen her, gloriously naked and panting his name.

"I'm not great at hitting," she corrected Chipper modestly. "But working on it."

"You're definitely ready for the U.S. Open," Pace said. "Maybe the Masters."

She cocked her head. "Those are golf tourneys."

"Yep. And that's what you look like you're playing." He went back for the bag he'd dropped in his misguided attempt to save her life and tossed it to the guys, who ripped into it with wild enthusiasm, pulling out Heat T-shirts and sweatshirts.

Holly was looking at him, silent and assessing, and he turned his head to meet her gaze, gently tapping up the bill of the cap to see her face. "What?" he asked.

"You are sweet."

Sweet? He was still on the instant replay of her naked, and moving onto the fantasy about how she might look with her legs sprawled wide enough for him to wedge his shoulders between, and she was thinking he was sweet? He let out a low laugh, and she stared into his eyes and blushed.

Yeah. There it was. Now she was on the same page. Which didn't help.

"There are kids present," she whispered.

"One of which nearly killed you last time. Wear a helmet when he pitches to you. In fact, always wear a helmet whenever you're up at bat." He reached into the equipment bag and found one, putting it on her head. Then he took her hips and turned her away from him.

"Been here before," she whispered, and he found himself grinning.

"Bat up, smart-ass." He ducked to avoid getting clocked in the head with it. "River, grab a ball."

"Yeah!" the kid said with enthusiasm and leapt back to the mound.

"Lob it softly," Pace directed. "Very softly."

"I can do it," Holly protested, and gave a little wriggle to get her stance right. A wriggle that put her butt right up against the button fly of his Levi's and very nearly had his eyes rolling back in his head.

"Don't hold back," she demanded of River with yet another wriggle.

Jesus. "Trying to keep you alive here," he said in her ear. "Go with me on this."

She craned her neck and looked at him, the kind of look that turned him on and upside down and inside out, and he had to laugh at her. At him. "Are you ready?" he asked.

"Yep."

"Don't try to kill the ball, just connect with it. And keep your eyes on it."

She rolled them first, then nodded to River as Pace backed out of the way.

"Wait for your pitch," he said. "Swing level, and follow through."

When she connected, she didn't drop the bat, she didn't run for first. Instead, she executed the cutest, sexiest little boogie dance he'd ever seen and whirled to him, nearly knocking him out with the bat. "See?" she asked, eyes lit with joy. "Told you I could hit."

It was a foul ball that any first baseman worth his salt would have caught in less than four seconds. Hell, Danny caught it, and he was nearsighted, farsighted, and had an astigmatism to boot, but Pace found that looking into Holly's wide, reveal-all eyes, he couldn't take it away from her by saying so. Tough as she was, smart and cynical as she was, when she looked at him like that, he also saw a flash of vulnerability, and it scared him.

He didn't want to be her soft spot.

So he turned from her and gestured to the guys to get into their positions. Since he couldn't even toss the damn ball, let alone pitch to them for hitting practice, he sat on his ass on the sidelines nursing his damn shoulder like a baby while he called out directions. "River, watch that foot. Remember, your foot is your lead."

And Jesus, now he sounded like Red.

Not a bad thing, he had to admit. He'd learned some of his best moves from Red, on and off the diamond. And it'd been from watching Red and Tucker together that he'd learned what a real father-son relationship should be like.

"You'll be a good dad."

He turned to look at Holly, who'd come to sit next to

him. She'd been playing left field, but since no one could hit that far, it was a waste of her dubious talents. But that she'd even tried had been . . . entertaining. Her nose was sunburned, and she had more freckles coming out. "I'm not planning on being a dad in the near future," he said as something clenched hard in his gut. "Unless you know something I don't."

"We used condoms, Pace. Don't worry, I won't show up with a baby and a request for a diamond ring." She took a look at his face and shook her head. "Okay, I'm teasing you, but clearly I hit a nerve. Did someone try to tie you down?"

"No."

She arched a brow, and he sighed. "I told you. I was with someone I gave brief thought to marrying, emphasis on the brief."

"You actually got down on one knee and everything?"

"I was young," he muttered when she grinned. "And I didn't get down on one knee because I'd pulled my ACL that season. Which was part of the problem."

"She dumped you because of a pulled ACL?"

"How do you know I didn't dump her? Never mind," he said when she opened her mouth. "Doesn't matter. It didn't work out. She refused to deal with me being gone for seven months out of the year, and I refused to quit playing ball. We were young and selfish, and love wasn't enough. We broke up. Mutually."

"It still sucked," she guessed.

"Yeah."

"I'm sorry if you got hurt."

"Part of life."

She lifted a shoulder.

"Which you don't agree with," he guessed. "Because you've managed to avoid such hurt."

"Not entirely," she reminded him.

"Right. Asshole Alex."

She choked out a laugh but fell silent.

"And if you were pregnant," he said after a long moment. "I'd want to know."

She looked at him. "Why?"

"Why?" He stared at her, stymied by the question, which he thought was obvious. "Because you shouldn't do it alone."

Her eyes chilled. "I could handle it. I can handle anything."

"I didn't mean it like that. Jesus." He shoved his fingers through his hair. "I just meant . . ." What, genius? You'd meant what? "That *no one* should have to do it alone."

She was running the grass through with her fingers, ignoring him, and he sighed. "There's one more thing."

"What?" Her voice was frosty as she lifted her gaze to his.

"I'd want to know," he said quietly. "Okay? I'd want to . . ."

"Run like hell?"

"Hey, give me a break here. New territory."

"Certainly." She rose to her feet, brushed off her hands, then cupped them around her mouth. "You guys about done? I'm springing for ice cream."

"Holly—"

She didn't hear him over the cheers. That, or she ignored him, which was more likely. Pace just looked at her, the woman who could do anything she wanted all by her damn self, and wondered how the hell it was that when he was with her, he sort of wished she needed him, just a little.

Chapter 19

Baseball is a game where a curve is an optical illusion, a screwball can be a pitch or a person, stealing is legal and you can spit anywhere you like except in the umpire's eye or on the ball.

—Jim Murray

Pace slept like crap and woke up before dawn, wishing he could skip the next few hours.

Surgery day.

To give himself a few quiet moments before facing that, he read Holly's latest blog entry. She'd written about the players' support teams—the wives, girlfriends, and significant others—and the pressures these people faced alongside their famous mates. She'd written about how those pressures led players to do things to keep up with other players that they normally wouldn't do.

Things like steroids and stimulants.

She pointed out how some of these drugs came in varieties so new and unstudied they weren't yet even on the banned list, but they would be added as the commissioner discovered them, in spite of the fact that these substances weren't mind-altering like other illegal substances. Nor were they as potentially dangerous as a few too many beers before going on the road, which put other people in danger, not just the athlete. She pointed out the irony of such contradictions, and then brought up drugs that weren't banned, like muscle relaxants and simple ibuprofen, and posed the question, should those things be added to the list as well?

As all her articles had been, it was incredibly well written and thought out, and, he was forced to admit, she'd nailed both the glory and the inherent problems of the sport.

He took a long hot shower, gritted his teeth at the movement required to towel off, then dressed and looked at the clock. Five thirty. He had to be at the hospital in thirty minutes, so he headed out, stopping short at the sight of Holly in his driveway, leaning on her car, arms and feet casually crossed, watching him. On her trunk sat a grocery bag, and she picked it up and held it out.

"What is it?" he asked warily.

"Well, it's not a hammer to hit you over the head with." Her lips curved briefly. "Which you look like you're expecting. The kids packed you a care package. Cookies and Dr Pepper, the apparent breakfast of champions."

"My favorites," he murmured, not even trying to hide his surprise.

"Interesting palette, but yeah, they wanted to bring you a comfort snack." Her smile warmed. "They love you. They're worried. I promised to take care of you."

"And in return they gave up all my secrets?"

"Yeah. And I only had to string them up by their fingernails and beat them to get those secrets."

Okay, so he no longer believed she was going to try to sneak one past him. He was just feeling a little raw, a whole lot scared, and he preferred to be vulnerable in private.

But she had his number. "You can try to piss me off all you want, Pace, I'm not leaving. As for the kids, they were worried about you. They wanted to get you something, so I drove them to the store. I also promised to bring them to visit you after your surgery, so brace yourself for that."

She'd eased their fears. She'd driven them to the store.

She was going to bring them to visit him. "Saint," he wondered aloud. "Or witch?"

"I use my powers for mostly good these days."

He looked into her fathomless eyes and saw her worry for him. "I'm going to be okay, Holly."

"I know. I also know I'm driving you to the hospital."

"I can—"

"Look, I know you'd rather have Wade or Gage, or just about anyone other than me take you because heaven forbid I see you weak, but we both know they're all in Baltimore for a two-game series and you're on your own."

A two-game series that he should be pitching. A two-game series that the Heat needed to take. He'd never missed games in the majors due to injury, never. It was a bone of contention, a point of pride.

"Get in the car, Pace."

He eyed her piece of shit and then his own Mustang. Again, pride warred with ego, even more so when she took one look at his face and laughed, making him scowl. "What's so damn funny?"

"You don't want to go in my car, but you don't want me to have to drive yours home from the hospital. You still don't trust me."

He winced. "Fine. I'm an asshole. We'll take my car."

"Good. I'll drive now so you can give me tips for later." She held out her hand for his keys. "Come on," she coaxed when he didn't move. "You can do it."

Yes, apparently he could do a lot of things. Such as crave her, the smart, funny, beautiful, warm woman who'd come to him when he'd needed her most. He couldn't have imagined that first day he'd met her, when she'd irritated him by wanting that interview, that all these weeks later he'd still be so intrigued and fascinated by her.

Contrary to his first impression of her, she was open and sweet and wildly passionate. In fact, he had nothing on her in the passion department. She was passionate about writing, about kids, about people, passionate about everything that crossed her path. She did nothing half-assed, not one single thing, and as a man who'd been passionate only about baseball all his life, he found the way she went about life incredibly . . .

Appealing.

It made no sense. His entire life was crumbling. He couldn't hold onto a damn pencil much less pitch a ball at ninety-six miles per hour. He was going to let everyone down from the Heat's owners to the fans . . .

And it was killing him.

Killing.

Him.

And yet just looking at Holly, some of the pain and confusion and anger seemed to fade away.

Even if she wanted to drive his car. "I was going to call a cab."

"Listen, I've only had one accident," she said. "And it wasn't my fault. It was an old car and I ran out of brake fluid on a hill in San Francisco and I rolled into a house. That's all."

Jesus. "That's all, huh?"

"Well, there're the three speeding tickets, which really, if you think about it, just proves I can handle myself."

That choked a real laugh out of him. A laugh, when he was on his way to being cut open.

She held out her hand, palm up, looking quite sure of herself and, dammit, hot. "Want to know something else?" she asked.

What the hell. "Sure."

"I'm wearing a bra, but since you still have the panties that match it, I'm commando."

His mouth fell open, and she twirled for him to see. He drank her in, but she was wearing cargo pants, low on her hips but too loose so he couldn't tell. Not that it mattered, the view was mouth-watering regardless. He dropped the keys into her hand, dropped his whole damn life in her hand just to watch her walk around the car.

* * *

Holly paced the hospital waiting room, unaccustomed to the pit of anxiety in her gut. One thing about the way she moved in and out of people's lives for her job—she hadn't done a lot of worrying about them.

This time was completely different. She worried about the people she'd come to care about, a lot, but she also worried about herself because here was something new to obsess over, something that had never bothered her until now—she was halfway through her series and had no idea what she'd do when she was done. She'd always known by now, but this time she had nothing.

Because this time, she didn't want to leave.

Pace woke up from his surgery feeling no pain thanks to a pretty nurse shooting some very good stuff into his IV. "Hey, is that MLB sanctioned?" he quipped.

She smiled and patted his arm, and when he woke up again, Holly was sitting by his bed, tapping on the keys of her laptop. She looked up at his movement and offered him one of those fake smiles people gave to people who are dying.

Uh-oh. "They operate on the wrong shoulder?" he asked.

"Of course not." She got up and put her hand to his cheek. "How are you feeling?"

"No pain." In fact, the room was spinning pleasantly, centered by her hand on him. "What's the matter?"

"Nothing." She plumped the pillow behind his back when he tried to sit up, fussing over him.

Stalling.

"Holly."

She was busy straightening his covers now, like he was a damn invalid.

Which he wasn't.

In fact, he was feeling the exact opposite of an invalid because every time she leaned over him, her button-up T-shirt gaped open and revealed a white silky demi-bra that had her breasts nearly spilling out over the top.

Which reminded him—she wasn't wearing panties. He had no idea why that fact so fascinated him. He'd seen her body. It was fantastic, but he sure as hell shouldn't be drooling to see her again. "It's the meds."

Her eyes met his. "What is?"

"The reason I'm getting a boner looking down your top. Nice bra."

She narrowed her eyes. "Are you hallucinating?"

"If I say yes, will you take off the bra? It would complete my collection."

"Okay, that's it. I'm calling the doctor."

He snagged her wrist with his good hand, which still had an IV in it. Because yeah, he wanted to see her breasts again, but mostly he wanted to know what had put that look in her eyes. The one that said he was fucked. "Tell me what's wrong."

"I told you, nothing."

"You're a shitty liar, Holly. Spill it."

"I snooped and read your chart."

He just gave her a long look.

"I wanted to make sure you were really okay. You were sleeping so heavily and I was worried."

"Concern or a reporter's cutthroat curiosity?"

"It was concern," she said tightly. "And your curmudgeonly cynicism is really getting old. Pace—"

"Just tell me. I'm dying, right?"

"No. You're—"

His doctor entered. "Look at you, awake and alert. Perfect." He looked at Holly. "I need a moment with the patient, please."

Holly gave Pace an indecipherable look and left the room.

And for a guy who prized his alone time, who craved it

like some craved water, he experienced the oddest sense of loneliness he'd ever felt.

And fear. Let's not forget the fear, because there was plenty of that, too. "So. What's up, Doc?"

Chapter 20

Strikeouts are boring—besides that, they're fascist.
Throw some ground balls. More democratic.

—Crash Davis in *Bull Durham*

Pace's surgeon didn't answer right away, waiting until
the hospital room door shut behind Holly, until he'd opened
Pace's chart. "How are you feeling?"

"A little uptight, actually, which is ruining my happy
drug buzz. What's going on?"

"Good news and bad news. Are you in pain?"

Pace turned his head and looked at the door that Holly
had just left through, thinking that when it came to her he
felt plenty of pain. She made him ache like hell. "I'm fine.
Tell me the bad."

"No. Good first. You didn't have a tear to the rotator
cuff. You had an inflamed bursa."

"A what?"

"Yeah, it's almost impossible to see on an MRI in the
position you were in. You have 160 bursae in your body,
located adjacent to the tendons near large joints, such as
your shoulder. You had one become inflamed from an injury, in this case probably your strained rotator cuff, and it
got infected. I removed the fluid, cleaned it all up a bit. You

should be good now. Relatively simple fix, at least compared to a torn rotator cuff."

Relief made his head swim. "Jesus, really?"

"Really. I know those suckers are a bitch on pain but the
recovery is going to be a hell of a lot easier than a repaired
tear would have been, and you can cut the down time in
half—maybe three weeks instead of two months."

Pace felt the rush of emotion clog his throat. "Okay,
now the bad."

"Yeah. That's not going to be as easy." The doctor sat
back on his little round stool and eyed Pace.

It was the same expression Holly had been wearing, and
he braced himself. "I wish people would stop looking at
me like that."

"Yesterday you had the standard operating procedure
presurgery lab work done. Per the request of your commissioner, and with your permission, you had your drug testing done at the same time."

"Yes."

"You tested positive for stimulants."

"That's impossible."

"I'm afraid it's fact. And I've got to report it."

"There's been a mistake. Test me again. I don't use."

"Look, you'll need three weeks off anyway for recovery, which should cover a good part of your discipline,
which I believe can be a twenty-five game suspension."

"No." No fucking way. "You have to retest."

The doctor rose. "You'll be released in a few hours. I've
prescribed pain meds to take you through the next seven
days, after which I'll need to see you for stitches re-
moval."

His doctor didn't believe him. Hell, who would? "I want
a retest. I'm within my rights to request one."

"Pace—"

"And I want my lawyer and agent, too." And for some
reason, Holly. He wanted Holly.

* * *

Holly drove a virtually silent Pace home from the hospital. He was dressed in his warm-up sweats, sitting very
still in the passenger seat next to her, his long legs stretched
out, his right arm held to his chest by a complicated sling
and sprint, both covered in a huge ice pack. She knew he
was still fuming over the drug-test results and the back-
lash that was liable to hit him over that. His agent and attorney had come to the hospital and they'd talked, which
had included a conference call with Gage, but she had no
idea the outcome other than they'd demanded a retest.

Pace hadn't said one word to her when he'd gotten off the
phone with Gage or when his agent and attorney had left. In
fact, he'd called a cab, but she'd sent the cab off and had put
him into his car, which she was enjoying the hell out of.

He sat in the passenger seat, head back, eyes covered in
his mirrored Oakleys, giving nothing away. She even
revved the engine to try to get a rise out of him. Nothing.
He was silent and pale, and after a few minutes, also a little
green, so she slowed down. "The doctor said nausea was
normal after anesthesia."

He didn't respond.

"He also said you'd feel like crap for a few days, but that
you'd be fine in a month."

"Two weeks."

"Ah, I forgot. You're Superman."

He didn't respond, but it didn't take a psychic to sense the
irritation level, which was rising, possibly due to the fact that
his phone kept beeping from some mysterious depth in one
of his pockets. "You want me to play secretary for you?"

"No."

He wasn't just hurting, he was angry. Vibrating with it.
"Are you mad at the doctor, or the lab, or—"

"Pretty much everyone, thank you," he said with silky
ire.

"Including your driver, I'm guessing."

"You snooped and read my chart."

"Out of concern."

"The test results are wrong," he said flatly. "So I'd better not be reading about this in your next article."

"Ah, so we're back to the mistrust." She sighed. "I'm going to cut you some slack since you're hurting."

"I'm not hurting. High as a kite, but not hurting."

Okay, then. Good to know where she stood with him.

Or didn't.

His phone rang again and he swore roughly, making her realize it was in his right pants pocket. With his arm freshly cut open and sewn shut and completely protected, he had no way of getting to it. She pulled over to the side of the highway and put her hand on his thigh.

"Fine," he said, unhooking his seat belt and taking off his sunglasses. "Angry sex works for me. But you're going to have to do all the work."

"Shut up, Pace." She frisked him for the phone, indeed finding it in his right pants pocket.

"A little to the left."

A little to the left and she'd be wrapping her fingers around something else entirely. She slid him a look.

"Hey, I'm drugged up nice and good," he said. "Go ahead, take advantage of me. I'll suffer through it." His voice was low and hoarse, not with passion but pain. The ass. She wanted to hug him.

Or smack him. "I prefer my men willing and able."

"Move your hand over a little and you'll see I'm both."

She pulled out the phone, and then because she couldn't help herself, glanced to the left of his zipper. He was hard. Her eyes met his glazed but amused ones. "Seriously?"

"Apparently you have the touch."

His phone rang again and she eyed the ID. "It's Wade."

"Tell him I can't talk right now, I'm in your hands." He laughed at his own joke.

Rolling her eyes, she opened the phone and assured Pace's best friend that he was okay. Or as okay as he could be under the circumstances of having just tested positive for stimulants. Then she handed the phone to Pace, and listened to him proceed to tell Wade that he hadn't had a rotator cuff tear after all, that he'd be good to go in a few weeks. He shut the phone and acknowledged her soft gasp of surprise. "Guess you didn't read far enough."

"Oh, Pace," she breathed. "That's amazing. I'm so happy and relieved for you."

He looked at her, clearly saw the emotion in her eyes, and closed his. "Thanks."

When she got them back on the road and pulled up to Pace's house, there were flowers on his doorstep. "From Tia," she said, reading the card. "Yours, forever."

"Good to know some things don't change. I'm good," he added when she followed him in.

Meaning don't follow him in.

She didn't listen. His house was huge and sparsely but decently furnished with big, soft, comfy-looking furniture, a plasma TV the size of an entire wall, a bunch of sports equipment everywhere, and the sense that this place was a real home, not just an MTV Cribs showcase. "Let me help you into bed, make sure you have food—"

He turned to face her, revealing that he was pale, and also now sweating. There was pain in his dark gaze, and plenty of other things to go with it. "I'm good," he repeated, so tough and strong, so utterly alone and vulnerable that he broke her heart.

"Pace." She shook her head and took a stand. "I'm not leaving you."

The doorbell rang, and then Tucker poked his head in. "Hey. Dad wanted me to check on you." He dropped a duffel bag to the foyer floor near a heap of other duffel bags, the only distinction between his and the others being that his had a tear in the bottom corner. "Looks like maybe you're already being well taken care of." Tucker smiled at Holly before turning back to Pace, who'd sunk to the bench right there in the foyer. "You need anything? Anything at all?"

"Better drugs."

"I can do that."

"Jesus." Pace let out a mirthless laugh and leaned his head back against the wall, eyes closed. "Don't say another word in front of the reporter who doesn't know that you're kidding. I'm fine, really. I just want to be alone." He opened his eyes and shot Holly a long look.

Tucker nodded. "Understood. But since everyone's in Baltimore, how about I go meet up with some friends for a couple of hours and then come back here and crash on the couch tonight in case you need anything later. Okay?"

"Yeah. Okay."

When Tucker walked out the door, Pace eyed Holly.

She eyed him back.

"Don't make me call 9-1-1 on you," he said.

"You didn't call the police on Tia and her flowers, so you're not going to call on me. Besides, I still have your cell phone." She pulled it from her pocket, held it up for him to see, then slipped it back into her pocket.

"Give that back."

"Tell you what. You take it from me and I'll leave."

His gaze dropped to her jeans pocket, and he gritted his teeth.

"Go ahead, Pace. Prove you're fine enough to be alone. Wrestle me down and take the phone."

"If I wrestle you down, I'm going to do something other than take my phone back."

"Promises, promises."

With a growl, he stood up and took a step toward her, then wavered on his feet and clutched the wall, letting out a tight breath. "Fuck."

"Okay, that's it." She slid her shoulder beneath his good arm to take his weight and led him out to the living room. "Which way?"

"To?"

"Your bed."

"What's wrong with right here?"

"Shut up, Pace. Which way?"

He sighed. "Down the hall."

His bedroom was as supersized as the rest of his house. The masculine oak furniture included a huge four-poster bed piled with sheets and blankets all askance from what looked like a restless night.

"I want a shower," he said, kicking a pile of clothes aside.

She looked at his complicated sling. "I think it's going to have to be a bath."

"Whichever." He headed into the bathroom, which was nearly as big as his bedroom. She flipped on the water in his Jacuzzi tub, then looked at him. "Do you really think I'd write about your test results?"

He toed off his shoes.

"Or that I'd expose you before the results were made public?"

"It's as good as public now. Gage's going to try to keep it quiet until I'm retested, but I don't know if he can." He leaned against the wall. "A stimulant isn't as bad as steroids. I'll probably only get a wrist slap, but if they retest and I show positive again, I'll get a twenty-five game suspension." His good hand went to the tie on his sweats, which was knotted, thwarting his best attempts.

She watched him struggle a minute before she stepped close. Holding his gaze, she untied the sweats and then nudged them down. His sweatshirt zipped and was easy enough to get off him, leaving him standing there in navy blue knit boxers and a sling and nothing else, which gave her an upfront and personal view of his torso and shoulder, already black-and-blue and hugely swollen. He had three incision sites: one where the microscopic camera had gone in and two where they'd done the actual work, and the abuse he'd taken today went straight to her heart. "Oh, Pace."

"I'm guessing that wasn't an 'Oh, Pace, you're so sexy, take me.'"

Throat tight, she put a hand over his heart. "You really don't need any pain meds?"

"Oh, on top of all the shit Tucker's supplying me with, you mean?"

"Pace."

"The tests were wrong, Holly." He said this in a low, tense voice. "I didn't take anything. Be sure to put that in your article."

She stared at him, hard. "First of all, I happen to believe you. And second of all, if you weren't already hurt, I'd hurt you myself. You know—dammit, you'd better know—that I wouldn't report you're on stimulants when it hasn't been proven."

"You saw my results. *Proof.* Which means you have me with my pants down." His smile didn't meet his eyes. "Literally."

She could scarcely speak past the lump in her throat. "Believe it or not, my personal morals mean something to me. Honesty means something to me, especially after how I grew up. I thought you knew that about me by now. And the fact that all along you've expected me to leak the story about your shoulder, and now the drug test, pisses me off. I'm damn tired of proving myself to you, Pace, and I'm . . ." Afraid to give any more of herself away than she already had, she simply turned and headed to the door.

"Holly."

She kept going.

"Holly, I'm— Please look at me."

When she turned back, he was just standing there in those knit boxers and his splint, the personification of big, edgy, testosterone-fueled male. "I'm sorry, okay?" His voice was tense. "I don't think you'd expose me in any way, any more than you'd bash my head in, even though I'm close to begging you to do just that." He closed his eyes. "But you should really go because I'm an ass today."

"Today?"

His lips actually quirked. "Yeah, yeah."

Dammit, he was gorgeous and hurting so much, but she shook her head. Not going to be moved by that. "I think I'll just grant your first request and leave you alone for your bath."

One of these days, she told herself as she headed into his kitchen, someone was going to accept her at face value. Not for what she did for a living, but for the woman beneath, the one who maybe didn't believe in love or happily ever afters, but secretly, desperately, wanted to.

She opened his fridge to get him something to drink to combat the tell-tale nausea that was making him green, and settled on toast and tea, which she brought back down the hall.

He emerged from the bathroom with a towel around his waist, pale, wan, shaking, and looking like death warmed over. He headed directly toward his bed, all dark eyes and stubbled strong jaw and edgy attitude, with droplets of water scattered over his long, tough body. She watched one fall from his hair to the tense muscles of his back, then run down the indention of his spine before vanishing into the towel. Her tongue would like to make the same trek.

"Thought you walked," he said.

"Is that what you'd do? Walk away?"

"No, that's what other people do to me."

Her heart squeezed hard. "Well, I've never been very good at walking away, even when I should. Lie down, Pace, before you drop. I'll go get the pills."

He unhooked his towel and let it fall to the floor. Naked, he hit the bed, sprawling half facedown, half on his good side. He didn't cover himself up—either because he didn't care or because he couldn't. Choosing to believe it was the latter, she pulled the covers over him, over those mile-long powerful legs, over the buns of steel she wanted to lean down and bite, over the sleek, smooth, sinewy expanse of his back.

"Thanks," he muttered into his pillow. "Fair warning, my stomach is considering revolting."

"Eat the toast." She sat it down by him, then went back to the foyer for her purse, where she'd stuffed his pain pills.

There on the tile floor was the duffel bag Tucker had left. It'd opened a little when he'd tossed it down, and a foil pack was sticking out. Two of them, actually, one a vitamin packet, the other a powder labeled a long name she didn't recognize.

She picked it up and flipped it over to read the ingredients, and recognized none. Grabbing Pace's pills and the packet, she went back to his bedroom to ask him about it, but he was out like a light. She covered him with another blanket and went back to her bag, where she pulled out her laptop. With one ear cocked for Pace and anything he might need, she set about doing some research, while also doing the other thing she'd promised—not walking away.

Chapter 21

> It's no coincidence that female interest in the sport
> of baseball has increased greatly since the ballplay-
> ers swapped those wonderful old-time baggy flannel
> uniforms for leotards.

—Mike Royko

By early evening, Tucker had gone back to Pace's place. Sam dropped by as well, and Gage's sister, and a few other friends. With Pace still sleeping, showing no signs of waking until morning, Holly left him in good hands. She went home to call a contact of hers in LA, who worked at a pharmaceutical company and could identify just about any substance.

"Yeah," he said, confirming her fears on the powder she'd found in Tucker's bag. "Those ingredients are made to pour into a water bottle and be taken by mouth, like the vitamin pack. They're natural, plant-based, with no manufactured derivatives, but it's a stimulant, no way about it, and just as potent. They've been taking that stuff for several years in Europe now, and interestingly enough, it's virtually undetectable unless looked for in the urine almost immediately after consumption. Going to be popular, that one is, once word gets out."

Holly had a feeling that word was already out—at least on the Heat. And damn if she didn't finally have her secret.

She just wasn't sure she still wanted it.

She asked her contact to e-mail her the information so she'd have it in writing, and then, while she was doing things she shouldn't be, early the next morning she used her press pass to get into the Heat facilities. There she sought out some of the support-team members and learned in casual conversation through two different trainers and an equipment manager that there were only two players Tucker was supplying with daily supplements on top of the vitamin enriched water everyone drank: Henry and Ty.

Which meant that the two players who'd had the DUI and disorderly conduct run-in, which had started this whole wave of bad press for the Heat, were the only two players being supplied by Tucker—a guy she'd just discovered carrying banned substances.

Coincidence? Maybe.

But Holly didn't believe in coincidence. She called Pace. "How are you feeling?

"Like I was hit by a truck."

"Can I come see you?"

"You're asking? What happened to demanding and bossy?"

"I'm trying something new."

"I'm in bed," he said, his voice going silky. "You bringing TLC?"

"I am." She sighed, knowing she had to break the mood and say something. "Pace?"

"Uh-oh. I know that tone. I'm not going to like this, am I?"

"Is Tucker still there?"

"Sleeping. Why?"

"I took a foil packet that was falling out of his bag in your foyer."

"A vitamin pack?"

"No. Something else. The contents are basically the equivalent of a stimulant, which is the same stuff you tested positive for. The same stuff you didn't knowingly ingest."

"What?"

"Yeah, it's an herbal, all-natural version, but still a stimulant."

He was silent.

"Pace? Don't you think it's odd that Tucker has it in his bag? A known banned substance? When he deals vitamins and protein supplements to professional athletes?"

"How do you know what you found?"

"I went to a friend, a pharmaceutical expert."

"Jesus, Holly."

"It was off the record, Pace. He has no idea where I got it, or why. He says the stuff is undetectable after a few days in your system. Which means—"

"I know what you think it means." He let out a long breath. "It means a player could certainly risk a few days without being tested, because we have that much warning, at least."

"Yes. It also means that there's going to be athletes who use it to cheat the system. Which in the long run means falsifying records, encouraging kids to—"

"Whoa, hold up. Tucker isn't a professional athlete."

"No, but he's likely supplying them with this stuff." And here's what was bugging her. "Why don't you sound surprised at this?"

"Holly." He sounded tired. Frustrated. "You're thinking you're sniffing out a story, but you don't have one."

"Yes, I do."

"You have no proof that he's given the stimulants to anyone."

"You tested positive, Pace. And you don't know how."

"So, what, you're suggesting that a lifelong friend drugged me?" he asked incredulously. "Without my knowledge?"

"I don't know what I think. All I'm saying is that you tested positive for a drug you don't use, a drug he has in his possession."

"Okay." Pain was clear in his voice, and she knew it

wasn't all physical now—her fault. "I'll get to the bottom of this, Holly. You—"

"Stay out of it?"

"Please."

"Pace, this isn't something I can hold back on like I did your injury. This crosses the line."

"What line?"

"My personal line of right and wrong. And hopefully yours, too."

"Don't, Holly. Don't even try to line my morality up with yours, because I'm not sure I could measure up. I'm not sure anyone could measure up."

"I have to do this," she said quietly.

"So what was that line you fed me about not walking away? Because to do this, you aren't just walking, you're running."

"No, I'm not. I'm just doing my job. It's what I'm doing here, Pace. I have to. But I'm not walking away from you."

He was quiet a moment. "I guess that's a matter of opinion," he finally said.

"Pace—"

"I've got to go."

She shut her phone, throat so tight she could barely breathe. She'd been right to tell him, right to insist that she had to do this. She just hated that she did.

And that was very new.

And very unwelcome.

Pace tossed the phone aside. Swore. Then struggled out of bed and staggered to the spare bedroom, where he slapped on the light.

Tucker blinked like an owl and sat up. "Dude."

"Wake up."

"You okay? You need something?"

"You have anything to tell me?" Pace asked.

"What do you mean?"

He had fire burning through his entire body. He'd skipped the meds, on purpose. Now he wished he hadn't as he had to grip the doorway through a wave of pain. "I need you to swear to me that the vitamins you've given me are just vitamins."

Tucker scrubbed a hand over his face, squinting sleepily through the bright light. "What?"

"Is it possible I got the wrong packet from you, say a day or two before my surgery?"

"No."

"Tuck—"

Tucker sat up and leaned back against the headboard. "The vitamins are pills, Pace." He paused. "Anything else is a powder. You couldn't have mistaken the two."

Okay. So he had two pieces of news, one bad, one worse. One, he hadn't accidentally ingested anything from Tucker. Two, Tucker did have the illegals. Shit. He turned off the light and went back to bed.

The news of Pace's drug test hit the sports world and blew up. Gage had promised to try to keep it undisclosed until after the appeal and subsequent second testing, but he hadn't succeeded.

Sam swore she had no idea how it'd gotten out of the Heat's office, and though she didn't bring it up, Pace knew everyone was thinking it'd been Holly.

He preferred to think someone in the testing office at the MLB commissioner's office had gotten his pockets greased instead. Still, it was yet another betrayal, and already hurting and pissed, Pace went back to bed to try to sleep it all off.

He couldn't.

Because he'd been hard on Holly, unfairly, and he knew it. He tried calling her, but she didn't answer.

He wouldn't have either.

The commissioner claimed innocence in putting out the

test results. Pace's agent and attorneys were on it, but it didn't matter. The damage had been done.

The news was everywhere, and when Wade and the guys brought him a loaded pizza three days later, they ate in silence as they watched all the sport shows tear into him, until finally, Ty turned off the TV. "Assholes."

Henry reached for his beer and thought better of it. "I'm driving," he said glumly.

"I'll drive you," Wade said. "We're not taking any more chances with anything. This is our year, goddamit."

"Our year," Ty repeated firmly, and they all toasted.

Then Pace slept for two more days, staggering to the door when someone knocked, staring bleary-eyed at the woman who'd woken him. He was hurting pretty good so he didn't speak. Instead, he just soaked up the sight of Holly as though she were a balm for his abused senses. Her hair was in a ponytail, and she wore sweats—Heat sweats, with his number on them. He tried not to be moved by that but failed.

She appeared to be having the same trouble, staring at the only thing he wore, the only thing he could put on by himself—loose basketball shorts.

"Hi," she said, sounding a little unsure of her reception.

"Hi. I thought you were on the job."

"I'm more than the job, Pace."

He didn't say anything to that because her point slammed home hard. She *was* more than her job.

He was not.

"I know you have doctors and PTs and a million people looking out for you," she said. "But I thought I'd come do some stretching with you, the ones your doctor recommended when I checked you out of the hospital."

"There's no point in rushing, not if I got suspended for twenty-five games. Or worse."

"Don't give up, Pace. We can get to the bottom of it, expose who did this to you, and—"

"And then what? Destroy someone else instead, some-one I likely know and—" Care about.

"Yes," she said softly, clearly understanding. "If that's what it takes."

Wishing he was still dead asleep because being awake hurt like hell, he moved aside for her to come in.

"I've been researching, writing," she told him. "I just wanted you to know. I want to be upfront with you on this."

Ah, hell. "Sounds argument inducing."

She turned and looked him over. "It won't be. I'm not here to argue. I'm here to help you stay in shape. Don't worry, I'll be gentle. And you're already dressed for what I have in mind."

Okay, that sounded a lot more promising than he'd thought. Especially when she put her hands on his belly and gently pushed him past the living room toward the hallway.

"Your doctor suggested a lower-body workout for circu-lation."

He was game for a lower-body workout, only she didn't go as far as his bedroom, pulling him into his home gym. She turned on the light and looked at him as she pulled off her sweatshirt and then her pants, leaving her in a pair of bicycle shorts and a sports bra. She pointed to the leg-press machine. "Sit."

He did, only because she looked exceedingly hot. He put his legs up and pushed.

"Good," she said, leaning over him. "Keep going."

He liked her workout outfit. A lot. He reached out to touch, but she slapped his hand away. "Sorry," she said, not sounding sorry at all, "but people who don't trust me don't get to touch me."

"It's not that I don't—"

"Shh. This is a workout." She sat at the bench press next to him. "I bet I can do more reps than you."

He eyed her gorgeous, curvy body, which had probably

never seen a gym, and pulled out a smile he didn't know he had in him. "No, you can't."

She gave him a sidelong look. "Prove it."

"I'd rather kiss you."

"Of course you would. I'm very kissable. Oh, and FYI . . ." She cocked her head. "I can see up your shorts."

She didn't sound too impressed, and he felt the need to defend himself. "Yeah. I don't think I'm . . . working. I think it was the anesthesia." Or so he'd told himself.

She raised a brow. "You're not . . . working? You mean you can't get an erection?"

Giving up with the weights, he lay flat on his back trying not to be embarrassed. So he couldn't get it up. He could live with that.

No.

No, he really couldn't live with that. "It's probably only temporary—" He broke off when he felt her finger outline his anklebone, then run up his calf. His basketball shorts were low on his hips and long to his knees, and she easily skimmed beneath the loose material to stroke his thigh.

"Did you ask the doctor about it?"

"No. It said something about it in the paperwork they gave me. In the fine print." Specifically it'd said that erections might be tricky for the next week or so. He hadn't gone a day without his dick at least twitching on its own since he'd turned twelve, but it'd been over a week now and nothing—

She stroked his leg again, with her entire hand now, then added the other to the mix in an intoxicating massage that felt so good he groaned, deep and heartfelt.

"You're tight, is all," she murmured. "Stressed." She dug her fingers into the muscles of his thighs. "That's not good for your recovery."

He opened his eyes and found her leaning over him, her ponytail hanging forward, lightly grazing his skin as she rubbed his legs. Her eyes locked on his and she smiled. She ran her gaze over his chest, then his lap, checking for success, which had him letting out a low laugh. "Don't bother. I told you—"

Her fingers skimmed back up to his hips and lightly stroked over his belly, then caught on the waistband of the shorts, which were so low they'd probably be too indecent to wear out of the house. Especially since, hello, her magic was working.

Things were stirring.

She smiled. A cat-in-cream smile as she played with the tie at the waistband, pulling lightly until it gave.

"What are you doing?" he asked hoarsely, not wanting to scare off his erection.

"You're far too tense. I'm going to fix that."

"I—" God, her hands were heaven. "I thought we were barely speaking."

"This won't involve speaking," she promised, and tugged. He lifted his hips to help, and then the next thing he knew, he was bare-ass naked and she was still fully dressed.

But then she remedied that by standing so that he could see her fully, and slowly stripped out of the rest of her clothes, then dropped to her knees between his.

"Holly—"

She licked him, and he choked out her name again, but he wasn't sure it was audible. He couldn't find his tongue. Jesus, he couldn't even find his brain as she slowly took him in her mouth and sucked.

At the low, inarticulate sound he made, she paused. "I should tell you, I'm not that good at this. Should I move on to something else?"

His good hand came up to tangle his fingers in her hair. "Please don't," he said with all his heart as she drew him into her mouth again. Oh Christ. Christ, it felt so good to feel. "Holly—"

She ignored him. Something he should have been used to when it came to her. She ignored him and kept at her leisurely pace of driving him right out of his ever-loving mind, which at the moment, was a fine place to be. "Two-minute warning," he gasped when his toes curled.

Her eyes were half closed, a dreamy, aroused smile playing about her lips as she worked him, and he had to reassess. "Make that ten seconds."

She reached up and put a finger to his lips, reminding him that this wasn't going to involve speaking. "Okay, yeah, but Holly, I'm going to—"

She didn't stop.

And he came.

He came from the tips of his toes and beyond, and when he'd relanded on planet earth, he was still flat on his back on the bench, blinking at the ceiling, feeling as if he'd taken the entire bottle of pain pills that he hadn't touched in days.

She kissed his inner thigh while he tried to find his tongue, which was currently stuck to the roof of his mouth. "I don't know whether to thank you or apologize," he murmured, unable to even muster up the energy to lift his head when she shifted away.

"Are you hungry?"

"I don't know." He reached out for her and got nothing but air. "Maybe a little."

She picked up a sweatshirt he had hanging over one of the barbells and slipped into it, which came down to her midthigh. "I'm going to find you something to eat," she said, zipping it up between her breasts. "Wait here."

As he'd expelled every last ounce of energy, that wasn't a problem. He couldn't have moved to save his life. So he waited.

With an undeniably dopey grin on his face.

Barefoot, wearing nothing but Pace's sweatshirt, Holly padded into his kitchen.

And let out a startled scream.

"Sorry," Wade said quickly, turning to face her, blinking at her attire, or lack of. "Didn't mean to scare you."

Henry had been in the middle of guzzling a Dr Pepper, but when his gaze ran down her body, he choked.

Wade simultaneously slapped him on the back and covered his eyes.

Holly tugged self-consciously at the hem of the sweatshirt. "What are you guys doing here?"

"We came to feed the poor, beleaguered, whiny patient," Wade said. "But it turns out he's not so beleaguered."

Footsteps came down the hall and then Pace appeared in the doorway. He took in the situation, which was the guys looking at Holly standing there in nothing but his sweatshirt, and with a low oath pulled Holly to him, protecting her from view of the others with his body as he turned the two of them to the door. "Wait here," he directed the guys over his shoulder as he led her out of the kitchen and into the hallway. "I'm so sorry."

"Not your fault. But I feel very naked."

"My favorite state."

"Yeah, but not mine." She headed back to the gym. He followed her, still wearing only those basketball shorts and his sling, extremely comfortable in his own skin. As he should be. If she had a body that fine, she'd be comfortable naked, too. At least some of his color was back, and she smiled as he put a big, warm hand on her hip.

"Hi," he said.

"Hi."

"Let me get rid of the guys."

"No, don't. I have to go work anyway."

At that, she expected him to rush her along, but he stayed still, dropping his forehead to hers. She just closed her eyes, breathing him in, lifting her arms to wrap around his neck. They stayed like that for a moment before she pulled free to slip into her sweatpants. When she started to unzip his sweatshirt to replace it with her own clothes, he shook his head. "Keep it."

So she left it on and slipped into her shoes. "I should go."

He came close, playing with the hood ties on the sweatshirt, the one that smelled like him. "I owe you."

Her knees knocked together. "Yeah. You do."

His mouth curved and his eyes were hot as he leaned in and kissed her good-bye, a kiss that made her wish things weren't so complicated, that they were just a man and a woman with a simple attraction for each other. An attraction without any messy emotions, attachments, or obligations to stories that needed to be told. But she'd never been that lucky, and she didn't see that luck changing any time soon.

Chapter 22

It's hard to win a pennant, but it's harder losing one.

—Chuck Tanner

Holly had left Tucker multiple phone messages, trying to arrange an interview, but he'd proven hard to get ahold of. She knew Pace had asked her to let him handle it, but he hadn't done so, at least not to her knowledge.

Plus, there was the little matter of this being her job, and she always did a thorough job.

When Tucker finally called her back, they arranged to meet at an outside burger joint in the center of town. Surrounded by tourists doing some summer shopping and college students on break, Holly pulled out the e-mail she'd gotten from her contact, the one that outlined the contents of the mysterious powder packet.

Tucker read the e-mail, then pushed it back across the table toward her, his face inscrutable. "What are you asking?"

"I got the packet out of your duffel bag. The duffel bag you brought to Pace's."

"Did you?"

"It . . . fell out."

He laughed. "Uh-huh."

"What do you use it for?"

"That's not any of your business."

"You don't play ball," she said.

Something in his eyes changed at that, chilled. Hardened. "I do not, no."

She knew his background, that he could have been a great player himself except for his accident, so she tread carefully. "I just don't see why you'd be taking stimulants."

"No? I have a bum leg, Holly. The powder in that packet is a natural growth stimulant, from plants and herbs."

"So you're saying you use?"

"It's not a manufactured drug, it's natural."

"Semantics, Tucker, and you know it. If the commissioner had known of its existence, it'd have been put on the banned list. It will be put on the banned list."

He took a bite of his burger.

She sighed and tried another angle. "You and the guys on the Heat are all close friends."

"Yeah. So?"

"Ty had your vitamins on him when he was arrested."

"True. They're good. They really work for him and his needs."

"You're right," she agreed. "And I'm wondering what else works for him. I've done the research, Tucker. I know that with some of these new high-tech, drugs, if you're not tested in the first twenty-four to forty-eight hours after taking them, it won't register. Which means Pace must have ingested one to two days before his blood work."

His amusement faded. "Are you accusing Pace of using?"

"No. The opposite. I believe he tested positive only because he ingested by accident."

Tucker set down his burger. Leaning forward, his eyes filled with a genuineness that couldn't be faked, he said, "Pace and I go way back. I'd never do anything to hurt him." His voice cracked slightly. "Never."

She could feel his grief, just as she felt something else—he was holding back on her. Was he protecting himself, or someone else? "I know you care about them," she said softly. "That you'd never hurt them. But whether by accident or not, someone did. Someone hurt Pace. And it could happen again."

But that was all she could get out of him. Frustrated, she went to the Heat facilities, where she had a scheduled meeting with Sam for the charity event she'd agreed to help with. They consumed a bag of cookies while they planned the annual poker night, laying out the floor plan, how they'd place a different Heat player at each poker table, the food, etc. And though Holly wanted to, though she had plenty of opportunity, she didn't tell Sam about the packet she'd found.

On the way out, she ran smack into Red. "Have you been to see Pace?" he asked.

"Yes. Earlier."

His mouth tightened. "Distracting him from his recovery?"

"No, I'm distracting him from his pain." She instantly wished back the words, especially when he started coughing. And coughing. "Red? You okay?"

"Inhaler," he gasped.

But that didn't work, so she ended up driving him to the ER and the entire time all she could do was picture Pace's face when she called to tell him she'd nearly killed his pitching coach.

But after a round of oxygen and some meds, Red was fine. Holly tried to take him home, but he refused to go, insisting on being dropped back off at the stadium, where he was meeting Ty for a pitching practice. "Damn stubborn men," she muttered, pulling back into the Heat's parking lot. "All of you."

"That's right, missy. We are." As he got out of her car, he reached into her backseat for his bag and she went utterly still, frozen in shock as she watched him walk away carrying the same torn-in-the-corner bag Tucker had left that night at Pace's.

She threw her car into park, turned off the engine, and followed him into the stadium and then to the bullpen, where Red had met up with Ty.

When she'd seen Tucker at the burger joint, she'd gotten the feeling he was protecting someone. What she'd never even imagined to think was that the person he might be protecting was his own father.

Red saw her approach, sighed, then gestured to Ty to keep throwing as he sauntered over to Holly. "What now? You not done trying to kill me?"

"Are you doling out stimulants to your players?"

He narrowed his eyes. "What the hell are you mumbling about?"

Ty stopped throwing and ambled up. "What's up?"

Holly was done tiptoeing. "I was just asking Red about the natural stimulants Tucker supplies him with, and who he's given them to."

Ty's eyes slid to Red.

"This is a private practice," Red said, and turning his back, he walked off.

But Ty didn't. He didn't move.

"I know the players on this team," he told her quietly. "Inside and out. I want you to know that none of them are using. Not a single one."

Very carefully worded, she noted. "And how about you?"

He looked away.

"Ty—"

"I take vitamins. Lots of us do, but me more than the others because my body has taken a hit from the leukemia, and I get run down faster. I take added supplements and proteins." He met her gaze then, his own earnest. "We've talked about this, Holly. There's nothing wrong with making your body as fit as you can get it, especially for an athlete in a sport where you're considered old at the age of thirty. You have to be fit for as long as you can be."

"I understand that. Vitamins are one thing. But stimulants—"

"Natural ingredients," he maintained. "All from plants. Nothing manufactured."

"But—"

"Is eating celery and carrots all damn day long considered strength building?"

"Okay," she said, nodding. "But smoking opium is dangerous, isn't it? Because that's a plant, too, Ty. A natural ingredient. It doesn't make it right."

"Look, I'm not saying I'm taking anything, but you should know, I don't see a problem with it. I think the rules are too strict."

"Can I quote you?"

He stared at her a long beat. "I guess I don't see a problem with that."

"Thank you for your time." She went home and called the other players on the roster, one by one, asking each of them their stance on undetectable and banned substances. She got a variety of answers, but the bottom line was the same. Unlike Ty, each of the rest of them viewed a banned substance as unacceptable, in whatever form it took.

She stared at her blank computer screen, then started typing. She wrote the article she wanted to write. Well, not quite the way she wanted to write it, but close enough. She started with how the MLB and the commissioner's office had forever changed the way athletes viewed banned substances by putting in mandatory testing, which was great, except that testing wasn't always accurate, and there were athletes still managing to use. There would probably always be certain athletes who managed to use.

She went on to explain that so much was expected of athletes in this day and age, the pressure not only to beat long-standing records but also to shatter them, and to do that, the athletes needed to constantly increase their strength. With conventional steroids and enhancers closed off to them, some were turning to less tried-and-true methods. Herbal and natural remedies, for one. But just because a drug was made from a plant extract didn't make it any safer than the manufactured ones had been.

Or any more accepted.

The bottom line, she wrote, was that the players had to take responsibility for themselves, their own actions, and the consequences, and that while most were doing exactly that, there were always going to be the ones who didn't. That even on a young, talented team like the Heat, this was the case. And it wasn't necessarily just the players to be blamed for turning a blind eye, but management as well. She quoted the guys themselves, each of them, including the fact that Ty was the only one who thought the rules were too strict.

Just as she finished the rough draft, Tommy called. "What," he said, irritated. "You don't return calls or e-mails anymore? Makes a guy nervous, doll. Especially a guy with a deadline. What have you got for me? Tell me you have something."

She e-mailed him her article and waited.

"My God," he whispered a few minutes later when he'd called her back after devouring her words. "So how does Ty get the stuff?"

"I didn't say he's using."

"Oh, he's using." He paused. "I'm going to guess there's a whole story here you haven't yet told."

She'd left Tucker and Red out of the equation, not for their sakes but for Pace's—her own concession to what he meant to her.

"No worries," Tommy said. "You've taken it far enough for now. The commissioner can deal with the fallout. You're brilliant, doll. Did I tell you that? I'll run it tonight."

"No, I need a day." She couldn't let Pace read this without warning. She had to find a way to tell him what she'd done. "Promise me."

"I have to admit," he said instead. "I thought you might be losing your touch. Crushing on one of your subjects, taking your sweet-ass time getting to the meat . . . Can't blame me, though; it's been weeks and weeks. I figured you'd gone soft."

"I mean it, Tommy. A day."

"Fine. But this new you? The kinder, gentler version of my hard-assed, hard-nosed Holly Hutchins? I don't know her. And I don't like her either. Let's meet next week and talk about what's up next. See you in LA, doll."

When she hung up, she stared at her computer screen. Tommy was right. She had changed. She was no longer a reporter who cared only about her story. She cared about the people she was writing about, deeply. She cared about the fact that someone was going to get hurt. Ty. The Heat.

Pace.

She'd been the catalyst for that, though not the cause, and she couldn't save him from the hurt.

But she'd be there for him. If he could forgive, that is. She just hoped like hell he could.

The next morning, Pace woke up and actually felt halfway human. It was either the orgasm, or the fact that the Heat had won last night with Ty pitching. Yep, things were looking up. Or they would be, if the media wasn't still crucifying him for testing positive for drugs.

Red and Wade stopped by as they had every day they hadn't been on the road, and brought McDonald's.

"Your damn woman put me in the hospital," Red said.

"But not the fifty years of smoking?" Pace asked. "It was the damn woman?"

"That's right."

"You know it's your lifestyle," Wade said.

"Bullshit." Red munched defiantly on a hash brown patty. "She's nosy."

"It's her job," Pace reminded him. "And you know you're not supposed to eat those."

Red popped the rest into his mouth with defiance. "You defending her?"

"I'm just reminding you that we all have our jobs to do and she's doing hers. If someone on the team is up to something that they shouldn't be—"

"Like what?" Red pushed back from the table. "You got something to say, say it."

"Actually, I have plenty to say—"

"Okay, whoa," Wade said easily. "Don't make me put the two of you in separate corners."

"She's just doing her job," Pace repeated to Red, as stubborn as the old man. "And the rest of us should remember that. If someone needs more strength and endurance, they need to try the gym instead of whatever new trick Tucker has for sale. And if someone, even a coach, has a fucking disease that's threatening his life, he needs to fucking stop smoking and retire before he fucking dies and pisses me off."

Red set down his food and crossed his bulldog arms. "I don't like where this is going."

"Yeah? Well, neither do I. And I sure as hell don't like wondering how the hell I got tainted with a stimulant."

Red stared at him for a long moment, then slowly stood. "I'd do anything for you," he said. "Anything."

Pace's chest tightened hard. "You don't think I know that? But I didn't want this."

"Are you blaming me?"

"Should I be?"

Red jerked as if he'd been sucker punched, and Pace immediately opened his mouth to apologize, but with a shake of his head, Red slammed his way out the door.

Pace felt the wave of helplessness and frustration roll over him, and picked up the McDonald's bag to chuck it across the room.

"Wait." Wade rescued the last Egg McMuffin before handing the empty bag back to Pace. "Okay, go ahead."

"Goddammit."

                              *   *   *

Wade stayed for the day, probably to keep him sane. He
fielded the phone calls from pushy reporters and the one
from Pace's father calling to ask how Pace could have been
so stupid as to get involved in a drug scandal. That was
fun. They had to ring the cops twice to chase away the
paps hanging around outside. When Pace's physical therapist came by, Wade worked out while Pace got tortured, a
process which left him a shaky, sweaty wreck. Wade stayed
and watched TV with him, and they ate some more. It was
early evening when the doorbell rang. Wade got the door,
raising a brow at the gorgeous, elegant, sophisticated crea-
ture wearing a satiny royal blue evening gown cut up to her
thigh. "Pace," Wade said slowly, staring at Samantha as if
stunned. "Did you call for a stripper?"

"Funny." Pissy, Sam breezed in past him, carrying a
garment bag.

Pace felt as stunned as Wade looked. "Holy cow, Sam.
You look amazing."

"Yeah, yeah." She turned to Wade. "Okay, strip down,
big boy. You're this stripper's date."

Wade blinked. "What? Me?"

"Did I stutter?"

Wade whipped his head toward Pace with a what-the-
fuck expression, but Pace merely lifted his good shoulder.
Wade and Sam had been growling at each other ever since
their single, disastrous night together.

"You don't want to go anywhere with me," Wade told
Sam. "You can't even look at me."

"No shit, Sherlock. But I don't have a choice."

"Are you sure?" Wade was sounding a little pissy himself. "Because there's got to be someone else, anyone else,
that you can get drunk and take advantage of this time."

Sam's eyes narrowed. "Okay, let's be clear on who the
ho is in this room, Wade O'Riley. And it is not me."

Wade opened his mouth, but Pace shook his head at him. "Okay, kids, let's all just try to get along—"

Sam put a hand in his face to shut him up.

"Fine," Wade said to Sam. "You want me again? Suits me. Let's go, Princess."

"Oh, I am so not your Princess." Sam unzipped the garment bag, revealing a tux. "Pace was supposed to go to this auction gala with me as the guest of honor, but now that's out of the question. I can't go dateless, Jeremy's going to be there with some hot, famous Brazilian model, my father will blow a gasket if I show up alone." She lifted her head and smiled grimly at Wade. "So I'm stuck with you."

Pace looked at the tux and grinned. "Ha."

Sam glanced at him. "You're not going to be smiling when you read these." She dropped some newspapers on his table. "If it was up to me, I wouldn't have brought them to you, but Gage insisted that you were a big boy."

"That I am." He grimly eyed the latest sports news, more of him being a druggie. Perfect.

Sam put her hands on her hips. "I want to offer you some advice."

"I don't—"

"Get over it. You're getting your appeal and the retest tomorrow, and when the results come back, you'll be proven right. End of story."

"Only if I'm truly clean. But if that first test was accurate and I somehow really ingested, I could conceivably test positive again." He shrugged. "Either way, people will always remember that I was accused of using."

"People are idiots. We'll get past it—somehow. I promise." She turned to Wade, who was still just standing there. "And since when are you allergic to big fancy fund-raisers with all the fixings including sexy woman and good food?"

"I'm not." Wade snatched the tux and headed toward

the other room to change. "But we're taking the stairs, even if it's to the roof. No elevators."

"Done."

Later that night came yet another knock at the door. Tired of people, Pace considered not getting it, but on the off chance it was someone bringing him food, he made his way through the house. He pulled open the door and came face-to-face with the woman of his dreams.

"Two things," she said quietly. "Well, three. One—I've never lied to you. Not once. Never will. Do you believe me?"

He looked into her eyes, which were filled with frustration, exhaustion, and a genuine warm affection for him. "Yes, I believe you. Actually, I believe in you, I always have, I just happen to be an ass when I'm in pain. I'm sorry for that. It comes naturally to me."

"Not going to disagree with you there. Can I come in for thing two and thing three?"

"Sure."

She walked into his living room and turned to face him. "Thing two. I told you how I wrote about Alex, because what he was doing was wrong. I would never do the same to you because you've not done anything wrong."

"I know you wouldn't. Holly—"

"I wouldn't hold back, though, if you had. You should know that."

She was looking at him, really seeing him, like so few did, and right then and there he realized something. She was one of the few people in his life who didn't want anything from him, didn't expect anything other than complete honesty at all times. Added to that heavy fact was that he really cared about her, deeply, perhaps more deeply than he'd ever cared about anyone before.

Ever.

He knew she was nearly done here in Santa Barbara,

and in spite of him doing everything in his power to push her away, he didn't want her to go. "I'd never ask you to hold back, Holly."

"Good." She took a deep breath. "Because I can't hold back on the Ty thing. I won't hold back. Thing three—he's using, Pace. And it's wrong."

"You don't know that for sure."

"I talked to him. I also talked to Red."

"I heard. Tried to kill him, did you?"

"That old stinker is too stubborn to die. You remember Tucker's bag, the one he dropped on the floor right there?" She pointed to the corner of the foyer where there were still a stack of duffel bags, minus the one she was talking about. "The one I got the packet from?"

"What about it?"

"It was Red's. I don't know why Tucker had it," she said, watching his face carefully. "I'm guessing he was bringing it to his dad."

"Actually, yeah," he remembered. "The next morning."

"I told you that I think Tucker's vitamin company also sells natural stimulants. I think Tucker is supplying Red, who is supplying Ty. I still don't know how you accidentally got some, but—"

Pace put a hand to his suddenly throbbing temple and backed to the wooden bench in the foyer, sitting heavily. "I know how."

"You do?"

"If I hadn't been so out of it from the surgery, I'd have remembered sooner . . ." He was quiet a moment. "I drank Ty's water." He lifted his head and met her gaze. "The day before my surgery, at the team meeting, right before my pre-op work. We're always grabbing each other's drinks, and Wade had said . . ." Wade had told him to go for Holly, to let her into his life to give him something more than just baseball. "I was unnerved about it," he said now, softly. "And I downed Ty's entire water bottle."

"He didn't tell you what he had in it?"

"He made a crack that it was a good thing we'd already been drug tested earlier in the season. He didn't know I was to be tested again. Hell, I didn't know then either, not until after the meeting."

"He joked about it?"

Pace let out a heavy breath. "Yeah." He looked at Holly, who was clearly thinking that Ty should have told him the truth, or at the very least, warned him. If not then, then certainly when Pace had tested positive.

Tucker could have said something, too.

Or Red.

She remained silent, not saying that if they'd all been so close, then what they'd done had been a huge betrayal. She didn't say any of it, but it was there in her eyes, along with a soft compassion and worried affection.

For him.

He closed his eyes. "So what you're saying is that you're going to write about this."

"I did write about this."

Well, hell.

"You know it's what I am paid to do," she said quietly. "Ferret out a secret and expose it. It's my job."

"I don't think I like your job."

"I'm sorry you feel that way. I never meant to hurt you."

He let out a low laugh.

"What Ty's doing is wrong." She came right up to him, put a hand on his chest. "But I didn't reveal where Ty got the stimulants."

He paused. "You didn't expose Red?"

"Or Tucker. Because I don't have specific proof that that's where Ty got it from."

"Am I supposed to thank you for that?"

"You're supposed to understand that it was going to get out anyway, that I'm merely doing my job. Ty is guilty, Pace."

"Jesus." He jammed his fingers into his hair and turned away from her. "So what do you want from me?"

"Truthfully?" She walked around him to look into his eyes, her own solemn. "I wasn't sure until you opened the door and looked happy to see me in spite of the fact that I've pissed you off. I want this thing that's happening between us. I really want it, more than I could have fathomed. But I can see now that's a silly little dream."

His heart seemed to swell against his ribs. "Why?"

"Because you say you don't want anyone to walk away from you but you're not . . . available. You're baseball. No room for more. Certainly no room for a girlfriend who dares to question some of the practices of your sport."

No. She was wrong. He *was* more than baseball. Or so he'd wanted to be. But she was gone, out the door, leaving himself feeling like he'd somehow just screwed up the best thing that had ever happened to him.

Chapter 23

Poets are like baseball pitchers. Both have their moments. The intervals are the tough things.

—Robert Frost

Holly's article came out the next morning, and by noon, her cell phone was full of unhappy messages.

"I thought better of you than this," Sam's said. "I gave you access to these guys for your articles thinking you'd get some great new angles on the sport and we'd get some coverage, and this is how you repay us? I thought we were friends, Holly."

Gage's was no easier to listen to. "I need you to explain to me what the fuck you thought you were doing when you wrote this article. You might as well have put a big fat red circle around Ty, whose been ordered for drug testing tomorrow instead of pitching for us."

Wade wasn't much happier.

Or Henry.

But perhaps the toughest message was the one that didn't come at all.

Pace remained silent.

Everyone was upset with her, and she didn't blame them. It was Florida all over again. "I've screwed up," she said to Allie via phone.

"Really? So it's your fault that Ty was using?"

"It's my fault that the whole world knows."

"We make our own destiny, Holly."

True enough. And she had a feeling she'd just made hers.

Pace slept in, and when he finally rolled over, he wished like hell that Holly was here with him. Warm. Smiling.

Naked.

The sun was pouring in the wide windows and it was nearly noon. He'd actually slept, really slept all night, no pain. He very carefully rolled his shoulder. Twinges, but he no longer felt as though someone was stabbing him with a sharp, fire-hot poker. Cheered by that, he headed toward the shower.

The house felt . . . empty. Other than a physical therapy session later, where he hoped to do a little throwing, something he was anxious to get back to, he had nothing going on.

A day off.

He could do whatever he wanted. Take a drive up Highway 1. Call the kids and coach them. Sit on his ass, if he wanted.

And yet all he really wanted was one carefully organized, slightly obsessive reporter who'd turned his world upside down.

And then left him.

No, he thought, getting into the shower, letting the hot water pummel him—she hadn't left him.

He'd left her.

And he'd been wrong, very wrong.

"We had so many hits that our server crashed," Tommy told Holly when he caught her by cell phone later that morning. "Plus three threatening phone calls," he said proudly. "Oh, and I hear talk of a lawsuit from Ty."

"And you're happy?" she asked incredulously.

"Hell, yeah. Listen, no one's going to sue, not success-fully. And the threats are just icing on the cake. But I'd watch your back in dark parking lots for a few days, doll."

"Gee, thanks." She remembered how it'd felt to listen to all those messages, all the people she'd disappointed, peo-ple who had been her friends.

"Don't worry, you're protected. It's a blog, for God's sake. It's an opinion."

"I quoted the guys," she reminded him. "All of whom said they weren't interested in banned substances, and then the one who said he doesn't see a problem with it. In Gage's words, I put a big red circle around him."

"Ty drew that circle himself."

"And if he tests positive, he faces a suspension."

"Maybe he'll learn to play by the rules. Listen, Pace's retest results came in, inconclusive. Thought you'd want to know, he's in the clear."

"Thank God."

"Jesus Christ, Holly, are you listening to yourself? What's happened to you?"

She sighed. "I don't know. No, I do know. I want to do things differently next time. I want to do something softer. Something that helps people."

"Uh-huh."

"I mean it. And I want to stay in Santa Barbara, and grow roots."

"Roots? Are you not a brunette?"

"Roots like a tree, Tommy. A solid, happy, healthy tree. I want a home base, a place of my own to settle down into."

"Crazy talk, but fine with me. I don't care where you live."

"I want that in writing."

"The crazy-talk part?"

"Tommy."

"Doll, you can have whatever you want. Just keep writ-ing for me."

* * *

Three days later, Pace took himself to the bullpen to throw, improving his confidence and renewing his hope that he didn't totally suck. He wasn't done playing ball. Hopefully he wasn't done with a lot of things. Or people—like Holly. Turning, he found Red quietly watching him. He looked uncharacteristically solemn.

"Looking good," Red said.

"Thanks." They'd been avoiding a real conversation all week, but Pace was done with that. "You saw Holly's article."

"Whole world saw it, didn't they?"

"Is it true?" Pace asked him. "And are you the one supplying Ty?"

A muscle jumped in Red's jaw, but he said nothing. His damn pride. One of these days he was going to choke on it.

"Jesus, Red."

"You gonna believe the word of a reporter over me?"

"You didn't give me *any* words. I'd love to hear your words."

"You've already judged me. I have no words for you." And with that, he walked away.

Damn, if Pace wasn't tired of that. He went home, showered, and called Holly. "Can we talk?"

"I'm in LA."

"When are you coming back?"

She paused, and his heart dropped. "Are you not coming back?"

"Tomorrow night," she said.

Ah, hell. "I leave with the team in the morning." He let out a breath. "When I get back then?"

"Yes," she whispered. "I'll be here."

A sentiment that meant far more than he could have imagined.

Chapter 24

You can't sit on a lead and run a few plays into the line and just kill the clock. You've got to throw the ball over the goddamn plate and give the other man his chance. That's why baseball is the greatest game of them all.

—Earl Weaver

The Heat went on both the road and a losing streak. Holly watched the games on TV, hoping for glimpses of Pace on the sideline, and for a change in their luck.

She got neither.

She kept busy. She still owed Tommy one more article on her baseball series, and needed to be working up her next series idea, but she was so unsettled and unsure. She couldn't concentrate on anything. She knew that the guys were still pissed at her, leaving her in a state of . . . suspension. As for Pace, she was even more uncertain. He'd wanted to talk, she just didn't know if that was a good or bad thing.

"Get a kitten," was Allie's suggestion when Holly called.

"A kitten? Are you crazy?" Holly looked around her leased condo. "This isn't even my place."

"Sure it is," Allie said calmly. "You're happy there. You love Santa Barbara. You love the people. You love it all."

"I've screwed it all up."

"No, you haven't."

Holly opened the sliding back door of the condo and

looked out at the Santa Ynez Mountains, the glorious, craggily, beautiful peaks that made her sigh every time she caught a glimpse. She did love it here. So much.

"Get yourself a kitten," Allie said again. "Make plans. Stick around awhile. Just try it, Hol. There's more to you than being an investigative secret hound."

"Yeah." For the next few days, she thought about little else, especially as the Heat lost four more games in a row.

The press was still clobbering the team. She hadn't gotten any more death threats, but neither had anyone from the team spoken to her. On the morning of the Heat's first home game in ten days, and also the poker night event, Holly got up early. The guys had probably gotten home late and she wasn't sure what that meant for her, having them back in town. They were only going to be in Santa Barbara for one day, and then they were off again on another road trip.

One day.

Having no idea what the day would bring, she killed some time in the grocery store getting some comfort food. On impulse she grabbed a cute little plant from the garden aisle.

Not exactly a kitten, but hey, it was alive.

She went back to her condo, set the plant next to her laptop on her kitchen/office table and opened Word. She looked at her next article—or the blank page masquerading as her next article. Giving up, she closed the document and opened iPhoto instead. The first picture that came up was of her and Pace back in Atlanta. The Heat had just won. Holly was up against Pace, all snuggled in like she belonged there, and he was grinning down at her with an abundance of emotion in his eyes.

Throat tight, she hit Print, then leaned the photo up against the plant. Her own little corner of home, she decided, and forced herself to go back to her Word program.

Two hours later she'd gotten a great start. She drove to the stadium where she paid for a general admission seat. At the sight of Pace in the dugout, her heart seemed to swell in her chest. He wore warm-up sweats, not his uniform. He didn't have on a sling, but from beneath his T-shirt she could see an elastic bandage around his bicep and shoulder, a horrible, gut-wrenching reminder of what he'd been through. Using his right hand—it was working!—he shook someone's hand and then turned to look in the stands as if he felt her eyes on him. He looked a little leaner than when she'd seen him last, and he had at least a day's worth of stubble on that strong jaw. He looked so good her heart kicked hard. She waved, but the sun was in his eyes. He couldn't possibly see her.

Or so she told herself when he didn't wave back.

The game was a rough one. Henry took a fly ball to the chest and got the air knocked out of him. Wade got kicked in the face when a player slid home, causing a tussle that the ump had to break up. The game ended at a painful fifteen zip, the worst in Heat history.

Holly went home, grabbed a change of clothing for the poker night fund-raiser and headed to the hotel where it was being held, knowing Sam would need help setting up. Indeed she found the publicist looking a little harassed and most definitely overworked.

"Hey." Holly's heart pinched at the way her friend looked at her, as if Holly had run over Sam's dog. Twice. And then backed over it.

"Holly. You didn't need to—"

"I thought you could use help."

"That's . . . generous of you," Sam said softly.

"Not generous. Greedy. I wanted to see you and the others." Holly stepped close and reached for her hand. "How are you?"

"As you'd expect after a horrific nine-game losing streak and a wave of bad press that always seems one step ahead of me."

"I'm sorry about the losses, more than you know." It'd been devastating to watch from afar; she could only imagine how it felt from the inside. "I looked for you at the game today. I'd hoped we could talk."

"Yeah. I was with Jeremy, actually. He's in town for this thing tonight." Sam's face twisted in indecision. "Holly—"

"No. Listen," Holly said quickly. "I get that you're hurt and furious, and I understand how bad the press has been, how ruthless. I know, and I'm sorry. But I miss you, Sam."

"I miss you, too," Sam whispered, squeezing her hand. "So damn much."

"I know you think I betrayed you, but all I did was expose a truth that would have come out eventually. I'm not your press leak. I'm not a spineless coward. I sign my name to my writing."

Sam rubbed her eyes, looking so weary she could hardly stand. "I want to believe that."

"Then believe it. You were my first real friend here in Santa Barbara, Sam. Please believe that, too."

Sam looked away for a moment, then turned back, her eyes shiny. "It'd be great to have another set of hands right now, especially someone who created the floor plan and knows what she's doing."

"Done."

Sam closed her eyes, then opened them and hugged Holly hard. "Thanks." She pulled back. "I believe in you. I do, but you should also know that others aren't so sure."

Even though Holly had known this, it still hurt. "I understand."

Sam squeezed her hand and walked off, and with a deep, fortifying breath, Holly turned to face the ballroom.

In a way that guys were masters at, Pace and Red had avoided talking about anything too personal since their last conversation at the bullpen. But when Pace pulled up to the hotel for the poker night and got out of his car right next to Red, he knew they couldn't keep it up. Not when he was about to see Holly for the first time in too long, not when it was sitting like a block of ice in his gut. "Got a minute, Red?"

Red looked over, clearly saw the determination on Pace's face, and sighed as he tossed aside his cigarette. "Yeah."

"You ever think about what'll happen when you leave baseball?"

"Not until recently." Red shrugged. "I have nothing but the game, son."

Pace nodded. He knew that feeling all too well. It didn't change a thing. "Did you do it? Did you give Ty the stimulants?"

Red closed his eyes. "Why shouldn't I?"

"Because it's wrong."

The older man, the only man to have been there for Pace through thick and thin, shook his head, then slowly nodded. "I know."

"You have to stop."

"I know that, too." Red paused, never one to use a lot of words. "Ty's tests came back positive this morning. He's not going to appeal."

Which was as good as an admission of guilt, and meant he'd be suspended, leaving the Heat without a strong pitcher to cover Pace until his return at the tail end of a season that had been touted as The Season. "He's young," Pace said. "He'll get through it. We'll all get through it."

"Yeah." Red looked at the hotel. "About that woman."

"Holly," Pace said wearily. "Her name is Holly."

"I know. Dammit, I know." He started coughing, forcing him to pull out his inhaler. "She makes you happy. That pissed me off. I thought baseball was it for you, but it's not. It's her." He looked pained. "I'm going to get used to that. I'm retiring, Pace."

"Red—"

"Jesus, I'm doing it your way, and you're still fucking arguing with me." He clasped Pace on the shoulder, his eyes serious. "Thanks for not ratting me out. Thanks for letting me do this with my dignity intact."

Pace stared at him, his throat tight. "I didn't do that for you. Holly did." And in return, Pace had been hard on her, too hard. She'd deserved better from him. Much better. He was going to do his damnedest to make it up to her.

Holly had assigned jobs to the volunteers and was putting up the decorations when the guys started to arrive. Once the event began, they'd each be manning a table, available for fun and laughs and whatever else the people who'd paid a thousand bucks a head to be there wanted. For now, they were volunteers like the rest of them.

When Henry came in, Holly smiled, but he didn't. Joe arrived, and she showed him to his table. He quietly thanked her, but without his usual smile. Mason came through without stopping to say hi.

Holly took a deep breath and kept working.

Red stood in a corner with Gage, talking. When she needed help moving a huge table, she turned to them. "Can either of you help?"

"Of course," Gage said, nudging her out of the way. "It's our team."

Right. Message received. They were helping the Heat, not her. Her chest ached, and her eyes burned, but she kept her chin up. "Thank you."

Wade walked by, looking his usual California-surfer-boy gorgeous. He was the first to stop. "Hey," he said quietly.

"Wade." She swallowed past the lump in her throat and looked at the bruise on his jaw from the earlier fight at home plate. "How are you?"

He let out a breath. "Keeping my head above water. You?"

"Same." She paused. "How is he? How's Pace?"

"On or off record?"

Her heart squeezed. "Off."

"Missing you," he said bluntly, his green eyes meeting hers. "A lot."

Oh God, this was tough. Holding it together was tough. "Good."

He smiled at that and tugged a loose strand of her hair. "Hang in there."

"I'm trying." When he left, she looked around the ballroom at the people she'd come to know and love, all working their butts off for a charity event, all giving back to the community, all united together. She'd never really had that; she'd always been on the outside looking in.

But there for a little while, she'd gotten a taste of being on the inside, and . . . and she'd loved it.

Loved them.

Throat even tighter now, she forced herself to keep busy. Because busy, she couldn't think too much. Or so went the plan, and she was in the middle of adding a gold streamer to the silver ones already strewn between two huge chandeliers when she felt someone steady her not-quite-steady ladder. She glanced down, and her heart lodged in her throat.

Pace.

He stood there looking fit and relaxed and so good that she nearly lost it. He was in faded Levi's and a Cal State sweatshirt, laid-back and casual.

But she couldn't pull off laid-back and casual, not with his eyes drinking her in. "Hey," she managed, gripping the top of the ladder.

"Hey."

He wasn't favoring his shoulder, and there was no sign of any pain as he held the ladder for her, eyes locked on hers.

She'd imagined what it would be like to see him again, what she would say, how she would try to make him want her again.

But she couldn't do it.

Not after the past hour, seeing how the guys saw her, what they thought of her. She couldn't, wouldn't, beg him to want her. "You're healing."

"Getting there. Come down, Holly."

Her throat burned so badly she could hardly breathe as she backed down. He kept his hands on the ladder so that she ended up climbing right into the crook of his arms. She slowly turned to face him. "No pain?"

"None. I'm day-to-day again."

"Oh, Pace," she breathed, knowing that meant he could play again as soon as he was ready. "I'm so glad."

He shifted his hands from the ladder to her hips. "You look good," he said very quietly. "You've gotten some sun."

Her heart gave one hard kick against her ribs. One more kind word, and she really was going to lose it. "I've been playing ball."

"With River and Chipper and the other guys?"

She nodded, and he arched a brow. "They didn't tell you?" she asked.

"No." But he didn't look irritated. He looked . . . pleased.

"I'm getting good at hitting," she informed him. "And I think pitching might be a calling."

He smiled, and dammit, she nearly melted.

He noticed the streamer in her hand, the one she hadn't been able to get up high enough. "Need some help?"

Her throat tightened even more, completely blocking off her air supply as her chest constricted hard. "Why are you being so nice?"

Clearly surprised at the question, he took a slow look around the room, his gaze touching on each of his teammates as if taking in the situation. There was understanding in his gaze when it landed on her again, which in itself nearly broke her. "Listen, they opened up and talked to you about the banned substances, and one of us pretty much admitted to fucking up. It's easier to blame you than Ty. They'll get over it."

"Will they?"

"Yes."

"You got over it?"

"You've done nothing wrong," he said firmly. "Ty did. Tucker did. And Red. They all screwed up, and during my pity party, I blamed the wrong person."

She met his soft, warm gaze. "Yeah?"

"Yeah." His hands tightened on her, one sliding up her back. "I'm sorry it took me so long to say this, but you were right. Red's retiring."

"Oh, Pace. I'm sorry."

"Also not your fault. But he's going to get to leave with his pride still intact, and that's thanks to you. He knows that, too. It took guts to come here tonight, Holly."

"Pace—"

"I've always had a thing for guts." He ran a finger over her jaw.

She closed her eyes to absorb his touch, which she'd missed. "I'm not brave. Just stubborn."

"I'll give you that, too. Holly . . ." He waited until she opened her eyes. "You accused me of being all baseball. I—"

"Okay, guys," Sam said through a microphone to the entire ballroom. "All the Heat players need to go change pronto. Fifteen minutes before you have to be in your places!"

Pace let out a frustrated breath.

"It's okay, Pace."

"No, it's not." He turned his back on the room and looked into her eyes. "I'm not all baseball, Holly. Or I'm trying not to be." He shifted a little closer, bending to put his mouth to her ear. "I missed you."

His voice was low and sexy as hell, which had her eyes drifting shut in pleasure. "Pace—"

He kissed her, soft and warm, and it felt real. So damn real. Then with Sam barking into the microphone again, he slowly pulled back.

"You have to go."

"I know." He kissed her one last time, then turned and headed toward his team, most of whom were watching.

She let out a breath, knowing he couldn't have given her a better gift than the one he just had, the one of undeniable acceptance.

Chapter 25

Baseball is life. The rest is just details.

The Heat's Third Annual Poker Night was a huge success, and the hotel ballroom was packed to the gills with the rich and famous. It was late by the time Pace got a five-minute break from his table, and he immediately went looking for Holly. Instead, he found Tia.

For the first time since he'd first met his tiny stalker, she wasn't wearing his jersey. She wore a long siren red evening gown and actually looked quite amazing. He couldn't even tell she was crazy as she smiled. "It's not what you think," she said immediately. "I came here tonight to break up with you."

He blinked. "You did?"

Stepping close, she cupped his jaw. "Aw, Pace. It was beautiful while it lasted, but frankly, you're a little skittish for me. I need more of a real man, someone not afraid to go after what he wants." That said, she pulled him down and kissed him on the cheek. "I'm moving on. Don't mourn me, love, it just wasn't meant to be." And with a last smile, she walked away.

Pace watched her go, torn between relief and terror for whoever her next love was. "Tia?"

She turned back to face him. "Don't try to sweet talk me back into your life, Pace. You can't."

"I'm just wondering who the real man is, the guy you're leaving me for."

She sent him a dreamy smile. "Wade O'Riley."

He blinked, then grinned. "Excellent choice." When she was gone, he headed back to his table, making a quick stop at Wade's. "Watch out for the lady in red."

Wade was running the five-card stud table, entertaining a packed crowd. "Is she hot?"

"Gorgeous but bat-in-the-cave crazy."

Wade slid him a look. "Tia? You're giving me Tia?"

"The one and only." He slapped Wade on the shoulder and moved toward his table, craning his neck in search of Holly. Every once in a while, he caught a quick glimpse of her moving through the crowd in a black cocktail dress that revealed her shoulders and back, hair piled high, sparkling earrings brushing her shoulders, emphasizing that sweet spot that once upon a time he'd kissed just to hear her shaky inhale of breath, but he never got close enough, and his table was packed.

When the evening finally wound down, he once again went searching. He thought he saw her near the doors, but when he got there, she'd vanished. He ran out into the hot summer night, heading down the middle aisle of the parking lot, searching right and left.

"Fother mucker!"

He felt his heart lighten as he followed that voice down the second row of cars. There she was in that sexy little black dress, kicking her tire with her black, strappy heel.

"Problem?" he asked.

She whirled around so fast she nearly fell on her ass. Her hair, so carefully piled up on top of her head, bobbed, and some strands slipped into her face. "No." She forced a smile as she swiped her forehead with her arm. "No problem."

"It won't start, will it?"

"Of course it'll start." She leaned back against the car and folded her arms in a casual pose that wasn't casual at all, looking uncharacteristically rumpled. " 'Night, Pace."

She'd rather be alone in a parking lot than accept help from him. "Was the kiss that bad?"

"What? No." She smiled again and shook her head. "I understand what you did, showing the guys your acceptance of me, and I appreciate it. But I don't want you to feel obligated—"

"Okay, whoa." He shook his head. "Damn, you think too much. That wasn't obligation, Holly."

"It wasn't?"

"No." He stepped closer. "It's nearly two in the morning, and I realize you're probably exhausted, but let me give you a ride."

"Honestly, Pace. You don't owe me anything, okay? I don't need a pity friendship from you."

He slipped his hands in his pocket and came up with his keys, which he dangled in her face. "How about a pity drive?"

She snatched the keys so fast his head spun. With a grin, he followed her to his car and got into the passenger seat, enjoying the flash of leg as she took the wheel.

"I want you to know, I'm not usually so easy," she said as she whipped them out of the parking lot in an impressive exhibition.

He gripped the dash. "Furthest thing from my mind."

She slid him a look, but he kept a straight face as she drove. At her condo, she turned off the engine, grabbed her purse, and turned to him, an inscrutable look on her usually wide-open face. "Thanks for the ride. Thanks for being there when I needed you tonight."

Then she was gone so damn fast that he barely caught her at her front door, putting a hand on her waist as she fumbled with her purse. "I wasn't always there when you needed me," he said quietly. "But I'd like to be there for you now."

"Thank you. But I don't need anything at the moment."

"Nothing?"

Her gaze dropped to his mouth and gave him a rush, but then she moved inside. He followed her, looking around as she flipped on the lights. "Interesting."

"What?"

"I just realized. You said I was all baseball, but you know what? I don't see evidence of a full life here in your place either."

"Yeah." She looked around. "I realized that, too." She gestured to the kitchen table, to the plant there, and a picture of them nearly two months ago now. He looked at the smile on her face and knew he wanted to see her look that happy again.

"I'm making some changes," she said with a lift of her shoulder. "Making a few moves."

"Ah." He nodded. "Me, too." Slowly he tugged her in, loving the way her breath caught. He skimmed a hand up her back, nudging her closer, and—

And his phone beeped. "Ignore it," he whispered against her lips. "Whoever it is can take a flying leap."

She put a hand on his chest. "It's two in the morning. It's got to be important."

True. Dammit. Still holding her close, he pulled out his cell, only to have his gut tighten as he answered. "Chipper?"

"Come to the park, Pace," the boy said, sounding harried. "Quick!"

"Are you all right?"

"No. Hurry!"

When the kid hung up, Pace immediately turned to the door. "Something's wrong. He's at the park. Come on."

They got to the park in seven minutes flat, and as they got out of the car, Pace saw the three shadows standing at the park's entrance, which was blocked off by a chain-link fence.

"It's locked," the tallest shadow said in disbelief. It was Chipper.

The other two shadows—River and Danny—nodded glumly.

On top of that, the For Sale sign had been nailed back up, and there was a new sign that read, Stay Off, Private Property.

"Can you believe it?" Chipper kicked the dirt in a perfect imitation of Pace on the mound. "Now we'll have to give up playing. And we were getting good, too."

Pace took in the three dejected kids. "No one's giving up playing. What the hell are you doing here this late?"

"It's too hot to sleep," River said.

"So open a window. Do not sneak out, ever," Pace told them. "It's not safe. As for the rest . . ." He looked at the new sign. "I'll fix this. Somehow."

"How?"

"I'll figure it out. Come on, I'll take you all home."

He and Holly loaded the three kids into the back of the Mustang, and Pace eyed them in the rearview mirror. "Who's first?"

The guys looked at each other guiltily.

"What?" Pace said, twisting around to face them. "What aren't you telling me?"

"My mom thinks I'm at his house." River pointed to Chipper.

"And my mom thinks I'm at his house." Chipper pointed to Danny.

"We can't go back this late," Danny said. "We'll get busted."

"Well, prepare to get busted." Pace turned to the woman he'd hoped to have in his bed tonight. "Holly—"

"I know," she said, her lips curved in understanding. "You have to take them to your house."

The gang erupted with cheers.

"Yeah." He blew out a breath. "Except . . . I'm going to need you to come, too."

She arched a brow.

"For propriety's sake. I—"

"I understand," she said. "Public image and all. I'll stay, Pace."

"A sleepover at Pace's!" Chipper said, and grinned. "Fun."

"No," Pace said. "Not fun. It's nearly . . ." He looked at his phone. "Shit, it's three and I have a six o'clock flight with the Heat." He sighed. "We're all going straight to sleep." He slid a frustrated look to Holly. He'd had other plans for those few hours. "I'll be gone when you wake up, I'll have a driver take you home whenever you're ready. The boys, too."

"Ah, man," River grumbled.

"After each of you call your parents."

"Ah, man," River repeated.

Exactly how Pace felt as he drove to his house with Holly in that hot dress that was not going to be coming off for him tonight. In his driveway, he turned off his car just as Chipper thrust his head between the front bucket seats. "So are you two back together?"

Holly shook her head as they all got out of the car.

Chipper looked at Pace as he unlocked the door. "Why not? You have someone else on deck? Is that it?"

"No." Jesus. "Look, Holly and I—"

"You balk?" Chipper asked right over him as they entered the house. "Or quick pitch?"

Pace didn't know whether to laugh or be annoyed that the kid was using pitching terms to ask how he'd managed to screw up a sure thing. He grabbed blankets and pillows and tossed them to the boys, pointing to the huge U-shaped couch in his den that would comfortably sleep them all. "Call your mothers while I walk Holly to her room."

"You two had a shutout going," Chipper said. "I saw it. Everyone saw it."

Pace reached for Holly's hand and offered a smile. "Yeah."

She didn't return the smile, but she did entwine her fingers in his. She was confused, he knew. She didn't know how he felt about her. He was reading that loud and clear, but until now, until this very moment, so close he could see her heart and soul reflected in her eyes, he honestly hadn't known.

"Holly," Chipper said earnestly. "Pace is the best guy I know. Whatever he's done, maybe you could give him another chance. Heck, even fly ball pitchers get another chance."

That made her smile, but it was a sober one. "It wasn't him, Chipper," she said with quiet grace. "It was me. I screwed up. I . . ." She searched for a term. "Threw a quick pitch."

Watching her try to explain to the kid what had happened in terms he'd understand, without going into more detail than he needed, cemented it for Pace. She was truly one of a kind, the most amazing, caring, passionate woman he'd ever met.

She started down the hall.

"Dude, don't let her go to bed sad," Chipper whispered.

"Working on that," Pace said, pointing at him. "Call your moms. I mean it."

"If it's a homer, I get credit for the assist, right?"

Holly choked out a laugh. "Yeah," she said over her shoulder as she left the living room. "You'll get the point."

"Sweet." He glanced at Pace with something close to hero worship, which made Pace damned uncomfortable.

And just a little bit proud. Holly had also looked at him as if maybe he was worth something, something more than what he brought to the diamond, and between her and these kids, he felt more alive than he had for a damned long time.

"Night," Holly called back.

"Dude," River said in a conspirator's whisper. "She's walking away."

"You're supposed to walk her to the door and kiss her," Chipper said in the same ear-shattering whisper. "Hurry."

Pace caught up with her in the hallway at the door to the spare bedroom and took her hand. "Ever notice that we meet in a lot of doorways?"

"The looks on their faces about the park," Holly murmured.

She'd set aside everything—including whatever emotions were putting those shadows in her eyes—in order to worry about the kids. If he hadn't already been half in love with her, that would have sealed the deal.

"There's got to be something we can do," she said. "They need that park, Pace. And they need it fixed up."

"I've got an idea for it."

She cocked her head and studied him. "You're in the middle of a recovery *and* a baseball season."

"I have time and room for more."

"Since when?"

"Since . . ." You. "Holly, I—"

"Pace!" Chipper yelled.

Pace ground his back teeth together. "Yeah?"

"Can we have ice cream?"

"If you call home," he said, not taking his eyes off Holly. "I'm sorry," he said quietly. "About this."

"No worries." She reached for the door handle.

"Wait." He slid his fingers into her hair, tracing her jaw line with his thumb. God, he'd missed the feel of her. "You know that up until now my entire life has been nothing but one hard fastball."

She gave a faint smile. "Now you sound like Chipper."

"Yeah." He let out a small smile, liking that. "What I'm saying is that I've rushed through my life. I've rushed through everything, just to play ball. I still love it, I do, I just . . ." His smile faded and he shook his head again. "After my surgery, after Red and Ty, after everything, I felt . . . a little empty. It's made me realize how much I needed something else in my life. Something substantial." Like her. She was substance to him. "Holly—"

"Pace!" This time it was River. "Ask Holly if she wants ice cream!"

Pace closed his eyes, then opened them to look into Holly's laughing ones.

"I'm good," she called back to them. "But thank you."

Pace leaned past her to open the door, gently nudging her inside, then followed her in and pressed her back against the wall to kiss her.

She melted into him, and the next thing he knew their arms were wrapped around each other and he was oblivious to anything else except her sweet tongue tangling with his, lost to everything.

But her.

What seemed like hours later, she pulled back and opened her eyes. "Interesting that that's still there."

He'd known it would be.

"You have to go," she whispered. "The boys."

He stroked a strand of hair from her face. "They can wait another minute."

At that, she bit her full lower lip, a naughty light coming into her eyes. "We've accomplished quite a bit in a minute before."

He was already hard, he'd been in that condition since . . . since he'd first seen her in that dress, the one that was now slipping off one shoulder. And those black heels with the ankle strap . . . "You have no idea how much I want that minute," he said reverently.

She pressed her breasts into his chest. "Tick tock . . ."

"No." He gulped in air and put his hands on her waist, holding her away from him. "We're not rushing again."

"Again?"

"We were in a hurry last time. Good things come to

those who wait, Holly." And he planned on getting good things. Very good things.

She arched a brow, amused. "You sound like a fortune cookie."

"Yeah. And your fortune says the wait will be worth it."

"I'm not much of a waiter."

"I've noticed." He dropped his forehead to hers. From his vantage point, he could see down her dress, and he didn't think she was wearing a bra. "Got to go." He was talking to himself, reminding himself. "And in three hours, I fly to Arizona to watch us get our asses kicked by the Dia-mondbacks. But when I get back, we're both going to . . ."

"Get good things?"

"Yeah. Really good."

Her breath caught.

"You onboard with that?" he asked.

She could only nod, and he smiled grimly. It was going to be a long road trip.

Chapter 26

Baseball's designed to break your heart. The game
begins in spring, when everything else begins again,
and it blossoms in the summer, filling the afternoons
and evenings, and then as soon as the chill rains
come, it stops and leaves you to face the fall alone.

—A. Bartlett Giamatti

Holly woke up the next morning to find a note on the bedroom door.

*I'm off, taking the boys with me to drop them at home.
Your car's out front. You left the lights on and the bat-
tery needed a charge. See you when I get back.*
Pace

She peeked out the window. There was her car. Pace
had promised to be there for her, and he'd come through. It
was a first for her with a guy, and it did something to her
heart, something she wanted to attribute to lust but had to
admit, was more.

The Heat broke even in the Arizona series. Better than
losing, but still, not a record to be proud of. Not for them.

The Bad News Bears, the news reports mocked. Holly
read them all, and by the time the team came home, they
had to win their next game or be knocked out of the wild
card position for the run at the National League pennant.

She couldn't imagine the pressure.

But she had her own pressure. Pressure to make a living. While trying to find her next series, she went over the pictures she'd taken all summer, and as she played with the shots, she realized her own next series was right here in front of her—a slice of American life.

While she played with that, Tommy called. "Doll, I've got an idea. How about you extend the baseball series, figure out what's going on with all that bad press the Heat is getting?"

"The series is over."

"I don't think so."

"What do you mean?"

"Well, seeing as you've turned this new leaf and gone all conscientious on me, I might have something interesting for you."

"What?"

"The bad press isn't generated by your article, or from the Heat's play record. Sure, they've lost some games, but they're still at a winning record, and in fact, if they win today's home game, they're a cinch for the wild card position to go into the pennant for National League champions. Not too shabby. Plus, there's one undeniable fact—other teams have far bigger losing streaks going on."

"I know. Sam's been going crazy trying to figure it out."

"It's an inside job."

"No. No one would—"

"Would and did."

"Who?"

"Buzz is that it's coming from their own PR department."

"Samantha? That's ridiculous," she said firmly.

"Her brother's the publicist for the Charleston Bucks."

"Yes, Jeremy. So?"

"So the Bucks have a bigger losing streak than the Heat's. In fact, they've been big losers all season. They have a shallow bullpen and no solid hitters."

"Are you suggesting that Sam's creating bad press for the Heat to deflect from the Buck's losing streak?"

"Among other things, like causing the loss of advertising dollars and game-day revenues, yeah."

"Tommy, come on. That doesn't make sense."

"Actually, it does. We're talking millions and millions of dollars, and you know the saying: blood is thicker than a paycheck."

"How do you know this?"

"I know all."

"Not good enough."

"I was contacted by someone who wanted to sell me proof."

"Oh God," she breathed. "How much is that worth?"

"I don't know, I didn't take it. I have *some* scruples."

Whether or not that was true, Holly's head was spinning. Tommy was a greedy, sneaky, manipulative bastard, but the bitch of it was, he *was* always right. "You're sure?"

"Listen, doll, we both know my faults. Sniffing out an untrue story is not one of them."

"I'll get back to you." Holly shut her phone and stood still for a moment as the shock filled her. Sam, the bad guy? She grabbed her keys and headed out into the staggering heat, driving straight to the Heat facilities, where she found the pretty publicist in her office. "Sam? Can we talk?"

Sam barely looked up from her desk, where she had two laptops going and a handheld fan blowing right in her damp face. Her cell phone was ringing, as was her desk phone. "I'm sorry, the AC is out, the soaring temps are killing me, and I'm swamped. I don't have time to—"

"Are you feeding bad press to your brother so his team looks better than the Heat?"

At that, she had Sam's full attention. "What?"

"Are you?"

"I don't know what the hell you're talking about. I wouldn't feed Jeremy anything. He's a shark."

Holly sank to a chair. "Okay, here's the thing. My boss is a complete jerk, but he's got a way of sniffing out a story. He says your bad press is an inside job."

"Yes. Many think it's you."

"It's not."

Mouth grim, eyes worried, Sam stood up. "I know. God, I know. But it's not me either."

"So who?"

"I don't know— No one else has the info I have," Sam said.

"Then who's accessing your computers and information, besides you?"

Sam opened her mouth and then slowly shut it again, thoughts clearly racing. "I need a moment alone," she said tersely, reaching for her phone.

"Sam—"

"Please, Holly."

"Yeah. Okay." She was back in the parking lot, sweltering in the morning heat, when her cell phone buzzed with an incoming text from Pace.

I'm back. Come to the park.

It took her fifteen minutes in the morning traffic, in the damn heat wave with no AC in her car, during which time she went over and over the look on Sam's face. It wasn't her. Sam loved her job, loved the guys, loved everything about the Heat. She'd never have jeopardized that.

Holly parked next to Pace's Mustang in the parking lot and got out of her car and nearly melted. The fence wasn't locked today, and the For Sale sign had been covered by another that read, Sold.

She saw no one. With butterflies low in her belly over the thought of seeing Pace, she walked to the empty field and turned in a slow circle in the sweltering heat, coming to a stop at the abandoned building. It was a one-story structure, originally used to store equipment, with two high, long-slatted windows that she couldn't reach to see inside.

The door was opened. Dying for shade, she stepped

over the threshold and into a large room that was clear of everything but some drop cloths, a few buckets of paint on a lone table, two ladders, and one sexy-as-hell Pace Martin.

He stood at the top of one of the ladders, roller in hand. He wore loose cargo shorts, low on his hips, the hem past his knees, and a T-shirt, both smeared with baby blue paint. Just looking at him lightened her heart.

He had his baseball hat on backward, his hair curling out from beneath the edges, and an easy smile that pretty much galvanized her.

She'd go to the ends of the earth for that smile.

He backed off the ladder with easy grace, hopping down to the floor from the last few rungs. "Hey."

"You bought this place," she said. "You bought it for the kids."

"Yeah, but for me, too." He turned to shut and lock the door, then came close, his gaze touching her features. "I missed you, Holly."

Her heart caught painfully. The poor organ seemed to be getting quite the workout lately. He stood there with that melting smile, the promise there in his eyes, colliding with who he'd become—a man for whom baseball was just a part of his life.

Not the whole, but a part.

"I missed you, too," she said softly.

He smiled. "Good." He grabbed a second roller. "Want to help?"

"More than anything."

He cocked his head, holding the roller back from her now, his shirt stretching taut across his broad chest. "More than anything? That covers a lot of ground."

She caught the heat in his gaze and her tummy quivered, but she had to tell him what she'd just learned. "Pace . . . I talked to Tommy this morning."

"About today's game? Yeah, it's a big one. Do or die."

"No." She drew a big breath. "About what's happening in the press. He says it's an inside job." She told him everything she knew, including how she'd gone to visit Sam. "I don't believe it's her."

"I don't either." He looked pensive and quiet for a moment, then met her gaze. "But that's going to have to wait for a few minutes."

"Why?"

"Because baseball, and all that goes with it, is going to take a backseat, for once."

"But don't you think—"

"What I think," he said, taking her purse off her shoulder and setting it aside, "is that we've got a lot to do before the kids show up to see this place in an hour." He gave her a once-over. "How married are you to that shirt staying white?"

She looked down at herself. It was her favorite shirt, mostly because it was what she'd been wearing when they'd first kissed in the Atlanta locker room. "Pretty married." Compromising, she pulled it off, leaving just the red tank top she wore beneath.

His gaze took in the tank, and the fact that her nipples were hard and poking at the material. "Nice." He put his big hands on her hips and tugged her in. His hot eyes met hers, and then he kissed her until she couldn't remember her own name. Then, while she was still reeling, he backed away. To strip, she hoped dazedly. They had an hour, he'd said. They could do a whole lot with an hour—

He thrust the paint roller in her hands. "You know how to use that?"

She blinked. "Yes."

"Great." He grabbed the other roller, dipped it into the paint and headed to a wall, his game face on.

They were going to paint, not make love. Okay. Equally determined, she forced herself to head to the opposite wall. For the kids, she reminded herself. It was important and was a worthy cause, but damn it was hot in here, what with all the kissing and the added labor of reaching up and down . . .

Within ten minutes, she was a sticky, steamy mess.

"Hot," he murmured, echoing her thoughts, and pulled his shirt over his head, tossing it aside with no idea that now she couldn't take her eyes off him.

His surgery scars were prominent but no longer red and angry. His chest was deeply tanned, sinewy, and made her mouth water. Her entire body reacted, and when she looked up, his gaze was steady.

And scorching.

"Very hot," she agreed, thinking two could play this game. So she pulled off her tank top, tossing it aside as he'd just done.

His eyes darkened, his breathing changed, and he stepped close again, leaning in for another of those mind-bending kisses. Then, when she was panting for more, he simply stepped back and picked up his roller.

Dammit. She wanted to roll him. With her body quivering for his, she dipped her roller back into the paint. When she finished the wall, she turned to Pace.

Chest damp with sweat, he stared deep into her eyes and without a word, kicked off his flip-flops.

Unbuttoned his shorts.

Oh, thank God. She unbuttoned her shorts and let them fall off her hips. By some miracle of laundry and timing, her bra matched her panties today.

Pace let out an exhale of breath that conveyed heat, desire, and a need so strong her legs wobbled.

"Holly."

Now. He was going to take her right here, right now. "Yes?"

He pointed to the last wall. "We have one more."

She stared at him, then nodded. "You're right." Turning away, she bent over for more paint.

Slowly, in nothing but her bra and panties.

He hissed out a breath, but he didn't touch her. His shorts, already low on his hips, sank even lower. His bare back was sleek and strong, muscles rippling with his every movement. He joined her, reaching high on her wall as she painted low. A few seconds later, she felt his hand skim up her spine. When she straightened to look at him, her bra slid off.

She hadn't even felt him unhook it. "Smooth," she said, heart pounding.

His hungry gaze ate her up, from the tips of her hair, to her bared breasts, to her skimpy bikini panties. "Almost done," he murmured, and dipped his roller into the paint.

She let out a shaky breath and went back to the wall. Topless. In just panties.

Never in her life had she done anything like this before.

Thanks to all his stretching, Pace's shorts gave up the fight and slid down to his thighs. He kicked them off, leaving him in just a pair of black knit boxers with an interesting and mouthwatering bulge right in front.

By the time the last wall was done, Holly had a streak of paint on her shoulder, another between her breasts and belly, and one on her thigh. Pace had a long smear across his torso and abs, and another in his hair.

"Tell me we're done," she said, stepping close.

"Still always in a hurry?"

"Uh-huh." She slipped her fingers into the low waistband of his boxers as she pressed her lips to the scar on his shoulder.

He took her roller from her and set it aside. "There's no fire." He bent his head to nuzzle at her neck, one hand skimming up to cup a breast, his thumb brushing over her nipple.

With a low hum of pleasure, she arched to give him more access. "I feel like I'm the fire."

His soft laugh huffed against her skin, and the sound melted her bones.

"Slow," he murmured. "We have a better chance of finally getting satisfied."

The words penetrated her lust-ladened brain, and she went still. "I thought we were past the getting-this-out-of-our-system thing."

"We are. Way past." He made his way lazily to her shoulder, his hands skimming up and down her back, going lower each time until his fingers caught in her pale peach panties. "I like these."

She relaxed into him. "Do you?"

"Oh, yeah." He hooked his thumbs into the sides. "Every time you bent over to work the roller, they rode up. I got a lot of mileage out of that. But I'd like them even better . . ." He tugged them down to her thighs, and eyed the view he'd given himself with an appreciative groan. "Oh yeah. You should have painted like that."

"I couldn't have walked."

He smiled, a slow, sexy smile. And then he kissed her, opening his mouth over hers, the taste of him going straight through her, so familiar, so good, so . . . hers that she moaned.

In response, he pressed that hard, hot body close, so close that the paint on her belly stuck them together like glue.

"I'm a mess," she murmured.

"I know. I love you like this." He cupped her head, his fingers entangled in her hair. "I love that you've lost all that carefulness when it comes to being with me."

She really had. Which meant he had a direct route to the soft underside of her heart.

"That's the benefit to going slow." His mouth was at her ear, and he very gently sank his teeth into her lobe, enough to make her shiver in anticipation. "Drawing things out . . . you feel everything that much more. You feeling everything, Holly. Every little thing."

Oh yeah, she was. And bigger things, too, such as his erection straining against her. She slid her fingers into his hair and brought his mouth back to hers, that mouth that she could never in a million years get enough of, every slow thrust of his tongue making her heart beat even faster.

"Holly?" His tongue glided along hers as his hand slowly slid up her leg, catching on the panties still at midthigh, which he simply tugged all the way off.

"Yes," she managed. "I'm feeling every little thing. And the big ones, too." She pressed against him. "Especially the big ones."

He let out a low, rough laugh and backed her to the table, lifting her to it so she sat, gripping the metal beneath her. He nudged her legs open so he could step between, his eyes heavy-lidded and dark with passion, going even darker when she ran a hand over those mouthwatering abs of his. Freeing him from his shorts, she wrapped her hands around him and stroked, wrenching a satisfying groan from his lips as he thrust through her fingers, huge and silky hard, hot to the touch.

"Holly." His voice was raspy and thick as his fingers slid between her thighs, jerking a gasp from her. "God, you drove me crazy this past half hour, wondering if you were as hot as I was."

"I was. Am."

"Good." He dipped his head to watch himself touch her, and unable to stay still or quiet, she rocked her hips and let out a needy little whimper.

"Love the sound of you on the edge," he whispered.

And she was most definitely on the edge. A sweaty, paint-covered, on-the-edge mess. It shouldn't have been sexy, but with his hot gaze soaking her up, with his fingers taking her to new places, she'd never been more turned on in her life. "Pace."

"I know." Leaning over her on the table, he kissed her again, his mouth hot and just a little bit demanding as his tongue owned hers. Slowly. Achingly slowly, taking his damn sweet time, breathing her in, spreading hot, wet, open-mouthed kisses along her jaw, her throat, to a breast, and then, as he went down on his knees, over her belly.

Her inner thigh.

Between.

With a gasp, her head fell back, and she rocked her hips as he rasped his thumb over her, making her arch up for more. He gave it to her using his tongue now, and she lost her words, her train of thought. "Ohmigod, Pace—"

"Don't even think of asking me to hurry." His tongue made another slow foray over ground zero, and unable to keep quiet, she cried out, rocking mindlessly against him as his hands tightened on her, holding her still for his mouth.

She couldn't hurry him, which meant letting him do as he wanted to her, which was amazing, but she was programmed for fast sex, it was all she knew—

"Mmmm," he said against her skin, making her thighs quiver. He stroked them, soothing even as he nibbled at her in a rhythm designed to rile her up. Her belly quivered, too, and he stroked her there as well, all while slowly, tortuously driving her right out of her own mind. He held her on that edge, poised on the brink until she was panting, desperate to take the plunge.

And then he nudged her off, holding her as she burst, holding her through the shudders until she sagged back flat on the table, staring up at the ceiling, breathing like a lunatic.

He pulled a condom from his shorts on the floor. Straightening, he looked down at her with heated, glittering eyes as he lifted her leg and wrapped it around his hip, pulling her body up against his hot, hard one.

And everything that had kept her heart protected from him flew right out the window as he protected them both and entered her, a deliciously hot glide that had her wild again in seconds. She arched, rocking up so he'd move within her.

But he still couldn't be rushed. No, the man who could throw so fast he made her head spin took his damn sweet time giving her another long, slow, perfect thrust. And suddenly, instead of racing for the finish line, she wanted it to never end. "Don't stop," she gasped, holding on for dear life as he pushed into her. "Oh God, please don't . . ." Her toes curled, and she could feel herself letting go, really, fully, utterly—letting go.

"Feel it, Holly. Feel me."

Yes. She was getting a real feel for him, thick and straining for release inside her.

"Yeah, like that," he whispered gruffly in her ear, and it hit her like a freight train, making her cry out again, hearing him do the same as he pumped into her one last time. It was earth-shattering, and her mouth, disconnected from her brain, let three little words slip right out of her as if it was the most natural thing in the world. "I love you."

Above her, Pace went utterly still, and oh God, she did, too.

Then he lifted his head, slipped his hands into her hair, and tilted her head to his. "What did you say?"

"Nothing." She shook her head, still gasping for air. "I said your name. And then . . . and then I just stopped talking."

Eyes locked on hers, he slowly shook his head. "No, you didn't."

She squeezed her eyes shut. "Okay, then pretend I said nothing, the way we used to pretend that this was just an odd, inexplicable chemistry."

He stayed still, holding her against him as he supported the both of them, his arms still quaking faintly, his torso damp, his eyes opaque. "Holly—"

"Please," she whispered. "Please, Pace."

Looking staggered, he leaned in and kissed her softly, whispered her name, and then nuzzled her throat.

And very slowly, she relaxed. He was going to let it go, and in relief she curled into him.

"Okay, first," he murmured, "I hope you got the license plate of whatever that was that just hit us."

Yeah. That's exactly how it felt. A damn big truck. See?

It wasn't her fault. The next time they were together, she'd simply tape her mouth shut first, that's all. Or maybe she'd do it starting right now—

"And second—" he said, much more seriously, meeting her gaze.

Oh God. Oh shit. Shit, shit, shit—

"Holly, I—"

The knock at the door startled the both of them. As did Chipper's voice coming through it.

"Pace?"

Suitably distracted from wondering what he'd been about to say, Holly looked at Pace in horror because she was naked. Naked, with a twelve-year-old boy knocking on the door. "We lost track of the time!"

"Yeah." He helped her off the table. "The minute you took off your top, I lost all control of my thought processes."

No time for her bra, she grabbed her tank top as Chipper banged on the door. "Pace? You there?"

"Hold onto your shorts, buddy," Pace called back, tossing Holly hers.

"I am not going without panties again!" she hissed, but then slid on her shorts sans panties for speed. Dammit.

"I'm sorry," Pace whispered softly, giving her one last hard kiss as Chipper kept knocking. "So sorry."

She could do nothing but laugh in disbelief as he slipped her panties in his pocket, looking so damn sexy as he smiled at her in a way that had the love she hadn't known she felt brimming to the surface. Yeah, it'd really snuck up on her and grabbed her by the heartstrings.

Which meant in spite of her best intentions, she had a world of hurt coming her way.

Chapter 27

The charm of baseball is that dull as it may be on
the field, it is endlessly fascinating as a rehash.

—Jim Murray

Chipper and the guys were ecstatic at the news that Pace
had purchased the park and were arguing over who was going to help him fix up the building while Pace struggled to
get his head on straight. Not easy, because Holly stood there
in her shorts, once again wearing no panties.

"I'm great with power tools," River said. "I helped my
older brother tear down a car once."

Jesus. "Stay away from stolen cars, River."

"'Kay. So can I use the power tools?"

"Me, too," Chipper said. "I'm helping, too."

"You're all helping," Pace told them. "And then we'll
put out the word about baseball clinics, and more kids will
come, and maybe we can start a league."

"Who's going to coach us?"

"Me. I'm going to coach you, and by the time you get to
high school, the coach there will be begging you to try
out."

Chipper grinned and followed as Pace walked Holly out
to her car. The others came, too. Pace's legs were still wobbling from the climax that had nearly blown his hair off.

The lack of underwear wasn't helping, but there was a bigger reason he couldn't catch his breath or balance.

She loved him.

She.

Loved.

Him.

Never in a million years would he have guessed that they'd get to this point. He felt unprepared and disoriented and . . .

Well, he wasn't sure exactly. But he had butterflies in his stomach, and somehow his heart had gotten on the outside of his ribs. He might have mentioned these odd symptoms to her, but he had five kids hanging on their every word and a game to get to.

A game he was going to have to prepare for, somehow.

"Okay, well . . ." Holly turned toward her car. "I'll see you later."

"I'm glad you took Pace back," Chipper said. "I'm glad you're his girlfriend again."

Pace could tell by the look on Holly's face that she was trying to formulate a denial, a denial for his sake, to protect him, and that killed him. She was smart and sweet and loyal as hell, and she loved him—not because he was a baseball player, but in spite of it.

His own miracle. "Me, too," he told Chipper, grabbing Holly's hand. "I'm glad she's my girlfriend, too." He felt her stiffen in surprise at his side, and he looked into her eyes, which were warm and filled with things that somehow warmed him, too. From inside his pocket, his cell phone rang, and he pulled it out "It's Sam," he said.

"Pace," the publicist said in a voice that told him she'd been crying, possibly still was. "Holly isn't the leak. She never was. It's Jeremy."

"What? How did you find that out?"

"I lied and told him I had proof it was him, and he caved like a cheap suitcase. He'd stolen my password and was accessing my computer for privileged information. He's turned in his resignation at the Bucks."

"Are you okay?"

"Not really, no. I tried to turn in my resignation but no one would take it."

"Good." He couldn't imagine the Heat's PR department without her running it. "This isn't your fault, Sam. Any more than it was Holly's."

"I'll work on believing that."

"Good. You and Holly both deserve better." He slipped his phone into his pocket and found Holly looking at him. "What?" he asked.

"Nothing." She leaned in and kissed him. "Everything. You stood up for me."

"That's what boyfriends do," Chipper said. "Right, Pace?"

Pace found himself smiling into Holly's eyes. "Right."

She smiled back, and for the first time ever before a game, he felt light as a feather. Like he could do anything.

With her at his side.

In the stands, Holly distracted herself with her camera, taking shots of the guys warming up and interacting on the field. As practice ended and the stadium began to fill, adrenaline seemed to run high. From where she sat, she could see straight into the Heat's dugout, and she turned her camera there, zooming in for some great shots. She hadn't gone online to see the lineup today, and she wondered who was pitching as she got pictures of Gage talking to Pace, and then she went still, her eyes locked on the lens as Pace looked up and unerringly found her in the crowd.

He was a hundred yards away and yet in her lens he was right there, eyes warming. He smiled and mouthed her name.

And then, oh God, and then he mouthed three little words.

I love you.

Staggered, she sank to her seat, lowering her camera to take in the real Pace, but he was nothing more than a blur so she went back to the lens.

Because surely she'd imagined it, just a funny little trick her brain had decided to play. Ha ha. Funny.

Her eyes soaked him up, willing him to say it again, but Gage got in her way, squinting out into the stands to see what Pace had been looking at.

Holly sucked in a breath, painfully aware that she was probably still persona non grata around these parts. And it was then, while trying to lie low, that her cell phone buzzed. "You coming?" Gage asked in her ear.

"Um, what?"

"Get your ass down here. You have a player to kiss."

She dropped her phone, stuffed her camera in her bag, and raced to the clubhouse, passing by several of the training staff and maintenance staff, all of whom greeted her. At the door to the clubhouse, Gage pulled her in for a hug.

Stunned, she hugged him back.

Henry smiled at her. All the guys smiled at her, some even hugging her as Gage had. Hell, Wade gave her a smacking kiss right on the lips, lingering over it until she was yanked out of his arms and into another pair that she knew like the back of her hand.

"Hands off," Pace said over her head to Wade.

Wade grinned broadly. "Aw, that color of green looks so hot on you."

Gage pushed Wade clear. "You two have a shower room to get to in a damn hurry." He pretty much shoved them inside. "You know the drill."

When the door shut, Holly leaned back against the tile wall, her heart so full she could scarcely stand it. "I think we've had our quota today already."

Pace grinned as he came in close. Trapping her against

the tile with a hand on either side of her face, he stepped into her. "Maybe we're due for more than our fair share."

"I'm game." She was still smiling when he kissed her, but at the first touch of his lips all humor faded, replaced by a familiarity that was as natural as breathing and a heat that never failed to amaze her. She wound her arms around his neck, loving the feel of his bigger, stronger arms pulling her up against the body she planned on nibbling every single inch of later. He smelled like soap and deodorant and Ace Wrap and she inhaled him in—

"Okay, that's all we have time for, thank you." Gage fisted his hand in the back of Pace's jersey, pulling him free.

"Wait," Pace told him. "I've got to—"

"Later."

And just like that, he and Pace were gone.

A little dizzy, Holly made her way back to the stands, where just before the first pitch, Sam appeared at the empty seat next to her. "Is this seat taken?"

Holly looked up at the woman she'd become such good friends with and felt her throat tighten. "Yes. By you."

Sam sank down next to her. "I'm so sorry, Holly. I've given you such a hard time, and it wasn't your fault and I'm just so . . ." Her eyes filled. "Sorry."

Holly hugged her. "You were only protecting your team. I get that. I heard about Jeremy. Are you okay?"

"I'm shocked and hurt and pissed off, but I'm okay. And we're going to kick ass today to prove it."

When the announcer called out the starting lineup, the pitcher walked onto the mound.

Pace.

Holly gasped as the home crowd went crazy. "What?" she whispered to Sam. "He's pitching?"

"Yes."

He stood on the mound looking tall, tough, and a little lean after all the rehabbing he'd done.

And ready.

He pitched a tight seven innings and left the game with the score tied three all. By the bottom of the ninth, the Heat was down two. Henry, a power hitter, came up to bat with two men on base. He singled.

And then Wade came up to bat. Holly began to sweat. Sam was chewing her nails. "He can do this, he can—"

He hit hard, bringing all three runners home, and the crowd went wild with the win.

The players and management poured out of the dugout, all tumbling over each other right there at the home plate. Holly stood up, watching them from eyes that burned with fierce pride and joy.

After a minute, Pace separated himself from the pack, and with cameramen and reporters dogging him, he climbed the fence, determination all over his face.

Heart racing, Holly stared at him in shock as he leapt lithely to his feet right in front of her.

"Hey," he said.

She grinned. "Well, hey yourself, and congratulations."

"Thanks." He eyed the cameramen trying to follow his route, stymied by the fencing, then looked at her wryly as he rubbed his jaw. "We've got maybe ten seconds of privacy, so I'll be quick. About what I said in the dugout. About what I'd been trying to say since the boys showed early at the park."

She brought a hand up to her chest to keep her heart from leaping right out. "I . . . I thought maybe it was my imagination."

"No."

Around them she was aware of the other spectators, how they were beginning to take notice of them, a few even pulling out their cell phones to take pictures. She didn't care, and tried to pull him in.

"I'm filthy," he said, then gave up the fight and hugged her back. "All this time," he said in her ear, "I thought I was the worldly one, that between the two of us, I was more experienced, that I was waiting for your heart to catch up, but I was wrong." Pulling back, he looked into her eyes. "Every single moment since you came to Santa Barbara, you've schooled me. On top of being smart as hell, loyal, passionate, gorgeous, you are the most amazing woman I've ever met."

Behind them, two camera guys finally made it over the fence. Huffing, they stuck microphones in their faces.

Pace turned his back on them and, still holding on to Holly, looked down in her face. "I fell hard for you," he said quietly, for her ears only. "And the only thing better than knowing it, is going for it. Going for something other than baseball, something that means even more to me."

"Me?" she asked with a smile.

"You. Only you. I love you, Holly, so much."

"Hey." One of the camera guys behind them pushed his way around to look at Pace in horror. "You're not retiring, are you? You just got back."

Pace glanced at him with irritation, and the camera guy lifted his free hand. "Sorry, man. You're trying to get laid. Carry on."

Pace looked like maybe he wanted to shove him back over the fence, but then yet another camera guy came running down the aisle and stuck out another microphone. "What's this about retirement?"

Pace shook his head. "Okay, all of you, back up. I need a second." He turned back to Holly. "I'm trying to propose here."

"Propose?" she gasped.

"Yeah. I—oomph," he let out as she flung herself into his arms.

He smelled like the dust and dirt and sweat that was all over him, and she couldn't get enough. "Oh, Pace. I don't need a proposal."

"You don't?"

"No. I just need you."

He let out a slow, heartbreaking smile. "You were right before, you know."

"When?" she asked, liking to be right, about anything.

"When you said baseball was everything to me. It was, until you. Now you're my everything."

"Love the sound of that." She melted against him and put her mouth to his ear. "I also loved your pitching tonight. It turned me on."

His eyes heated. His hands tightened on her. They might have been alone as he dropped his forehead to hers. "Yeah?"

"Yeah." She put her mouth back to his ear. "Now get me out of here, because you have another perfect game coming. This one private."

He tossed his head back and laughed out loud as the flashes went off all around them. And that was the shot of him that made it into all the papers the next day, and later into many books on the sport.

And only Holly knew that the special light in his eyes at that moment wasn't for the game the Heat had just won, but all for her . . .

Turn the page for a preview of
the next novel by Jill Shalvis

Perfect Game

Coming soon from Berkley Sensation!

She'd read somewhere that the way to a man's heart was through his stomach, but Samantha McNead knew better than that—in certain men the stomach was aiming just a bit too high.

Wade O'Riley was one of them.

One of the most celebrated catchers in Major League Baseball, he had women lining up to meet him wherever he went.

And it wasn't home cooking that they wanted to give him either.

Not that Wade minded. Nope, even with all the constraints that went with the new big, fat contract he'd just signed with Santa Barbara's expansion team, the Heat, the guy seemed oblivious to pressure. Laid-back and easygoing, he took everything as it came, with a grain of salt and a slow, knowing smile that let everyone in on the joke.

Because life was one big funny to Wade.

She appreciated that, she just didn't live it the way he did. Didn't know how. As the publicist for the Heat and the lone female in a man's world, Samantha's life tended to be more work than fun lately. Hence her mission today.

The limo pulled up in front of Wade's big beach-cottage-style house, which was perched on a bluff over the ocean. From the backseat she could see the ocean froth and pitch.

The motion matched what her stomach was doing.

In the work aspect of her life, she was extremely comfortable. That was a given. She'd been raised by men: her father, her uncle, her brother, and her cousins were all tough, implacable, unforgiving alpha males. Failure had never been an option, which translated to Sam being very good at whatever she tackled. Unfortunately, all she'd tackled lately was her job.

Maybe one of these days a guy would sweep her off her feet and then into bed, but it wouldn't be today and it wouldn't be with the guy she'd been tasked with baby-sitting.

The Heat had played last night. It was the first week of April, and it'd been an exhibition game, a prelude to their season opener on Sunday. They'd played the Padres, and it'd turned out to be surprisingly down and dirty. Wade had hit a homer in the second inning then been beaned in the third when the pitcher had hit him in the thigh with a throwaway pitch. The game had gone two extra innings and way past midnight before the Heat had finally won on Wade's double, so Sam expected him to be exhausted and probably sore as hell. Maybe she'd even have to pull him out of bed.

The thought brought concern and a secret tingle to parts of her body that had been neglected for far too long.

Nice to know they still worked.

As she started to exit the limo to go get him, his front door opened. Six feet of rugged, leanly muscled male stepped out in Levi's and an untucked blue-and-white-striped button-down. A gust of wind molded his clothes against the body that tended to make her tongue stick to the roof of her mouth, and he stopped to slide on his sunglasses and take in the ocean, the picture of a California surfer.

He'd been a rock star in another life, she was convinced. She purposely let out a breath and leaned back, reminding herself he was just a guy. A *flawed* guy at that, though certainly none of his flaws happened to be showing at the moment.

He walked across the lawn with an unhurried, easy stride in all his scruffy gorgeousness and opened the limo door, letting in the chilly April afternoon air. With one hand on the roof, the other on the door, he bent down, peering in through his Prada sunglasses, merely arching a brow when he saw her.

Couldn't blame him. They weren't exactly on speaking terms.

His unruly sun-kissed light brown hair was either styled messy today on purpose or he hadn't bothered with a comb. His face was scruffy with at least a day-old beard so she was going with the no-comb theory. He should have looked sloppy and unkempt but nothing about him ever looked like anything less than God's gift. She'd seen him in uniform, in designer suits, in work-out gear, in all sorts of things, including absolutely nothing, and he always looked perfect.

Especially in the nothing.

"Hey," he said in that low, slightly raspy voice of his, the one that never failed to immediately put her back up.

And/or turn her on.

"Hey yourself." He wasn't limping, and he sure as hell didn't look exhausted. The opposite, she thought a little breathlessly as his deceptively lazy gaze raked over her from head to toe. Deceptively, because behind that beach-bum facade of his lay a sharp-as-hell wit.

Given their . . . tense relationship at the moment, she didn't smile.

And though he usually smiled at anything female, neither did he.

"Are you okay?" she asked.

"Always. How about you, Princess? You ready to do this?"

She'd asked him a million times not to call her that. It drove her crazy, which was of course why he did it. "We need to talk."

"Sorry," he said with mock regret. "But we don't talk. We fight. And I'm not in the mood."

He hadn't been "in the mood" since what she called the Mishap.

The Mishap Never to Be Talked About.

Except . . . except Wade got along with the entire world, and she had to admit it was disturbing that they didn't. Couldn't. Fact was, the two of them rubbed each other the wrong way, always had, and there was nothing to be done about that now.

Nothing.

She had a job to do. *They* had a job to do. So she swallowed the little ball of nerves in her throat, reminding herself that as the estrogen quota in a world of testosterone, she'd made her place by being cool, calm, and implacable, just as her father had taught her.

Tough and composed.

No weaknesses.

None. And on the whole, it worked for her.

Ninety-nine percent of the time.

At least until that rare occasion when she had to deal with this *one* player, this *one* guy who had the singular, most annoying ability to get beneath her skin and make himself right at home. It wasn't even his fault. He simply threw her off by just being. He made it so she couldn't be professional, and that more than anything was worrisome.

Aka terrifying.

"I realize you probably don't want to go over the plan," she said. "But I think we should."

"I know the plan," he said. "One of the corporations endorsing the Heat has a new conservative CEO who has high 'family values' and is upset about our PR troubles—"

"*Your* recent PR troubles," she corrected.

He let out a tight breath. "Whatever. The fact is that you, the manager, the owner, hell, everyone but me, believes that the world cares about one more ridiculous baseball scandal, and they think that scandal is going to be me simply because some woman claims I've gotten her pregnant. I never slept with her."

"You can't blame people for thinking it. You do have a bit of a playboy reputation, and she had pictures of you and her on the beach by your house."

He just looked at her, clearly standing by his claim that this wasn't his fault.

"See," she pointed out. "This is why we have to talk about it."

"Look, I get what the powers that be want from me. From us. We pretend to be a couple in the eyes of the press so our endorsements won't be pulled. How hard can it be?"

"I don't know," she replied cautiously. "How hard?"

He gave her a look. *The* look. And heat seared through her belly. "You know what I mean," she mumbled.

"The plan is that I have to behave. And you're supposed to make me." He shot her the look again. "I'm looking forward to the 'make me' part."

Oh, God. "Okay, this isn't going to work," she said stiffly. She was fun. Lighthearted. Why the hell he made her sound so uptight and stuffy, she had no idea.

Wait. She did have an idea. An exact idea.

She'd slept with him.

Once.

On the one single night in her entire life she'd had too much to drink. Except there'd been no sleeping involved. To make matters worse, it'd been one of the hottest, best nights of her life. "Listen, I realize we've had our differences, but—"

"Differences?" He laughed, then shook his head, still amused. "I'm going to let you get away with that, Princess, because I'm in a hurry."

A friend of his was getting married. A close friend who just happened to be a big-time Hollywood producer, and Wade was one of the groomsmen. The wedding was an entire weekend extravaganza where there was sure to be tons of press. If he was going to attract any of it—and just by being Wade, he most definitely was—he needed to attract *good* press.

They had a two hour car trip ahead of them, and by the time it was over and they got out of the limo at the resort, they needed to be in sync and looking like lovers. Willing to do her part, she smiled, the smile that usually got her exactly what she wanted, and in this case, what she wanted was Wade's cooperation. Thing was, he didn't often feel the need to cooperate, which she knew all too well. "You're right, let's just get going, we can finish this on the way."

He looked at her for a long beat, all big and built and completely inscrutable, during which time she held her breath. For as laid-back as he was, he was also tough as steel. He had to be. Catchers had what was arguably the hardest position in baseball. They had to command the respect of all the players, as it was the catcher making the calls. He had to have good sequences in those calls, and the ability to change it up and keep hitters off balance. Which meant he had to be smart, sharp, and strong in both mind and body.

Wade was all of those things and more. Including quick to come to a decision. He tossed his overnight bag into the limo and followed it in. Leaning back, he stretched out his long, long legs and looked around. "So. We have any food in here?"

"No. Are you hungry?"

"Starving."

He was always starving. Probably because he burned God knew how many calories a day between five mile runs, weight training, and the game itself. "We can stop and get something to go. Rosa's?" she asked, naming the closest café. Look at that, she was getting the hang of taking care of him already.

"DQ is good."

She'd never met a grown man with such a love for fast food before. But whatever he wanted, she'd get. It would make him happy, and a happy Wade was hopefully a compliant one. With a nod from her, the driver started the engine, and they began their trek, heading through town.

Santa Barbara was a colorful blend of history and up-scale Southern California living. Wade was looking out the window, taking it in, giving her his profile as they turned onto Highway 1, heading south. The sparkling Pacific was on their right, the green, craggily Santa Ynez peaks on their left, both breathtaking.

They made a stop at Dairy Queen and got back on the road. Wade was quiet as he ate, watching as they left the affluent homes and ranches, and headed into the outlying county and the far-less privileged area. She knew he'd come from an underprivileged neighborhood himself. In fact, despite his many faults, he was surprisingly humble and quick to laugh at himself, and often joked he'd grown up so far from the proverbial tracks that he hadn't even been able to *see* them.

And her?

Well, she'd grown up with a silver spoon in her mouth, and everyone knew it. It was certainly all Wade knew about her, because it'd been the only thing she'd ever let him see. He had no idea that the two of them had a hell of a lot more in common that he'd ever guess.

He polished off two burgers and went to work on a bag of fries. "So . . ." His green eyes were relaxed but assessing as they met hers. "When are you going to tell me they want us to do this boyfriend/girlfriend thing for a whole month?"

"You heard?" she asked in surprise. She thought she was supposed to talk him into it.

"I work with a bunch of women. They tell all."

"Wade, you work with a group of professional athletes."

"Who gossip like women. Pace told me. He'd heard it from Henry, who'd overheard Gage talking to you."

Pace being Wade's best friend and the Heat's ace pitcher. Henry was their shortstop. Gage, their team manager. And yes, the supposedly *professional* clubhouse really was similar in nature to a high school locker room.

Wade was still looking at her. He was sprawled out, relaxed. She took a careful breath. "A month shows stability. It's more impressive than just a weekend wedding fling."

His brow shot up so far into his thick and unruly hair it vanished. "So you're okay with being joined at the hip for a month?"

"If you are."

"Are there benefits?"

"No!"

He sighed.

"Hey, it's not that bad. I'm fun, you know."

He just looked at her, which burned. "I am! And I just realized, there *are* benefits."

"I'm listening."

Seemed she'd managed to surprise him after all. "Maybe it'll be fun."

"How?"

"Well . . ." She wracked her brain. "I can be a pretty convincing bitch when I want to be."

"Nooo," he said with mock shock.

She ignored that. "I can scare all the crazy women that chase you around and thereby give you a break, and in return, you can just relax knowing you won't have to take care of me like your usual hanger-on, clingy type who bores you within the span of one date."

He slid her a look.

"Hey, just calling 'em like I see 'em."

He didn't say anything to that as he finished the fries, then tossed all the trash back into the bag and set it aside.

He rubbed a hand over his jaw and said another entire boatload of nothing.

"It's just a role, Wade. And it could have been worse. We could have lost the endorsement entirely, or they could have traded you."

"They're that desperate for good press." He shook his head in disbelief.

"Hey, baseball isn't exactly showing its best foot to the public lately. We need this. The Heat needs this."

"And your father's okay with it?" he asked carefully, with good reason.

Her father was one of the owners of the Heat. Her uncle owned their sister team, the Charleston Bucks. The McNead brothers were famous for getting their way, or more accurately, infamous.

And they were baseball royalty.

Or had been until Samantha's brother, Jeremy—her equivalent at the Bucks—had stepped over the ethics line, the moral line, and several other lines as well, and brought the wrath of the press down on the McNeads. "Yes," she said quietly. "He thinks it's a good idea."

"So they're willing to pimp out their princess as it suits them."

A McNead was expected to stick to the pack. "It's just an illusion, Wade."

"It's an entire month, Sam."

The reminder made her stomach quiver. An entire month of being his "girlfriend." "We're grown-ups."

"Really? Because we've not spent more than two minutes together without snarling at each other."

True.

"Well . . ." His smile turned sleepy and sexy. "Except for the elevator."

Also true, and her stomach executed a somersault as the memory flew back, hot and sexy, resurrected by nothing more than the sound of his voice and the look in his eyes.

It'd been last season. The Heat had just lost, bad. Her

family had been driving her insane, and she'd been in desperate need of a pity party for one.

Instead, she'd gotten stuck in that damn elevator on the way to her hotel room with Wade and a couple of little bottles of airplane Scotch. Adrenaline still racing, she'd found something she hadn't expected—a naked party for two.

And now erotic, alcohol-tinged memories came in slo-mo and without conscious bidding, and as always, *always*, sent her spinning between total and complete humiliation and an even more devastating aching hunger.

Neither of which she was comfortable with.

If she could erase from her memory bank the pictures of Wade taking her straight to heaven in under five minutes, she would, but those memories seemed to strengthen with time, teasing her. She darted a quick glance at their driver, who was currently sipping a seventy-two ounce soda and rocking his head to the radio as he beat the steering wheel like a drum.

Not listening. Good. "I don't want to discuss that night."

Wade shrugged. No skin off his nose. Hell, he'd probably had lots of nights like that since.

Dammit.

She concentrated on the view. Not a hardship. Santa Barbara wasn't called the American Riviera for nothing, and she watched as they passed 4,000 foot peaks covered in unique and beautiful chaparral and sandstone outcroppings. Their destination was the famous OC, Orange County, specifically Laguna Beach, for a "magical" weekend. "So we're good?" she asked quietly.

Wade smiled. It was his professional smile, the one that could melt a woman's panties at fifty paces and make men wish that they had half his athletic prowess, and it was a charmer. She knew its potency, braced herself for it, and *still* felt her panties begin to melt.

"What the hell." He stretched out farther, his thigh sliding against hers. "I'm on board. Girlfriend."

"*Fake* girlfriend," she corrected, shoving his leg over,

telling herself she was absolutely not noticing the heat of him, the feel of his rock-hard thigh . . .

He stretched some more, straightening his arms above him, for a minute exposing a brief flash of washboard abs between the hem of his shirt and the waistband of his jeans. Jeans that were faded to white at all the stress points. He had some very fine stress points . . .

Sam saw more men in a day than the average woman dreamed of, many—if she was in the clubhouse before a game—in various stages of nakedness. She was immune to tantalizing glimpses of male skin.

Completely.

Immune.

And yet her mouth went dry.

Wade finished stretching. "Maybe we should kiss on it."

"What? No!"

"Spoil sport," he said so good naturedly that she knew he was only teasing. He'd probably be shocked if she had said yes, which she absolutely wouldn't do. Even if he was the kiss master. Which he was . . .

His leg was touching hers again. He was hogging the backseat, albeit unintentionally. He was a big guy, and he smelled good. He looked good, too, which really didn't seem fair at all.

But he was here, not pitching a diva fit, and she owed him for that. "Thank you," she said. "For agreeing to this."

"You're welcome."

Well, that seemed surprisingly genuine, and she had to wonder if maybe she'd anticipated trouble with him simply because of their past. Maybe . . . Maybe deep down he really was a good guy.

It was possible.

Maybe they could laugh about this, someday.

This could possibly be funny. Maybe.

Sort of.

And maybe they could even become friends. That would be nice—

"You packing any Scotch today?" he asked, looking around the limo. "Should I brace myself for you to tear my clothes off again?"

With a sigh, she leaned back and closed her eyes.

Okay, so they weren't going to become friends.